A CORPSE IN THE CASTLE

A POLLY PEPPER MYSTERY

RICHARD TYLER JORDAN

OLIVERHEBERBOOKS

Published by Oliver-Heber Books

Cover art by Dar Albert at Wicked Smart Designs

0 9 8 7 6 5 4 3 2 1

 Created with Vellum

For Braden Wright.
This was only possible because of you.

PREFACE

Murdered bodies are found with regularity in places like New York, Los Angeles, and London. But killings in the wee village of Abbots Clover, England? Absurd! In this quaint hamlet of centuries-old houses, cobblestone streets, and narrow lanes bordered by thick, unruly hedgerows, one would more likely get hit with a flying teapot than the flip of a middle finger.

Abbots Clover is the sort of place where doggy poo is dutifully scooped away faster than a magician's disappearing rabbit. The theft of a garden gnome would be treated like an *Ocean's Eleven* sequel. And the residents would find it difficult to recall anything more sinister occurring in their midst than when Vicar Aylsworth quaffed the entire stash of communion wine on a Saturday night and then replaced it with red grape juice before the Sunday morning church service.

So when the Abbots Clover police constables examined a lifeless body on the cold stone floor of the larder at the castle known as Thistlethorne Lodge, they were as confused as a chameleon in a bag of Skittles. The idea of murder never entered their minds.

But murder was always on the mind of faded TV legend

Polly Pepper, and her sleuthing instincts kicked in faster than a bear to a picnic basket. Some people attract socks with holes. Others pull in dates who still live with their mother. But Polly Pepper? She had a knack for stumbling upon dead bodies the way a metal detector finds loose change on the beach—and figuring out how the heck they got that way.

With a star on the Hollywood Walk of Fame, a dozen Emmy Awards gathering dust in her trophy case, and an uncanny talent for bumping into murder mysteries the way others bump into their ex at the supermarket, American expat Polly Pepper is now angling for King Charles III to award her an OBE for her invaluable sleuthing services in the UK. His Highness may even deign to confer a damehood on her, too. That is, if she survives her latest and greatest role to date... starring in her own real-life reality show: *A Corpse in the Castle*.

1

___

The Southern California January morning was typical of La La Land: sunny and mild. It was breakfast time, and showbiz living legend Polly Pepper was seated poolside at Pepper Plantation—her fabled mansion in the bucolic hills of Bel Air. With her hair freshly dyed the color of a cherry-flavored lollipop, Star Lady was wearing a pink satin *PP* monogrammed bathrobe and matching slippers. Her sexy-for-sin, gym-built, adult-but-still-living-at-home son, Tim, was also at the table, clad only in the bottom half of his drawstring pajamas. Mother and son were best buds, and this morning routine was a sacred ritual.

Polly held a Bloody Mary in her hand.

Tim gripped his iPhone, which was open to Plunder, his favorite online dating app.

Both were nursing hangovers and debating the (mainly illegal) aspects of what Polly believed to be a win-win email invitation she'd received.

"I've been offered a bloody fortune just for helping that adorable Nigerian prince get his family's money out of Africa!" she said in a raspy, too-early-in-the-morning voice. "Prince

UnpronounceableLastName only requires a small amount of upfront capital—for admin expenses and such. Then I get a big fat paycheck as soon as his family's life savings are safely out of their corrupt authoritarian government's treasury!"

"When was the last time you got something for nothing?" Tim asked absently, dividing his attention between Polly and a new *like* on his dating profile. "Stranger danger," he said as he grimaced at the image.

Polly thought the warning was meant for her and the Nigerian prince. "Clearly not for nothing, sweetums. I have to wire twelve thousand US clams. But we get twelve million in return!"

"Twelve million years in prison," Tim cracked as he swiped the phone screen and cringed at another picture of a potential paramour. "I'm sure this is a crime."

Again, Polly thought the remark was meant for her and the Nigerian prince. "Oh, give it a rest, dear," she said with a sigh. "Dating apps are like a box of chocolates. But you never know if you'll get a nougat or a nut job."

Tim groaned in agreement. "Remember my date with the guy whose profile said he was a dog person? I thought that was a euphemism until he started licking his plate clean and growled when the waiter came to take it away."

Just then, Polly's maid and confidante, Tiara, came to the table with a fresh BM for her boss. Tiara was a petite woman with curvy features and caramel-colored skin. Despite her delicate features, she had a tough interior and a sharp wit that she often used to keep her boss in check. Wearing soft-soled shoes and the French maid's uniform that she hated—but that her pretentious boss had stolen from the costume department at Netflix and insisted she wear—Tiara set down the glass and picked up the old one. "Haven't you learned anything about online scams? You've forgotten the money you sent when you got an email that said Oprah was mugged and lost all her dough and identification while building a girls' school in Mozambique?"

Polly rolled her eyes, perturbed that Tiara had brought up the prickly subject of the time she'd been swindled out of $10,000. "That email was on her personal letterhead, for crying out loud!"

"Except she doesn't spell her name O-P-E-R-A," Tiara countered and sashayed back inside the mansion, shaking her head and muttering something about vodka, chemicals in hair dye, and brain cells.

"The thing is, my love," Polly said to Tim in an unusually somber tone, "we need money! Moolah! Dinero! Gravy! My agent hasn't lined up much of anything for the foreseeable future. I haven't wanted to worry you and Tiara, but I'm extremely concerned about our future!"

Polly Pepper was the quintessential faded star from yesteryear whose financial stability was about as precarious as her hillside mansion in this legendary earthquake fault zone. Her long-running television variety series from the 1990s, *The Polly Pepper Playhouse*, had been a megahit for a decade and was considered a music/comedy classic by fans and critics alike. But those were the high-flying good old days. Now, in the twenty-first century, the name Polly Pepper was a mere footnote in the annals of television history, and she was feeling down on her luck. Not down as in property-foreclosure time or anything like that. But her checking account balance had dipped below the $500,000 level, and she was terrified of receiving the next champagne bill from the Liquor Locker. A bunch of no-talent Gen Zers were raking in big bucks simply by making stupid videos on TikTok and being what they call influencers, and Polly wanted a slice of that easy-money pie.

"You have a TV commercial coming up," Tim reminded her. "You're the new celebrity pitch person for... what is it again?"

Polly waited a beat, then half-heartedly said, "Reverse mortgages."

"Right. Then I guess you've officially joined the Henry Winkler Has-Been Club."

Polly grimaced as she took another pull of her drink and looked around at her lushly landscaped surroundings. "I couldn't endure losing all of this to some predatory loan company. I'd rather cancel my next surgical fat transfer. We've got to figure out a way for me to earn big money again. I need a second act!"

For a long moment, Polly pondered multiple scenarios for improving her financial plight. She considered selling the rights to her life story for a major motion picture. But then she remembered that Simon & Schuster nearly went bankrupt after they published her memoir, *PP Through Life*, a few years ago and had been forced to shed half of their editorial staff. Then she thought about starting her own YouTube channel and creating videos of her day-to-day activities.

"Kardashian," she uttered with a tone of revulsion that triggered a shudder that vibrated through her entire body.

Then she considered marrying someone rich. *Sex for money and security would make me...* That last thought jolted Polly back to reality. "There must be a solution!"

As Polly wallowed in her sullen mood, Tiara returned to the patio and dropped the daily mail in front of her.

"Real live mail!" Polly squealed, her thoughts of get-rich-quick schemes scattering like sand on a windy beach.

"I had to sign for this one," Tiara said as she pointed to the top of the small stack and took a sip from Polly's glass. "It's from England. Looks important."

Polly's eyes landed on the profile of King Charles III

adorning the stamps. She picked up the envelope and looked at the return address. "Who do we know in London?"

Tiara made a face of impatient annoyance as she swiped the envelope, ripped it open, and withdrew the letter. "This is the only way you're ever going to find out," she scowled, handing it back to her boss.

Polly rolled her eyes and began to read. The patio area was hushed except for the sounds from a few tweeting birds, a helicopter in the distance, and the gurgling pool filter sucking in chlorinated water. Tim studied another potential date's profile on his phone, and Tiara watched as Polly squinted and moved her lips to silently pronounce the words in the letter. When she finally finished, Polly looked up with a puzzled expression. "A castle? Who gives away a castle?"

With the word "castle" hanging in the air, Tim looked up from his phone's screen. He took the letter from Polly's hand and scanned the page. "Who is... Alistair Drake?"

"A fan. Dead."

Tiara seized the letter and read it aloud. "It says... blah, blah, blah... Mr. Drake was an ardent admirer of yours, and as he once read an interview in which you said you had always dreamed of living in an English castle, he wanted to make that dream come true."

"He obviously got me confused with Madonna," Polly said. "A lovely idea, but couldn't they just sell the place and send me the money? I can hardly afford this pile, let alone a castle!"

Tim shook his head and made clicking sounds with his tongue. "I get it. We were just talking about scams, and this is one of the oldest in the book. How much do they want for the paperwork or filing fees?" he asked. "Nobody leaves a castle to a total stranger!"

"I'm hardly a stranger to millions of fans," Polly protested.

"Hundreds, maybe," Tim sniped.

"Hundreds of thousands!" Tiara deflected, standing up for her boss.

"But you're probably right," Polly admitted. "Fake news!" She looked at the letter again and studied the envelope. "Some crook took the time to get decent stationery with an official-looking letterhead," she said, admiring the raised and embossed type. "And what about these stamps? Postage to the States from across the pond ain't cheap. Registered, no less! I have a mind to phone up the FBI or Scotland Yard and report a crime. Or better still, I'll call... " She found a name printed below a handwritten signature. "Tristan Wainwright, Solicitor, and lecture him on the perils of scamming Hollywood icons."

"It's best just to ignore these people," Tim said. "You're probably one of many to get that letter."

"There's one way to find out," Tiara said, picking up Polly's portable landline phone from the table. She looked at the letter again and found a telephone number on the letterhead. "It's eight hours ahead in England, but if this is legit, they might still be in the office." Tiara dialed the UK and handed the phone to her boss.

Five minutes later, having disconnected the call and conversation with Tristan Wainwright, Polly was stock-still from shock.

"It's for real," she said numbly as she stared past the celery stalk in her glass and even past the buff, shirtless, sweating Mexican gardener whom she often spied on with lust from behind her bedroom window curtain and who was now making his way around the manicured property, pushing a lawnmower. Finally, she blinked her eyes and returned to the moment.

"We're going to England!" she said with all the excitement of a lottery winner. "This castle thing could be the answer to all my financial worries. And before you pooh-pooh it as another attempt to separate me from my hard-earned greenbacks, that nice Mr. Wainwright is arranging our first-class travel! Actually, business class. For me. You two are back in the seat-squeeze suite with the other cattle. We're meeting next Monday in his London office to go over the will and get the keys to—listen to this—the castle is called Thistlethorne Lodge."

"Sounds like something romantic out of Charlotte Brontë," Tim said approvingly.

"Or *Dracula*," Tiara shot back with skepticism.

"I've always thought of myself as royalty," Tim gushed.

"Court jester, maybe," Tiara smirked.

Polly raised an eyebrow. "Try queen."

It was an overnight flight from LAX to London's Heathrow Airport, but Polly barely slept for any of the nine and a half hours in the air. It wasn't just the thrill of being in the swanky business-class cabin that had kept her awake, but also her fantasies about making big money from her ownership of a castle in England. *Everyone wants a fairy tale! Tourists will pay me a mint to visit*, she'd scratched on the pages of her journal. *I could rent the place out for extravagant weddings or film shoots. Or I could turn it into a posh B&B, catering to wealthy tourists who want a taste of royal living.* Her thoughts conjured up images of visitors throwing their holiday money at her for guided tours and over-priced souvenirs. The possibilities were endless. *I've always been an Anglophile at heart, and it feels like I'm going home!*

When the airline captain announced the plane would be landing shortly, Polly smiled her famous toothy grin and peered out the rain-streaked window. As the aircraft descended below the heavy, gray clouds, Polly spotted some of the famous London landmarks: the River Thames winding its way through the capital city, Big Ben and the buildings of Parliament, Buckingham Palace, and St. Paul's domed cathedral. Polly thought back to an evening many years before when she had been onstage at the London Palladium for a charity royal command performance. Queen Elizabeth II and Princess Margaret had attended and briefly visited with her and the cast backstage. She smiled at the memory of her deep, wobbled curtsey. And then a slight jolt from the plane's landing gears being engaged snapped her back to the moment.

After the plane had rolled to the jetway and the passengers in Polly's cabin disembarked, she reunited with Tim and Tiara outside the terminal gate area. Like tributaries flowing into a river of multinationals, they joined the several hundred other passengers and made their way toward passport control. After presenting their travel documents to the customs agent, they moved to the baggage-claim carousels.

"That was easy-breezy." Tiara smiled. "He only asked me why I was in England and how long I'd be staying and then told me to enjoy my visit."

"Mine was definitely a toasty English muffin!" Tim said, feigning an exaggerated swoon. He formed a hand fan with his fingers splayed wide and waved it at his face.

"Don't let the Brits fool you with their accents," Polly said. "After that long flight, he probably saw you as a stale crumpet."

The trio collected their luggage, hefted them onto a cart, and then made their way through a long corridor and into the wide-open arrivals hall, where families and friends were waiting to greet loved ones. They quickly spotted a portly man wearing a black suit and tie and holding up an iPad with the initials *PP* in large-type red font on the screen. Polly gave a slight finger wave of acknowledgment.

With a nod and a smile that revealed he was missing a canine tooth, the man touched his index finger to the brim of his cap. "Welcome to England, mum," he said. "My name is

Kenneth. I'll be driving you to your hotel." He took charge of their cart. "This way, please."

Polly whispered to Tim, "The last time I was here, I was the talk of the town, and the car, a Rolls-Royce no less, was waiting at the curb."

Kenneth overheard the comment and insisted that Polly Pepper was still a big name in England (although he'd never heard of her before getting his driving assignment a few hours earlier), but that, thanks to ongoing threats from a bunch of international terrorists, he wasn't allowed to park any closer than the adjacent car park.

"Car park," Polly parroted the driver. "That means *parking lot* in American. And that," she said, pointing to the luggage cart, "is a trolley. And in England, they fill their tanks with petrol, not gas. And—"

"And a car has a bonnet and a boot instead of a hood and trunk," Tim interrupted. "I wear a jumper and a waistcoat instead of a sweater and a vest. Mother, I've watched enough Hugh Grant rom-coms to know that apartments are flats, French fries are chips, chips are crisps, and soccer is football."

"And you're a wanker," Polly snapped. "Need Google Translate?"

"We're two countries divided by a common language," Tiara added as the trio exited the terminal behind Kenneth.

As they stepped outside, Polly and her troupe were immediately assaulted by the biting cold and wind that whipped their hair into wild frizzy mops. Coming from sunny Southern California, they were unprepared for the damp-to-the-bone winter weather of England. They didn't even own umbrellas.

But Polly was undeterred. "I'm so excited! We're in the land of *The Great British Bake Off*, Paul McCartney, and Harry Potter."

"Don't forget Harry Styles!" Tim suggested, with a twinkle of desire in his eyes.

While checking into their hotel, the Chesterton, in the Mayfair district of London, the trio agreed to rendezvous in the lobby at 4:00 for a proper English high tea service. Until then, they were free to play tourists or rest. A porter escorted Polly to her suite while Tim and Tiara were abandoned to find their own rooms. The old-world charm of the building added to their excitement. Like many boutique hotels in the city, the Chesterton was once a private residence. Tiara tried to imagine what the life of a servant must have been like before elevators were invented. They had to run up and down four flights of stairs to serve their employers. Tim admired the architecture and wondered what the Victorian tenants would say if they could see their home in the twenty-first century and how much guests paid to stay there.

"Maybe this place has ghosts," he said with a thrill in his voice. "Anne Boleyn could be wandering around looking for her head."

The day passed in a blur of excitement. After enjoying a traditional high tea complete with trays of tiny crustless sandwiches and an assortment of delicate pastries in the hotel's posh drawing room, Polly and her posse retired to their rooms for the night. But sleep was elusive as their minds raced with thoughts of the castle Mr. Drake had bequeathed to Polly. Tiara tossed and turned, her thoughts filled with visions of her having to clean God knows how many castle rooms. Tim envisioned a life of regal leisure and maybe finding his own knight in shining armor. And Polly brainstormed how she could turn her inheritance into big bucks. When they reassembled in the lobby the next morning, they didn't know if their sleepless night was due to jet lag or their eagerness to see what Polly had inherited.

The engraved brass sign on the door read:

TRISTAN WAINWRIGHT
SOLICITOR

Polly expected the Hollywood version of a Victorian-era law office, but Mr. Wainwright's place of business was high-tech, modern, and completely lacking even the slightest hint of old-world charm. *Where are the handsome mustachioed men in three-piece tweed suits?* she lamented to herself. *And the heavy, dark wood furniture? And floor-to-ceiling bookcases filled with musty, leather-bound volumes of centuries-old British laws?* Polly silently clucked in disappointment as she looked around.

"Shall we?" said Mr. Wainwright as he ushered his clients into his glass-enclosed private office and motioned them to take the seats before his desk. He opened a manila folder and re-examined the contents for a brief moment before handing the file to Polly. "Mr. Drake was an ardent admirer of yours, Ms. Pepper. He loved the arts in general. As he had no living family as heirs, he wanted to express his appreciation for the pleasures you and your work offered him during his lifetime. He left quite a tidy sum to the National Theatre and the MacLaine Dance Company, among others."

"That's nice," said Polly in a tone that Tim and Tiara recognized as trying to be polite but eager to move on to the good stuff —like how much money she could get for the castle.

"He must have been an exceptional man," Tim said, trying to demonstrate an interest—however insincere—in their benefactor.

"Not really," said Mr. Wainwright, reaching for another file folder that contained a brief biography of Alistair Drake. "He inherited his fortune, but squandered most of it. Didn't do much of anything with his life other than travel, collect Hollywood memorabilia, and write fan letters to celebrities. I had his obituary copied for you. Perhaps it will offer a bit of insight into his life, such as it was," he said, handing the pages to Tim. "After Mr. Drake bought Thistlethorne Lodge about forty years ago, he became reclusive and hardly ever left the place."

"Yes! Thistlethorne Lodge!" Polly clapped her hands. "I'm sure you can't wait to tell me all about the castle's value!"

"It's actually the *ruins* of a castle, Ms. Pepper, but with a very lovely house inside the gated stone walls."

At the word "ruins," Polly's heart sank. "Why do I always inherit stinky stuff?" she huffed. "When Liberace passed away, all I got was a tacky candelabra. My beautiful Doris Day left me a doggie toy shaped like a fire hydrant. Now, I inherit a ruined castle. I'll probably have to pay inheritance taxes on a pile of rocks!"

Wainwright stifled a grin at the behavior of the Hollywood diva and handed her a sheaf of papers. "Sign next to the yellow tabs, and then the *rocks* are all yours," he said. "I'm including a list of several items reported as missing or stolen, but given Mr. Drake's age and diminished mental capacity, there's a good chance they may have been mislaid in the house. Call me if you find a gold watch and a couple of rings set with precious stones. They're bequeathed to specific people. Now, I'll summon a taxi to drive you to Paddington Station. You can get the train to the village of Abbots Clover to see Thistlethorne in person. It's a two-hour journey, but once you get out of the city, I think you'll enjoy the view of the English countryside." He handed her a large manilla envelope with the keys to the castle, the list of Mr. Drake's missing bits and bobs, and a few flyers describing fun things for visitors to see and do in the Abbots Clover area.

∼

Mr. Wainwright had been right that the train ride to Abbots Clover was a pretty one. Once the train left London and passed through suburbs with names like Woking, Basingstoke, and Ramsbottom, they marveled at the rolling hills dotted with sheep, horses, and cattle. The scenery reminded them of all the TV period dramas and movies set in rural England that they'd ever seen. The grass was greener than they'd imagined, and the sky was always dramatic, with cotton-ball clouds gracefully gathering and drifting apart. When the train finally arrived at the tiny Abbots Clover station, they hired the only taxi idling near the platform and set off to see their new home.

After a ride of only ten minutes, the car turned off the main road and trundled along a pitted narrow lane that was no wider than the cow path that it probably once was and bordered by tall hedgerows.

And then Polly suddenly squealed with excitement and pointed up ahead. "That's it! That's my castle!" She acted like a survivor on a desert island, pointing to a rescue ship. As the taxi gingerly made its way up a steep incline and onto a wide, graveled parking area, Polly's elation turned to dismay. "Castles are supposed to be like that one where Sleeping Beauty lives. Looks like Maleficent put a spell on this one!"

"You were expecting Windsor or Balmoral?" Tiara asked as they stepped out of the car and gazed with awe at Thistlethorne Lodge. It was an authentic—if smaller than expected—Norman castle.

"It's about a thousand years old, so maybe it shrank with age —like grandma." Tim grinned.

Thistlethorne was a modest little castle nestled atop a small hill and covered in ancient ivy and moss. The castle's two front towers were decidedly stubby, one round and the other square. A short, rickety bridge leading to an arched entryway and iron-studded wooden door spanned a shallow, muddy trench where a long-empty moat had been. A metal grate was suspended above the entrance to be dropped for protection from any onrush of fearsome invaders. Or Jehovah's Witnesses.

The group timidly approached the massive door. A thick, rusted, iron-ring knocker was centered on the left of twin door panels, and when Tim lifted and released it, the sound was a dull thud. They waited. And waited. Tim noticed a frayed rope dangling by the side of the door. He pulled on it. As he'd hoped, a bell clanged on the other side of the gateway.

In a short moment, a panel in the door slid open, and a middle-aged woman with a round face and tight curly brown and gray hair peered out. With red rheumy eyes bulging from sockets set too close together and a bulbous gin nose, she looked at the trio and snapped, "Is yous who I'm 'spectin?" When satisfied that the visitors were indeed the castle's new owners, she opened the heavy main door. "I'm Gwellyn Clogg. The household caretaker," she said matter-of-factly and without a trace of friendliness as she ushered them into the courtyard.

A scruffy-looking black cat with two white front paws, a scar over one eye, and an air of entitlement and superiority sidled up to Polly and rubbed its head against her ankle.

"Such a good bay-bee," Polly cooed as she stooped down to pet the animal. "Such a good bay-bee!"

"That there's Mr. Boots," Gwellyn said. "He's mostly an outdoor cat. For the mice and rats, you know." She didn't see the grimace of rodent revulsion on Polly's face.

The courtyard was a vast expanse of green lawn surrounded by tall stone walls and bordered by winter-dormant plant beds. A man was on his knees, tending to the soil.

"That's Merv, the gardener and handyman," said Gwellyn, "but I don't trust him to know a turnip from a tulip." Then she whistled like a New Yorker summoning a cab. "Bloody buggering bollocks!" she yelled. "Come and greet the new owners!" She turned back to Polly and, in a voice loud enough for Merv to hear, said, "He's an idiot. Don't trust him as fer as I can kick 'im. And I'd like to kick 'im to China!"

Merv was in his mid-forties, solidly built, and his brown hair was cut military short. Despite the cold air, he was clad only in a faded *Rolling Stones* concert souvenir T-shirt, khaki shorts, and brown leather boots with thick, brown socks. His knees and shins were soiled from kneeling in the muddy flower beds.

Mmm. Tasty, Polly thought to herself and lasciviously compared him to her hot Mexican gardener in California.

Tim went a step further when he reached out to shake Merv's hand. "I see there's no truth to the rumor that you Brits don't hit the gym." He grinned.

Tiara gave Tim a reproachful nudge with her elbow, then offered her own hand for Merv to shake.

"Mum," was all that Merv would say as he acknowledged Polly and company with a polite but sheepish nod.

"He'll give you a tour of the castle grounds after tea," Gwellyn said, volunteering Merv for an unexpected chore.

Merv looked at his wristwatch. "Meetin' me mates at the pub in an hour," he said apologetically.

Polly's heart swelled with excitement as she looked around and squealed, "My very own castle!" It was no longer just a pile of rocks to her, but a place of possibility and potential. Her eyes roamed over the house's exterior, taking in the details and imagining the history within its walls. She marveled at the multipaned windows of diamond leaded glass, each piece slightly different from the next, giving the house a charming and imperfect feel. She couldn't help but think of all the people who had lived and worked in the castle over the centuries. She imagined generations of families, each one leaving their mark and adding their own story to the rich tapestry of its history. Then, with her arms outstretched, she performed a dizzying three-hundred-sixty-degree Maria von Trapp-on-an-Austrian-mountaintop twirl and absorbed the surroundings with her eyes as she sang a verse from the old Carpenters song *Top of the World*.

The house, which shared a wall with the ancient castle, was two stories and very obviously several hundred years old. Gwellyn opened the front entryway door, and Polly's eyes widened with anticipation. As they moved through the hallway to the main reception room, the trio was immediately struck by the place's grandeur. Wood-beam ceilings towered above them, and antique furnishings dotted the room. Threadbare Oriental area rugs blanketed wide, dark hardwood floorboards, lending the space an air of faded elegance. The room was filled with furniture passed down from generation to generation, each piece imbued with nostalgia.

Tim, in particular, had always been drawn to grand old buildings and their history. He loved the idea of restoring something and breathing new life into a place forgotten or neglected. Thistlethorne Lodge was an ideal canvas for him.

Polly was especially intrigued by the place. She could feel the weight of history all around her. As she walked through the ancient rooms, she was bubbling with ideas for exploiting the castle to make money. She saw potential everywhere and rattled off her plans aloud: *A tearoom. Guided tours. A gift shop.* "I can picture this place as a romantic wedding venue with attractive couples exchanging their vows in the chapel," she said, already counting the truckloads of money pouring in.

"Ridiculous!" Gwellyn spat. "This is a private residence, not a bloody hotel. And besides, where would guests stay? We only have six bedrooms."

"Ever hear of Airbnb?" Polly retorted.

"A tearoom? Who's going to staff it? Not me," Gwellyn mocked.

Polly's enthusiasm wavered momentarily, but she refused to give in. "We'll figure it out."

"We don't need a bunch of strangers traipsing through the place. This is a home, not a tourist attraction," Gwellyn said dismissively.

"Watch and see," Tiara said, siding with Polly.

As the trio entered the main reception room, they were impressed with the large stone fireplace. Above the mantel hung a gilt-framed painting of a nobleman in formal attire. His red lips and page-boy hairstyle gave him an almost comical appearance, while a gold stickpin with a bright red ruby accessorized the lapel of his black jacket. Polly was fascinated by him.

"That there's the Duke of Droitwich," said Gwellyn, noticing Polly's interest in the painting. "He built this house back in the 1700s. Before that, the castle was just a fortress. Legend says his dog, Loki, was apparently so obnoxious that Old Nanny Grumbles, the castle witch, put a spell on him, and he disappeared into that painting of a fox hunt in the entry hallway. Sometimes, you can still hear him bark!"

Polly imagined the duke walking through these rooms, the rustle of his silk coat and the clack of his walking stick echoing off the walls. She wondered what kind of person he had been, what secrets he had kept, and what legacy he had left.

"And who's that?" Polly asked as a short, frail-looking young woman in her mid-twenties—wearing a dirty apron over jeans and a long-sleeve sweatshirt, holding a bucket and mop—entered the room.

Gwellyn's response was sharp and abrasive, causing Polly to recoil in surprise. "Are yeh bloody blind! Can yeh see we're busy?" she bellowed at the young woman, her voice filled with disgust.

The terrified girl looked like she was going to cry. "That there's Lily. The half-wit maid," Gwellyn said, as if apologizing for the woman's existence on the planet. "A good-for-nothing dogsbody, if you ask me. Barely good for scrubbin' floors. Can't remember her own name half the time, either. And she's a clumsy thing, too. I calls her the Terminator 'cause she's always destroying stuff. I swear, if you leave her alone with a feather duster for two minutes, she'll pluck it like a chicken." Gwellyn sniggered at her own mean joke.

Tiara smiled kindheartedly and moved to Lily's side. "I'm a maid too," she said, trying to let Lily know they were kindred spirits. "We'll grab a coffee one of these days and exchange horror stories about working for Leatherface from *The Texas Chainsaw Massacre.*"

Lily hadn't a clue what Tiana had just said and offered a tight, wary smile and sheepishly looked at Gwellyn for guidance. The household caretaker twisted her mouth and ordered Lily back to work. "Put the kettle on and don't be comin' into the reception room again unless you're called!" She turned and continued playing museum docent.

As Gwellyn led the group into the dark, shabby library, Polly was disappointed. The room looked as though it hadn't been decorated since at least the 1970s, with tattered wallpaper peeling off the walls and worn carpet underfoot. An ancient IBM electric typewriter from that era rested on a Victorian, double-pedestal partner's desk, as if it were the most technologically up-to-date writing implement imaginable. Tim couldn't help smirking at the sight of it. And Tiara thought it looked like something from a museum exhibit.

As Polly looked around the room, she noticed that instead of being lined with books, the library walls held a vast collection of framed original classic movie posters and autographed black-and-white glossy headshots of celebrities. There was Rita Hayworth's poster for *Cover Girl*, Bette Davis's *All About Eve*, and Roz Russell's *Auntie Mame.* She recognized most of the framed faces and signatures, and when she found her own image, she squealed with delight. "*Bacteria: The Typhoid Mary Story!* That was my first off-off-Broadway musical! The critics loved me. Brooks Atkinson said I was 'as infectious as tuberculosis!'"

Gwellyn didn't care.

Polly smiled again when she noticed that her picture was in a more expensive frame and more prominent position than Mr. Drake's signed photos of Marilyn Monroe, Judy Garland, and Helen Mirren.

After inspecting the memorabilia, they toured the kitchen with its vintage Aga stove and the formal dining room boasting a Waterford crystal chandelier. Gwellyn then led the group up a staircase to see the six en suite bedrooms.

As they walked down the long hallway corridor, Polly couldn't help but feel a chill in the air. The house seemed impossible to heat, and she shivered as she wrapped her arms around her chest. "No central heating?" she asked, her teeth chattering.

"Too expensive for this big place," Gwellyn said matter-of-factly. "We make do with hot water bottles. Lily'll fetch you one. You'll get used to it. It's all part of the charm of living in an old house like this."

Polly rolled her eyes. *Charm, indeed,* she grimaced to herself. *Another big expense for a boiler. This place screams money pit.*

As they entered one of the bedrooms—Gwellyn called it the Edward VII Suite—Polly felt a pang of anxiety. The room was spacious but shabby. She had been hoping for a luxurious bedroom but was faced with a dingy, uninviting space. The bed was old, and the mattress looked lumpy. The bedside table was chipped, and the lampshade water-stained and lopsided. She could see cobwebs in the corners of the room.

When the tour was over, and they were all seated downstairs

in the main reception room, Gwellyn served tea, and Tim gazed around with satisfied approval.

"A place this old and with so much history, surely there must be a ghost or two," he said. It was meant only as a wisecrack to start a casual conversation.

"Ghost?" Polly repeated with suspicion. "Better be Casper. I don't want some creepy Victorian child who died tragically and now spends eternity leaving wet footprints on the floors and crying for her teddy bear."

"It don't have no name," Gwellyn said as she tried to conceal an evil smile.

"How does he—I'm presuming it's a he ghost—manifest?" Tiara asked. "Is it spooky, like in *The Uninvited*?"

"The usual ways." Gwellyn shrugged. "Rattling chains. Strange sounds comin' from inside the walls. Stuff like silver candlesticks gone missing, then reappearing somewhere they shouldn't be. Especially that one on the sideboard in the breakfast room. It comes and goes as it pleases. Mr. Drake used to have a gold watch and some rings with precious stones that all went missing, too. Whenever something disappeared, he made the joke that Bloody Mary must've nicked it."

"Bloody Mary? As in the ghost that haunts bathrooms and mirrors?" Tiara gasped.

"Don't you get scared being here all alone?" Polly asked. "I'd be too creeped out to sleep at night."

"I'm only here in the daytime now," Gwellyn said, "but I wouldn't spend the night after Mr. Drake died. Anyway, the phantom—as I calls it—goes about its own business. Not much I can do."

"Sort of like sharing the house with a spider, I suppose. Like that one," Polly said, pointing to a long-legged beast on the fireplace hearth, waiting for a meal or a mate.

"Bloody hell!" Gwellyn cried out and leaped from the settee.

"How'd that bugger get past me? I hate spiders! I hate 'em! I hate 'em!"

"I've heard them say lovely things about you," Polly tried to joke, but it went over Gwellyn's head. Polly had reached a stage in her life where she was more apt to insist that Tim or Tiara play catch-and-release when it came to disposing of unwanted, crawling visitors. "Never mind the little fellow," Polly insisted. "You can put him outside later."

"He'll only come back in!" Gwellyn said defiantly. "They're territorial, you know. I don't go crawling around their woodpiles; they shouldn't come into my personal space!"

"When was the last time Mr. Ghost made an appearance?" Polly asked, returning to what was quickly becoming her new creepy obsession. She looked around the room and imagined an invisible specter watching her like someone behind a CCTV security camera. "Haven't you ever tried to get rid of it?"

Gwellyn sat back down on the settee and thought for a long moment. "The last time it showed up?" she said, smiling smugly. "I s'pose it was the night that old Mr. Drake died. That's right. I remember now. The French doors in the dining room blew wide open, and a gust of icy wind came rushing in from the garden. That's usually a sign, just like in scary movies. I think the devil was personally coming to claim the old man's soul. Then I heard someone weeping-like upstairs. I went to investigate, and when I was halfway up the stairs, I could see candlelight flickering somewhere up there in the corridor. But there wasn't nobody else in the bloody house. Just me and Mr. Drake's dead body lying cold in his bed."

"Definitely sounds like a ghost," Polly said with a quiver in her voice. "I don't like things that are weird and creepy. Like ex-husbands and their twenty-five-year-younger girlfriends who think I'm an idiot who can't see what's going on in front of my own eyes and trying to make me think I'm going cuckoo and then suing me for alimony and selling fake news stories about me to the *National Intruder* and *People* magazine and… " Polly ran out of breath and came up for air. "Oh hell, have you tried burning sage? Or hiring an exorcist?"

"Eh, live and let live, I always says," Gwellyn harrumphed. "Except for spiders! They don't deserve no mercy from me!"

"I say die and stay dead!" Polly retorted. "Especially previously alive people who have no business hanging around after their passports to planet Earth have expired." She took one last sip of her now-tepid tea and stood up. "Right-o! Time to toddle on. We've got to get back to the hotel. Then we'll move in here tomorrow. Doesn't that sound marvy?"

"Move in?" said Gwellyn, her voice suddenly filled with panic and her face changing from devious glee to distress. "Nobody said nothin' 'bout you livin' here! I thought you was just visitin' from America. Mr. Wainwright said you'd probably take a look around, then never set foot in the place again."

"That was the plan, but I like what I see," Polly said with a wan smile. "We'll have to go back to California eventually, but we can stay for up to six months a year without a visa. I don't have much in the way of specific plans for the near future, so we'll hang out with you for a while. A lovely plan, eh?"

As Polly and her crew walked out of the reception room, they heard Gwellyn making low-decibel, nonverbal noises suggesting that she could barely contain her rage and might, at any moment, burst out of her apron and transform into the Incredible She-Hulk. When Polly reached the entrance hallway, she turned around to tell Gwellyn how nice it was to meet her and to have a good day—and caught the housekeeper angrily squashing the spider by the fireplace.

3

———

It was nearly teatime the next day when Polly, Tim, and Tiara returned to Thistlethorne Lodge.

Tim was a white-knuckled, rattled wreck. He'd driven through the traffic-treacherous streets of London, then along the crowded M5 motorway, using a manual shift for the first time in his life—with Polly and Tiara constantly screaming, "*The left, the left!* Stay on the *left* side of the road, you boob!" He was shell-shocked by the time they reached the gravel forecourt of the castle and begged, "I need a drink. And a lobotomy."

The afternoon sky was gray and losing its light, and a chilly breeze was swaying the branches of leafless trees. It looked like it was about to rain, but as Polly and her team had quickly discovered, the weather in England was like a good mystery— just when you thought you'd figured out the plot, there's a twist. Blue skies could turn gray in a matter of minutes.

As the trio unlocked the main gate in the castle's curtain wall and walked through the stone portal, they found Merv pruning shrubbery. He offered a broad smile and nodded in silent greeting. At the same time, Mr. Boots sat nearby, absorbing the weak afternoon sunlight, ignoring the new arrivals, and contentedly grooming his private parts like a perverted contortionist.

Polly practically skipped to Merv's side. "Now would be a lovely time to see the rest of the grounds. Shall we have a bit of a wee tour?"

Merv checked his watch, then looked at the increasingly heavy sky. "Not much light left, mum," he said, hoping to stall her for yet another day.

"Not to worry," Polly said, presenting her smartphone. "We've all got flashlights, er, *torches*, in case we find ourselves tripping over hedgehogs." She opened the camera mode and took a candid picture of Merv, who smiled but seemed barely able to contain his irritation. Polly then started shooting frames of the castle courtyard with Tim and Tiara mugging for the lens. "These are definitely going to Barbra and Bette," she said. "And it's about time Cher was jealous of *me* for a change."

Reluctantly conscripted into service, Merv nonetheless offered a pleasant smile and ushered them around the castle grounds. He pointed out an ancient yew tree that he said was over five hundred years old and had been used for hanging witches and criminals. He escorted them through the ruins of the old chapel, the dovecote, battlements, and—finally—the potting shed. The shed was a dimly lit space with only a few rays of light penetrating the dirty windows. The scents of soil and fertilizer and the faint smell of cigarette smoke permeated the air. There, among the spades and shovels and bags of compost, Polly posed Merv at his worktable next to the grimy cobwebbed window. A glazed, hand-painted ceramic teapot with an ornate handle rested on the sill beside a coffee mug that said: *This Is My Happy Face Before Coffee.*

"And that, as they say, is the conclusion of the tour," Merv said, wiping his dirty hands on a dirtier rag. "It's been my great pleasure to show you around, mum. And please watch your step on the way out."

Polly suspected he was gently trying to get rid of her and the others as he offered a friendly wave, and they all headed back to the house.

At the entryway door, Gwellyn met them with an imperious attitude. They could instantly tell she wasn't in a chirpy mood. She seethed and noisily prepared the tea service. Polly flinched at the sound of delicate cups clashing with saucers, and she braced for what she suspected was an oncoming tense encounter. Gwellyn slammed a scone onto a plate and set it before Polly. Then she demanded to know what the plan was for her future service at Thistlethorne Lodge.

"Tell me right now what you're doing with this place and where I fit in," she said, arms crossed and her blood reaching a rolling boil. "We was told the estate won't pay our wages after the end of the month, and it's up to you whether we stay on or not."

Polly hated confrontations and glanced around for a diversion from the cranky housekeeper. "Oh, Tiara, sweetums! Drinky, please! Something bubbly," she sang out to her maid, who had wandered to the far end of the room expressly to keep her distance from what was a developing war of words. "Bring an extra glass of boob-*ly* for Gwellyn. And maybe some garlic or silver bullets or whatever you use when Harry and Megan visit."

Gwellyn's face was twisted into a snarl, her eyes flashing with anger. Her thin lips curled into a sneer, and Polly could see the tension in her jaw.

"I only want what's fair!" Gwellyn spat. "You, being a rich American, you can afford me. Sack Lily and Merv if you like, but I'm indispensable. I'm the only one who can make people in the village accept you. Get rid of me, and you may as well plan on not making any friends here. Arlene, down at the post office, is pretty creative when it comes to spreading mean rumors that I start."

Polly could feel the hairs on the back of her neck stand up. Gwellyn's anger was palpable, and she couldn't help feeling a bit of fear. She wondered what Gwellyn might do.

"Pitchforks and torches?" Polly gulped, taken aback by Gwellyn's attempt at intimidation. "Sweetums, seriously, I've never done well with ultimatums. They tend to make people realize my sugary-sweet image is pure baloney." Then she smiled and tried to give off a congenial air in a move meant to ease the tension. "Have a glass of sparklies with me, and we'll discuss this like intelligent international diplomats, shall we?" She hoped that she had a persuasive twinkle in her eyes.

"I don't do alcohol 'cept on New Year's Eve," Gwellyn hissed. "I'm just sayin' you need me. Old Mr. Drake said he'd provide... but he didn't mention one word about me in his will. And after all the work I done for him. And the secrets I kept."

Polly's mood softened just a trace. "Oh, goody. I love secrets almost as much as I love a fresh glass of bubbly." She held up her champagne glass and wiggled it at Tiara to remind her to hurry with the drink. "Are you telling me that Mr. Drake promised to put you in his will and then didn't?"

Gwellyn dabbed her dry eyes with the hem of her apron and fake-sniffled. "Not in so many words, I guess. More like, 'When I'm gone, you'll get what you deserve.' I just thought he meant that he'd leave me something. Maybe not the house, but a bit of money as a nest egg for me old age in Wales."

Polly took a sip of her drink, squared her shoulders, and regarded Gwellyn with circumspection. "Let me get this straight. You expected a windfall from dead Mr. Drake, and since the old man didn't cough up the dough, you think it's up to me to make amends?"

Gwellyn stood silent for a long moment, trying to figure out how best to make her case. "Not exactly," she grumbled. "Not when you put it like that, maybe. But it's not fair. And I'm right about being your ticket to people in the village acceptin' you." Her impudence returned. "This is how it works," she said, poking a fat finger into Polly's chest. "You treat me right proper, and I report that to all the gossipers down at the pub. Then they'll like you. You don't do so good and... well... " Gwellyn's voice trailed off. "Think about it. But don't take too long," she said, heading for the front hallway exit.

Polly took a deep breath, and her eyes narrowed. "Let me make something perfectly clear, Gwellyn. I will not tolerate any form of blackmail or threat, no matter how thinly veiled. I will treat you respectfully as long as you do your job and treat me the same. But if you ever try anything like this again, I won't hesitate to involve the authorities. Is that clear?"

Gwellyn turned around and crossed her arms. "You rich Americans think you're so entitled and can push everyone around and get your way. Well, you can't push me no further. I know what I deserve and won't rest until you do what's right. I'm tired and finished with being afraid of posh people just because they think they're important. Do you hear what I'm sayin'? Do you understand?"

Polly snort-laughed and rolled her eyes. "Oh, yeah, sweet-ums, I definitely understand. I understand probably better than you do. And I find it curious that this is how you negotiate a trade agreement. I have a larger-than-average aversion to bullies. Always have. If you're looking to retire early from your dusting duties, I'll happily arrange for you to sleep late for the rest of your life."

"And I don't respond so good to foreigners who come to my country and take away my job!" Gwellyn spat back. "It's time the king built us a wall like the one you had goin' on over where you come from to keep immigrants out."

"Out is exactly where you're going," Polly said. She opened the front door and shooed the housekeeper from the house. "Come back when you're ready to apologize... or resign."

Gwellyn's face was red with anger as she stormed away. She kicked a terracotta garden gnome, breaking it into pieces. When she reached the main gate, she raised a fist and shouted something unintelligible in Welsh.

"I'm rubber, you're glue... " Polly shouted back, confident that whatever Gwellyn said was probably mean-spirited.

The evening meal had been an uninspired combination of a margarita pizza and French fries that Tiara found in the freezer. They were all exhausted from the long day of traveling and still cheesed off from the altercation with Gwellyn. Although relatively early, when Polly decided it was time for bed, the others gladly followed her lead.

Instinctively appropriating the largest of the six bedrooms before Tim or Tiara could lay claim, Polly was lured by its antique four-poster mahogany bed with a moth-eaten embroidered canopy. She also admired the large Victorian chifforobe in the room, the elegant tri-mirror vanity, and the marble fireplace that looked not to have been used for decades. The chamber was carpeted with an ancient room-size but threadbare Oriental rug. The once-white vaulted ceiling was now a dull grayish color and literally falling apart, as evidenced by segments from the plaster-sculpted cornice littered on the floor. The faded and water-stained, rose-patterned wallpaper was peeling. Even the two floor-to-ceiling multipaned windows had wood frames and discolored and rotting sashes, and the glass was cracked in several places. The en suite bathroom boasted a deep Victorian clawfoot bathtub.

Polly looked around the room and rolled her eyes. She whispered in despair, "Only that Facebook billionaire guy has enough bucks to remodel this old dump and bring it up to date. I may as well rent it out to ghost hunters. So much for my stupid plans to haul in a fortune from tourists."

Tim's and Tiara's rooms weren't any better. Their beds were narrow and lumpy, with mismatched bedding that looked like it had been salvaged from a charity shop. Tiara's room was cluttered with old toys and stuffed animals heaped in the corner. Tim's room was even worse. The air was stale and musty, and the pillows looked like they'd been used as punching bags.

Despite the less-than-ideal conditions, it had been an exhausting day, and they were all too sleepy to care about anything more than setting their heads down on pillows.

Polly removed her makeup, brushed her teeth, and said her prayers. With her head bowed and her hands pressed together in supplication, she whispered, "Please, dear God, let me cash in on this pile and fly back to America with a trunk-load of cash." She sighed heavily as she switched off the light and lay down on her bed, feeling defeated.

As Polly lay in the darkness, she wondered how to turn Thistlethorne into the next *Escape to the Chateau*. She imagined the pots of money she could make with cameras following her every move as she transformed this dilapidated castle into a tourist hotspot. She could see herself wielding a rhinestone-encrusted hammer and looking glamorous as a team of sexy carpenters, painters, and stonemasonry people worked around her. As she drifted off to sleep, Polly felt a glimmer of hope. She smiled and thought, *Maybe this still can be my ticket to success. Or maybe Alistair Drake is laughing from the other side of life.*

4

———

"Which of you two chowderheads had the bad dream last night?" Polly sassed when she arrived in the breakfast room the next morning.

It was a dreary, gray day, and even with the light from the crystal chandelier hanging over the round mahogany table, the whole place seemed dull to the new mistress of the manor.

As she settled into her chair and lifted the glass of Prosecco that Tiara had set out, Polly said, "Is it too much to ask that Mr. Sandman fill your REMs with butterflies and puppies instead of axe murderers? You were loud enough to wake the zombies in the church graveyard last night!"

Tim and Tiara shared a look. "We were just talking about how noisy *you* were," Tim said. "What were you watching, *Federal Indictments: The Donald Trump Story*?"

"You're getting pretty good with the English accent, though," Tiara acknowledged. "The four-letter words were a bit unattractive, but you always sound that way when you're arguing with your agent about the paycheck for your next gig."

Polly pooh-poohed the idea that she'd been the cause of her

son's and maid's disturbed sleep. "I was dead until I got up for a wee at two. That's when I heard all the racket."

"I would have sworn it was from your side of the hallway," Tiara said, starting to rethink her initial accusation.

The trio looked at each other and simultaneously whispered, "Ghost?"

As Polly slathered boysenberry jam on a warm croissant, Lily came into the room looking as miserable as a Dickensian workhouse orphan.

"Excuse me, mum," she said, apprehensive about speaking directly to her employer. "Is Gwellyn taking the day off or something? She hasn't come in yet. I need someone to tell me what my duties are."

Polly rolled her eyes and picked up her Prosecco. "Maybe she's taking a mental health day—accent on mental."

"Or she's in the village stirring up trouble with the postmistress," Tiara suggested.

"Maybe raising a militia to storm the castle," Tim added.

"I called her phone, but she didn't answer," Lily continued. "Is it because she's mad that you won't give her any of Mr. Drake's money?"

Polly took another fortifying sip of her bubbly and turned to look directly at the young maid. "Is Gwellyn always as imperious as she was yesterday?" she asked, trying to sound nonthreatening and not frighten away the mouse Polly had decided was Lily's spirit animal.

"I don't know what that word means, mum. But if it's like malicious, malevolent, despicable, contemptible, obnoxious, vile, odious, and loathsome, then yeah, in that case, she is," Lily said as the others looked on in amusement at her thesaurus-like response.

"It's bad enough that our Tiara can be a bossy shrew. I simply can't work with another like her," Polly said.

"Shrew?" Tiara spat. "You're the dragon lady, not... "

"I said can be! *Can be!*" Looking again at Lily, Polly said, "I'll give Gwellyn a jingle. In the meantime, I'll be forever grateful if you'd be a doll and run along to the village and buy a bushel of white sage and a box of matches. This place needs a good smudging. There's too much negative energy hanging around."

With a quick curtsy, Lily retreated, and as Polly and her clan resumed their breakfast and chattered about ghosts, a sudden clap of thunder drew their attention to the window and the vile winter weather outside. Once again, Merv was wandering around the courtyard.

Too bad the climate here isn't more conducive to good-looking laborers taking off their shirts, Polly grumbled to herself. She felt drool forming at the corner of her mouth.

By noon, there was still no word from Gwellyn. Polly had phoned her a half-dozen times and finally called Solicitor Wainwright to get the lowdown on British law regarding the termination of troublesome servants.

"As a matter of fact, Gwellyn rang me yesterday," Wainwright said as Polly carped about the housekeeper's lousy attitude. "She accused you of being abusive and said she feared for her life. She wanted to know what recourse she had if you sacked her."

"She threatened me with extortion if I didn't hand over some of Mr. Drake's dough!" Polly said, dumbfounded by the accusation and denying the maid's allegations. "We had a disagreement," she said and clumsily tried to explain that Gwellyn was the one who instigated the row. When she'd finally hung up the phone, she looked up to find Lily trembling in the doorway.

"It's Gwellyn, mum," Lily said, wringing her hands and looking like she was about to wet her pants. "I know why she hasn't come to work."

"Yeah, yeah, I've heard all about it. She plans to file a lawsuit accusing me of harassment. But I'm a goddamned saint compared to some of my Hollywood friends. Tiara has chums in other houses whose employers wake them up in the middle of the night screaming for a bargain bucket of freakin' KFC hot wings, for crying out loud! One maid who works for a has-been talk show host was forced to wear a bell around her neck so her boss could hear when she was coming near. As if she were a cat or some sort of farm animal. If Gwellyn thinks she can assail my stellar reputation as one of the all-time nice people in showbiz, she has another thing coming."

"I think *another thing* already came," Lily said timidly. "Gwellyn's in the larder. She sorta looks like my aunt Maggie. My *dead* aunt Maggie."

5

The two-person Abbots Clover village police department, headed by twenty-something Constable Grayson Jenkins and assisted by Constable Ella Towers—who appeared old enough to be the younger policeman's grandmother—was still poking around the larder at Thistlethorne Lodge when teatime paused their investigation. Tiara brought in a tray with steaming mugs of tea and a basket of warm scones and set it on the larder's rickety workstation.

The larder was a small and dimly lit room, the walls lined with narrow shelves filled with jars of preserves and canned goods. The air was thick with the scent of mildew, and on the dusty and damp floor, like a macabre sculpture, was the body of Gwellyn Clogg, laid out serenely, as if she were merely sleeping.

Then they all watched as the medical examiner's assistants filled a black body bag with Gwellyn's corpse, zipped it up like a piece of soft-sided luggage, and lifted it onto a gurney. Gwellyn was rolled into the early evening darkness and disappeared behind the doors of a black van.

Everyone was silent, their faces grim. Polly could feel her heart pounding as she looked obliquely at the contingent from

Abbots Clover's finest. The police team and the American visitors took only a moment to size each other up. Constable Grayson Jenkins, the far younger of the two officers, looked nervous and uncertain. Constable Towers, a short, gray-haired woman who was at least seventy-something years old, looked stern and disapproving. Polly couldn't help whispering a quip to Tim and Tiara about the elderly constable. "Must be Bring Granny to Work Day," she said.

A provocative look shared between Tim and Constable Jenkins wasn't lost on Polly or Tiara. They could see the attraction between the two good-looking young men. Even Constable Towers's eyes darted between the two before sipping tea and offering disingenuous condolences to Polly.

Young Constable Jenkins stood in the larder, his uniform already collecting dust and cobwebs from the scene. Despite his grim task and trying to remain professional, his dimpled smile was wide and friendly.

"I love this castle!" he squealed with the enthusiasm of a kid choosing his first puppy. "I've lived in Abbots Clover all my life, and Mr. Drake hated us kids because we used to sneak onto the property and play on the battlements. We pretended we were kings and knights and invaders. I always wanted to see the inside of the house. It was my dream to get maybe someday rich enough to buy Thistlethorne Lodge for myself!"

Tim's smile matched Constable Jenkins's, and he eagerly offered to show the officer around Polly's new house. "It's no problem at all. Really! Right, Mom?" Tim practically begged.

"Cracking!" Jenkins said, as if he were excited to be invited for a sleepover at a friend's house.

"But don't be gone long; you've got a report to file," Constable Towers said with a smirk, knowing that her colleague was besotted with the castle—and obviously with one of its new residents, too.

"And make sure he eats his vegetables and washes behind his ears," Polly cracked as if the two young men were setting off to summer camp instead of a house tour.

Constable Towers set down her mug and carefully looked around the dusty larder. She groaned, her eyes drifting to cracks in the tiled floor.

"Looks like the old girl had been there for a good ten or so hours," she said, taking in the full view of the cold room that had once served the house as a place to keep easily spoiled foods preserved longer before modern refrigeration in the early twentieth century. "Heart problems run in Gwellyn's family," she continued, having formed a sense of Gwellyn's probable cause of death. "Her older brother, Clive, had a bum ticker, too. She buried him just last year. Poor thing hasn't been able to catch a break lately. Mr. Drake died and didn't leave her a penny. Then she lost her job 'cause you sacked her. Now she's dead. A pity."

"She didn't lose her job," Polly corrected. "I didn't fire her."

"That so? I was in for a pint at the Fox & Hare yesterday, and I heard you even threatened to kill her. Said she'd be sleeping in late for the rest of her life."

Polly's body tensed. "A figure of speech." She held herself upright as she spoke, her shoulders squared and her chin raised defiantly. She made eye contact with the constable, determined to demonstrate strength. "Truth be told, Gwellyn and I had a bit of a discussion about her job. She wasn't sure she wanted to stay on now that I'd moved in. But I didn't terminate her. If I had, why would she still be in the house?" Polly's words were measured and controlled, but her body language betrayed her anxiety.

Constable Towers shrugged. "Maybe she came back for a letter of reference."

"In the middle of the night?" Tiara scoffed.

"Just a guess," Towers said, ignoring Tiara's observation. "It hardly matters since the poor thing's dead."

Polly bristled at the constable's dismissive attitude. "It matters to me. I'm not wild about former employees entering my house in the middle of the night while I'm sleeping."

"You just said she wasn't sacked, so she wasn't technically a former employee," Towers reminded her, giving Polly a suspicious look. "But if it happens again, call us. Since she's with the angels now, she's probably done here."

"Probably," Polly parroted the policewoman and rolled her eyes. After a moment, remembering the corpse's condition, she asked, "What did you think about the red rash on the back of her right hand?"

"I noticed that. Probably just a scrape," Constable Towers said. "I had a case of dermatitis once, and it looked a bit like that. Or maybe she scratched it on the jagged edge of the workstation when she collapsed. You should get that fixed. It looks dangerous."

"Don't you think the body's position was a bit curious?" Polly continued. "She was lying on her back with her arms by her sides, laid out so neatly. I was on the set of *Hell's Bells* when Mark Grubin had his heart attack and died. He fell into a crumpled heap. Gwellyn looked more like she was taking a siesta."

"Well, it was nighttime," said Constable Towers, who seemed bored by Polly's layperson suggestion that something nefarious might have happened to Gwellyn. "We can leave it at that."

"You know best," Polly said, indulging the policewoman but not having the slightest belief in Towers's unsuspicious pronouncement. "When the boys are finished exploring the house—and whatever else grabs their attention—I'll summon the crossing guard to make sure Constable Jenkins gets escorted safely home," Polly added sarcastically. "Now, if you'll excuse us, we have a moat to fill."

6

"We've only been in England a few days, and already the UK welcome wagon has dumped a stiff on our doorstep," Polly pouted as she finished the toad in the hole that Tiara had prepared for dinner (to prove she could cook something typically English). She impatiently tapped her pink acrylic nails against her champagne flute, indicating it was time to uncork a fresh bottle.

"At least it wasn't another murdered body, like last time. And the time before that. And the one before that," Tim said vaguely, alluding to his mother's innate talent for matching dead bodies with homicidal maniacs back in Hollywood as he fruitlessly wandered around the dining room with his iPhone, searching for a Wi-Fi signal. "Gwellyn actually looked kind of good, in a buh-bye-to-life-it-was-fun-while-it-lasted sort of way."

"On the bright side, this time, you can simply send a sympathy card instead of a 'Go Directly to Jail... Do Not Pass Go' Monopoly card for a sentence of twenty-five to life," Tiara added.

"Don't be so quick to make cause-of-death assumptions like Constable Towers," Polly said as she replayed in her head the scene of finding Gwellyn on the cold stone floor, her vacant open eyes staring into the nothingness of death. "Gwellyn's heavy woolen coat had been buttoned up as if she had just arrived at the castle or was about to leave, her black leather purse by her side, and an umbrella rested against the wall next to the door leading into the courtyard. I'm still wondering what the hell Gwellyn was doing here in the middle of the night."

As Tiara began pouring Polly's liquid sunshine, she picked up her boss's line of thought. "Constable Towers had no interest in speculating about the whys and wherefores of Gwellyn ending up dead in our house. She probably just wants to close the book and move on to retirement. But that's sort of unfair to Gwellyn. Especially if you think a helping hand pulled her into the afterlife."

Tim smiled mischievously, sipped his bubbly, and said, "Grayson—I mean Constable Jenkins—confided in me that Constable Towers isn't really Constable Towers. I mean, she's Towers—Ella Towers—but she's not really part of the village police force. No one else around here wants to join the department 'cause it's so damn boring in Abbots Clover. So when he gets a call about hedgehogs on a rampage—or dead bodies in a castle larder—he calls friends to help. Ella gets a kick out of pinning on a badge. But he says she's pretty clueless and probably thinks that misdemeanor is a drag queen's name."

"She acted as if Gwellyn coming into the house in the middle of the night was no more unusual than plugging in the kettle and getting boiling water for tea." Tiara sighed with a hint of indignation. "I didn't appreciate her condescending attitude. If she's not a real policewoman, she has no business making official judgments about dead people and how they got that way."

"I should call Grayson—I mean *Constable Jenkins*," Tim said with a twinkle in his eyes, recalling the flutter of excitement he'd felt every time he accidentally on purpose brushed his arm against the constable. "He's the man in charge, and he can answer a ton of important questions."

"Like, does he have a boyfriend?" Tiara smirked.

Tim smiled rakishly. The two were adept at playfully teasing each other about their various paramours and offering tongue-in-cheek observations that made light of their respective hopeless romanticism—and utter incompetence in finding lasting love.

The evening had turned to night, and the dishes were washed and put away. As the lack of a reliable broadband connection made watching cable television futile, there was nothing for the trio to do other than read a book, play a game of solitaire, or go to bed. They opted for the latter.

As Polly and Tim went to their respective rooms, Tiara walked through the house, checking that the doors and windows were secured. The old castle seemed to come alive at night with creaks and groans that sounded like ghostly whispers, and she couldn't shake off the feeling that someone, or *something*, was watching her from the shadows. Along the way, she turned off lamps and tried not to think about ghosts and demons. As she wandered through the suddenly spooky reception room, her attention was drawn to the mullioned windows, and she nearly freaked out when she saw a flashlight beam moving through the courtyard. She froze in place as she cautiously watched it sweep the castle's courtyard and interior walls, like a lantern from a lighthouse guiding seafarers away from rocky coastlines. It was impossible to see who held the light, but she quickly decided it had to be Merv, the gardener and handyman, making his last rounds for the day. Tiara cautiously exhaled a deep breath she'd unconsciously held, then walked toward the lighted stairway leading to the bedrooms, wondering if she truly was alone. She ascended the steps more quickly than she would have in the daytime, then tapped on Polly's door.

"No loud dreams tonight about your nincompoop agent or killer maids gone berserk, please," she said. "We all need our beauty sleep."

"My thoughts exactly," Polly said as she tied the belt to her bathrobe and looked into Tiara's drowsy eyes. She paused momentarily, reluctant to say what was on her mind. "You know I don't believe in ghosts... but... "

"But something strange really did happen last night." Tiara was less skeptical about spirits visiting from beyond the grave.

They were suddenly distracted by the sound of a door opening down the hallway. It was Tim. Wearing only the drawstring bottoms of his PJs, he wandered to their side. "Mummy, I'm scared," he said in a little boy's sleepy voice. "I'm hearing strange noises in my room."

"Probably your stomach," Tiara said, taking the opportunity to pat Tim's six-pack abs and admire his young, gym-pumped physique.

"Seriously, sweetums, put on a bathrobe," Polly said, although she secretly appreciated the time and effort that went into making Tim clickbait on his dating apps.

"I'm serious about the scary noises," Tim insisted. "I thought they were from you two fooling around. But you're way down here, and the noises are coming from the room next to mine."

"There isn't a room next to yours," Polly said.

"Exactly!" Tim agreed.

"What sort of noises?" Tiara asked. "Like the ones from last night?"

"Those were more like someone begging for their life from Tony Soprano. These are more like angry rats. Or old plumbing.

Or that shouty lady who calls herself a judge and sounds like a chainsaw with a law degree I saw when I accidentally tuned in to *FOX News* one night. Whatever it is, it's freaking me out."

From the moment Polly and her troupe arrived at Thistlethorne Lodge, they'd heard odd sounds stored within the house. They'd chalked up the groans and whispers to its age and the peculiarities that came as standard features with older buildings, especially ones that were literally a thousand years old. The noises they investigated could usually be attributed to the old boiler, air in the water pipes, or tree branches scraping against windows. They knew there was a credible source for every tap, rap, and thump. The abnormal had quickly become normal to them.

Polly surrendered her longing for her pillow and glanced down the hallway toward Tim's room. "Mummy will check for monsters and deranged US senator types hiding under your bed," she said as she cautiously led the others to investigate the origin of Tim's anxiety.

Tim's room was lightly furnished: marble-top nightstands on either side of a four-poster bed, a dressing table, a chifforobe, and a large, gilt-framed mirror that hung above the granite fire-place mantel. When they entered the room, the trio stopped beside the bed and listened silently. Expectantly. They looked around at the peeling, water-stained wallpaper and the worn and deteriorating brocade curtains hanging in the window. They tried to tune their hearing to a frequency the undead might use to communicate with the living. Polly could hear her own heart beating. Tim looked at Tiara, whose neck clicked when she cocked her head. After several minutes of hearing only their own breathing and the distant muted tick-tock of the grandfather clock down the hall, they decided that whatever Tim had heard was only in his imagination. Tim admitted that he might have been in that state between consciousness and dreaming about Constable Jenkins. Now, he couldn't be sure that he'd really heard anything at all.

"False alarm. I'm off to Dreamland," Polly finally said, rolling her eyes and giving up the chase. "George Clooney won't come to me until my eyes are closed." She turned and started to move toward the door. Then an unexpected sound caught everyone's attention, and Polly abruptly froze mid-step. "What the—" She tilted her head toward a faint scratching noise that seemed to be coming from behind the fireplace.

"That's the sound!" Tim murmured. "I knew I didn't dream it."

Something was definitely behind the wall, and the scratching became bolder and more insistent. The trio stood rooted in place.

For the first time in ages, Polly was genuinely afraid of something other than a theater critic or a bill from the Liquor Locker. She looked at Tim and Tiara, then at the fireplace. "Remember *The Exorcist*?" she whispered. "The mother of the kid whose head twisted like it was possessed by a demented chiropractor thought the sounds over the ceiling were from rats in the attic? We know how that turned out."

Tim gingerly approached the fireplace and touched the stone mantel, as if he could better hear the sounds through his fingertips. He glanced up at the mirror and saw his own tense expression reflected, as well as Polly and Tiara, with their arms protectively enfolding each other. Listening intently, he followed the sound with his eyes. For a short while, the noise faded to near silence. Then it came to life again with a mad vengeance. He was fairly sure that the sound was coming from within the built-in firewood cabinet beside the fireplace. He glanced at the decorative fireplace tool set and lifted an iron poker from the stand. Tim gripped the handle tightly and fixed the hooked tip over the pull knob on the cabinet door. He gave a gentle tug, and the door squeaked open on ancient hinges. But the cabinet was empty of all but dust and cobwebs and probably hadn't been used for wood storage since the fireplace was closed off during the Victorian era.

With the cabinet door now open, the sound became slightly louder and more insistent. Cautiously and with beads of sweat forming in the cleft of his chest, Tim guided the poker rod into the space. He dabbed it to the back wall of the shallow enclosure and gently tapped the wall. The baffling sound stopped, as if whatever lay beyond was pondering how to respond to a potential threat. Tim sensed from the way the back wall moved slightly against the heavy poker that it was not very stable, more like a temporary or improvised barrier that might easily give way. Now, pressing with only a bit more pressure, he felt the barrier relax. Then it fell back.

In that very instant, exploding like the pop of an old flashbulb, a dark mass shot forward, forcing everyone to scatter and take cover. "Jesus, Joseph, and Mary!" Polly shrieked as she clutched Tiara and buried her face in her maid's bosom. Tim, too, freaked out and huddled in the fetal position on the floor next to the bed, making wounded-animal sounds.

For a long moment, no one moved. They were waiting for the beast or ghost or Satan himself to attack and maybe shred them to bits or drag them down into the fires of hell.

But then... slowly... cautiously... they risked opening their eyes a fraction and peered out from behind fingers splayed over their faces. And then they saw it.

Polly, Tim, and Tiara screamed in unison.

"Mr. Boots!"

"It's the damned cat!" Tim yelled.

"How did... He must have been trapped in the wall!" Tiara added.

The trio's relief at surviving what they had been certain was something rising from the Kingdom of the Dead was instantly followed by nervous laughter at the cat for exploiting their fears and proving them all to be cowardly sissies. They just as quickly questioned how Mr. Boots could have gotten trapped in the wall in the first place.

Tim grabbed his cell phone from the nightstand and tapped the flashlight icon. He returned to the firewood cabinet and directed the beam inside. He was astounded. A narrow stone corridor lay beyond where the cabinet's back panel had fallen away.

"I think it's a secret passageway! How cool is that?"

7

———

Morning arrived, and when Tim got to the breakfast table, Polly was already well into her second Prosecco.

"I had a restless night," he complained as he sipped orange juice.

"Lancelot or Galahad?" Polly taunted.

"Not restless *knight*," Tim snarled. "I didn't sleep a wink! I kept dreaming about never-ending mazes and Yeti-size cockroaches stalking me and that wacko Disney Studios exec you made me date last year because you thought he might give you a job."

"Then you obviously slept," Tiara said, setting a silver basket with warm muffins and croissants before him.

While stroking Mr. Boots on her lap, Polly drained her glass and looked at her son and maid. "I didn't sleep well either and came to a decision," she announced, setting the cat down. "No time to waste. I have a mission! We have to explore that passageway. Something tells me we're in for a big surprise!"

"You sound like you mean surprise, as when a piece of junk sells for big bucks on that TV antique auction show you watch.

Not like, surprise, Charles Manson is hiding behind the dresses in your closet," Tim said as he rejected his mother's idea and imagined all the potential horrors that awaited anyone foolish enough to venture inside the passageway. "What if it's cursed like Egyptian pharaohs' tombs?"

"Spirits never find it amusing when you disturb their eternal resting places," Tiara agreed, hoping Polly would reconsider probing the mysterious space. "It might be like one of those escape rooms with puzzles and clues, and you can't get out without the right combination of answers."

"Nonsense. It's a secret passageway, and you know how I love secrets." Polly pooh-poohed their fears. "We'll probably be the first humans to go there since the Dark Ages. It can't be any scarier than I hear it is working for Prince Andrew."

Once Polly Pepper set her mind to do something, there was no use in trying to dissuade her, and the trio ultimately assembled in Tim's bedroom a short while later. For a long moment, they timidly stared at the firewood cabinet.

"Don't be a snowflake," Polly said, nudging Tim.

Tim shuddered at the thought of what might lie ahead in the dark tunnel. He reluctantly opened the firewood cabinet door and felt a creeping sense of dread as the sound of ancient, rusted hinges filled the room. He tapped the flashlight icon on his phone and peered beyond the wooden closet. Tim ducked his head and set a tentative foot into the narrow space. The ceiling was low, apparently built to accommodate the shorter heights of people who lived many centuries ago. He marveled at the engineering that enabled the construction of something so clever in an age that didn't have twenty-first-century building tools, and crept along the passageway. In one hand, he held his cell phone.

With the other, he braced himself against the rough stone wall for support. Polly followed closely behind, her heart pounding as if she were about to go onstage before an audience of thousands.

"Steps!" Tim alerted his mother, his flashlight beam dancing along the rough, uneven walls. "They look steep." The rise between the stone steps was inconsistent, and mouse or rat droppings and candle stubs with blackened wicks were evidence that rodents and humans had preceded them in the not-too-distant past.

"Timmy, dear," Polly said, spitting and wiping her face with her sleeve, "I just got a mouthful of a spiderweb. Warn me if you see the fella that makes his home here."

As they continued their descent, Polly divided her attention between the steps and scanning the space for crawling things. She nervously started humming *The Time Warp*.

"*The Rocky Horror Show* probably isn't the best musical to think about in a place like this," Tim suggested. "Try something optimistic. '*I Will Survive*' comes to mind."

Suddenly, a bat flew out of nowhere, causing Polly to shriek and reach for Tim's arm. "Good Lord, I'd hoped we wouldn't run into any of those damned flying rodents!" she said with a shiver.

"They're harmless. I think. Unless it's Lestat." Tim tried to reassure his mother as he continued to scan the corridor with his phone's light.

Polly's heart was pounding as they moved forward, and her palms were sweating. "Why'd I let you talk me into this?" she said, as if the investigation had been Tim's idea. Just then, a rat scurried down the steps past them, and Polly screamed.

Tim shone his light on the critter as it disappeared into the darkness. "Only a rat."

"The size of a goddamned dachshund!"

A moment later, Tim excitedly announced, "I see something up ahead! It looks like... It's a door!"

Polly and Tim were soon standing on a stone landing facing an old arched door set into the passageway's thick stone wall. The tunnel continued down to the left, but they stopped to inspect this portal.

Tim trained the beam of light on the door's large rusted-iron hardware. There wasn't a knob, only a keyhole. He pushed against the door, but it didn't budge. "Locked."

"Knock and see if anyone's home," Polly said, just as another bat flew out of nowhere and grazed her hair. "Holy Mary, Mother of God!" she yelled and ducked to avoid being bombed again. Her heart rate increased. She began to sweat. She felt trapped. "Sweetums, I think I made a wee boo-boo. They've given us enough notice that we're not wanted here. I think you were right about pharaohs and mummy curses! Let's forget about what's behind the door! It probably leads to Harvey Weinstein's audition room. Get me out of here!"

Then they heard muffled voices from the other side of the door. Although they were eager to return to the safety of the bedroom up the stairs, they froze in place and listened. They couldn't decipher much, only muted fragments of a conversation. The only words they could distinctly comprehend were *Gwellyn... dead... murder*.

"Someone is definitely home," Polly said.

By the time they retraced their steps and returned to Tim's bedroom, Polly was hysterical. She was panting and blowing their experience out of proportion.

"Dead people coming alive!" she gasped breathlessly to Tiara. "Vampires and rats this big." She opened her arms in wild exaggeration. "A door that probably leads directly to Donald Trump's bathroom!"

"Actually, sort of a letdown," Tim said, dismissing his mother's drama-school histrionics. "Mainly cobwebs and mice."

"Easy for you to say," Polly spat. "You weren't the one with tarantulas crawling up your nose!"

Tim rolled his eyes. "But we found a door that could prove interesting," he said. "Judging from the direction we traveled, I'd say it probably opens into the larder. By the way, you weren't just down there talking to Merv, were you? We heard voices on the other side of the door."

Tiara shook her head and said she hadn't moved from the bedroom the whole time they were gone in case she was called for assistance. "Perhaps Lily was singing along to the radio. You know how she fancies herself the next Masked Singer."

Soon, they were all back at the scene of Gwellyn's death in the larder, looking for the door Polly and Tim had discovered in the passageway. A dim light leeched through the dirty, cobwebbed window. In their respective memories, they could see Gwellyn's plump body lying lifeless on the floor.

"If only Mr. Spider over there could talk," Polly commented absently, pointing to the upper-left corner of the filthy window frame.

Polly's eyes suddenly caught the reflective glint from a shiny piece of lacquered ceramic lying on the floor next to tall wooden shelving containing jars of homemade pickled vegetables and assorted soup cans. Stooping down to examine the glossy white fragment, she could see it was intricately painted with tiny blue flowers.

"Perhaps part of a handle to something," she said. "Broken off from something like a serving dish, maybe." She absently placed it in her cardigan pocket and then noticed scrape marks on the stone floor in front of the shelves. "What do you make of this?" she said, pointing to the grazing that looked like the arc made by a wiper blade on a windshield.

"It looks as if something heavy has been dragged over the floor. Like maybe these shelves were moved," Tim said. He looked at Tiara and, with a shrug, indicated that they should see if it was possible to move the shelves. They put their shoulders into it and forced the heavy furniture away from the wall. It wasn't easy, but it was well worth the effort.

"A door!" Polly exclaimed.

"I knew it!" Tim noted. "It's gotta be the one we saw from the passageway!"

"There's something scratched in the wood," Tiara said, moving closer to the door and squinting at the letters. "*Abandon all hope, ye who enter here.*"

"Not very original," Tim added. "Dante came up with that first. Let's find the key."

Although they searched behind institution-size bags of rice and potatoes and under empty plant pots and small wicker baskets scattered about the room, no key was found.

Tiara left the larder to fetch Lily. When they returned, the young maid looked confused. "Sorry, mum, I don't know anything about a key to a hidden door," she said in panic. "But you might find what you want on here." From the deep pocket in her apron, she produced a jailer's key ring containing a dozen keys of various shapes and sizes—some ancient and rusting. "They're Gwellyn's."

However, after trying each one, Polly scowled. "Keys for everything but my heart and this damned door!"

"Who else has keys to the doors at Thistlethorne?" Tim asked. "Merv surely."

"He's off today," Lily said.

"Call him," Polly insisted.

Lily shook her head. "He doesn't have a mobile. He says cell phones cause lower sperm counts and brain tumors. Plus, he doesn't want to be at anyone's beck and call."

"Maybe he keeps the keys in the potting shed," Polly suggested as she left the larder and ventured into the courtyard. She made a beeline for the gardener's outbuilding, with the others trailing close behind. When she reached the old, vine-covered wooden structure, the door was unlocked, and she noticed that the hasp and padlock that would have secured it had been removed, leaving empty holes in the door frame where the screws would have been.

Polly pulled the door handle and peered inside. The dusty interior was cold and garnished with cobwebs and a few wayward snails on the walls. Among the shovels, hoes, and assorted gardening tools were several pairs of Wellington boots and half-filled bags of compost. For a flash of a second, Polly asked herself what was different about the shed from her first visit. She just as quickly dismissed the idea that anything was out of place. After all, she'd only been there once before and couldn't possibly know if a rake or a watering can wasn't in its usual place. Still, her impression registered in her thoughts.

Polly turned around and threw her hands up. "There's a key to that darn door somewhere! And why is Merv taking the day off?"

"He's always off on Wednesdays," Lily said. "And Sundays, too. He says he visits his mum, but I think that's just his name for the pub because he says that beer is like mother's milk. And I know he doesn't go to the village graveyard. That's where his mother really lives."

"Raising a glass to mum, is he? I think it's time for a pint for me, too!" Polly said.

The wooden sign hanging above the front entrance to the pub read:

Fox & Hare
Public House
Est. 1728

As Polly and her troupe entered the establishment, they were met with the comforting smell of old ale and smoke from a crackling fire. The lone patron, Merv, sat perched on a stool at the bar, his handsome face illuminated by the warm glow. The space was cozy and populated with a dozen wooden tables and an assortment of mismatched chairs. Molded wood-panel walls were adorned with paintings of hunting dogs, crowned royalty, and framed photographs of famous footballers at championship matches. All of this added to the vintage charm of the place.

Polly sidled up to the gardener. "Unwinding on your day off, eh?" she said, looking at Merv, who was nursing a pint of Guinness.

A warm smile instantly spread across Merv's unshaven face, crinkling the corners of his bright blue eyes. He quickly set down his pint and rose from his stool.

"Hello, mum!" he said enthusiastically. "Oh, I hope you don't mind me takin' me usual day off. I know we hadn't discussed it."

"You deserve a day off now and then." Polly smiled and assured Merv she didn't want to disrupt the status quo.

"Oh, thank you, mum. I shouldn't have presumed. But I did have a lot of personal chores to do."

"Absolutely. And no one deserves a day of rest more than you and God. I see how hard you work."

Merv nodded gratefully. "I appreciate that, mum. Is there something you need me to take care of for you?"

Polly plowed on. "Look," she started again, "I know it's your day off, but I wonder if you would please let me borrow the key to the door in the larder."

Merv stopped to think for a moment. He twisted his mouth in contemplation. "You mean the door to the outside? We haven't had a key to that door in ages. Don't really need one since we're behind fortified walls."

"No, not the door *into* the larder. The door that was hidden behind the shelves of pickled veg. Nothing stays a secret from me for long. You'll find that out in due course. I just need the key to unlock it. I'm the curious type."

Merv considered the question again and finally shook his head. "A door behind the shelves of pickled veg? Mum, I've been at Thistlethorne for twenty years. I would know if there was a hidden door to a secret passageway. It's news to me."

"Then you should be super excited to see what we've found," Polly said. "Come back and have a look."

For a fraction of a moment, it was clear that Merv was weighing his loyalty to his Guinness and to his job. Finally, he smiled and said, "I'll just get my coat."

When Merv walked into the larder and saw the exposed ancient wooden door, he offered a short whistle of surprise. "Cor blimey," he said, then added a "crikey" for good measure.

"The key?" Polly suggested. "We tried the old 'Knock, knock, who's there? Lettuce. Lettuce who? Lettuce in, it's cold out here!' But no one answered."

"I'm sorry, mum, but I don't have no key. I didn't even know that the door was there. Isn't that amazing?"

Polly's face fell with disappointment. "Yes. Amazing. You're the gardener and handyman for Thistlethorne. If you don't have the key, who else would?"

"I don't rightly know, mum. Maybe the key was lost a long time ago, and someone decided since they couldn't get in there, they'd just put the shelves in front so they wouldn't be reminded of it. And then, eventually, they forgot. Or maybe it was the ghost again. It likes playing hide-and-seek with us mortals. Keys and candlesticks are its favorites."

"Of course. Right after dinner, we'll hold a séance!" Polly snapped in frustration. She caught herself and apologized for being so impatient. "I'm sorry," she said. "I just confirm where I think the door leads."

Merv smiled, relieved that Polly wasn't angry with him. "I'm happy to help however I can, mum, but this one's a head-scratcher for sure."

With that, Merv made his way out of the larder and back to enjoying his day off. Polly stood there momentarily, lost in thought, wondering about the door and its secrets.

8

It was nearly teatime when Polly's thoughts drifted to the secret passageway again, and she remembered that it hadn't stopped at the larder door but continued farther down into the depths of the castle.

"Sweetums," she called out to Tim, "do your loving mummy a *flavor*? Take me back into the passageway."

"Now?" Tim had just found a Wi-Fi signal and was absorbed in his Plunder dating app. He was texting with someone in London and was irritated by having to divide his attention between his mother and *PrinceAlbert4U*. He looked at Polly, incredulous. "You were terrified of that place this morning."

"You've forgotten the bats and rats the size of Mack trucks?" Tiara reminded her. "I don't want you to get hurt. You're like Dorothy wandering into the Wicked Witch of the West's castle."

Polly sniggered. "Please, I'm more like Elphaba than Dorothy. And let's be honest, I'm no stranger to danger," she said, channeling her inner Indiana Jones. "I faced Karl Stephen's halitosis when I did *The Phantom of the Opera*. And I survived those two talentless twits who played Roxy and Velma in that road production of *Chicago* I did a few years ago. After those experiences, everything else is a walk in the park."

"But you were scared out of your wits this morning!" Tiara said.

Polly's mind flashed back to the hair-raising ordeal of navigating the castle's secret passageway earlier in the day, and she could feel her heart racing as she contemplated returning to the unknown depths below. "Hell, life in general scares me! But I'm like Patti LuPone when an audience member took a photo during a show, and she snatched their phone out of their hand and kept on going. She didn't let a minor distraction stop her from delivering a killer performance. I won't be deterred by a scary castle."

Tim clapped his hands in approval. "That's the spirit! Like my hero Hugh Jackman when he injured himself while onstage in *The Boy from Oz*. He kept going until the end of the show!"

As the family's factotum, Tiara was expected to support Boss Lady in every way, regardless of her preferred agenda. Whatever Polly wanted, Polly got. And at this moment, Polly wanted to know where the passageway led.

Polly dismissed Tiara's suggestion that they wait until morning, and re-entered the narrow passageway with Tim. When they reached the landing by the door, Tim pointed the light beam from his smartphone farther down into the maw and felt a shiver move through his body.

"What's so scary about a place where no one's been for probably hundreds of years?" Polly tut-tutted to drive away their nervousness. "The door in the larder was locked, so the boogeyman obviously hasn't gotten in."

"Or maybe never got out," Tim said, not the least bit comforted by Polly's faux optimism.

Farther down the steps, they soon reached a vaulted chamber. The place smelled of mildew, and the light from his phone showed that the dirt floor was damp. Looking around, they discovered two jail cells with rusted, flat metal bars.

"The dungeon," Tim surmised, anxiety coating his words.

As they examined the stone walls and domed ceiling, Polly was drawn to something totally unexpected in one of the cells. "Who knew they had plastic a thousand years ago?" she said in amazement.

"They didn't," Tim said, following his mother's gaze and shining his light into the cell. "And certainly not a plastic grocery bag that says *Sainsbury's Finest*. Your theory that no one's been here for centuries is slightly off."

Polly cautiously approached the orange bag and poked it with her finger. When nothing inside moved, she slowly pulled it open.

"Hold the light steady," she complained. And an instant later, she shrieked, "Buried treasure!"

Tim brought the light closer and peered into the bag. "Looks like the stuff Solicitor Wainwright said went missing from Mr. Drake, and Gwellyn claimed the ghost had taken."

"A ghost with the eye of an insurance appraiser," Polly said, examining each item.

She retrieved an antique gold pocket watch, a diamond stick-pin, an antique brooch inlaid with precious gems, an engraved gold cigarette case, a pair of onyx cufflinks with diamonds in the center, and a postcard-size oil painting of an arched wooden bridge over a pond of water lilies.

"What are all these things doing way down here?" Polly asked.

"Phantoms need a safe place to stash stolen loot, too. Like the toilets at Mar-a-Lago," Tim said.

"Phantoms, my ass," Polly scoffed as she quickly refilled the bag and led the way back up the steps with her spoils.

"We found the Crown Jewels!" Polly squealed to Tiara as she dumped out the bag's contents like a haul of Halloween candy. "Finders keepers!" she insisted when Tiara challenged the idea of turning the items over to the police. "Mr. Drake's will explicitly said that Thistlethorne Lodge was all mine. That includes everything inside. So I don't see any reason to tell Mr. Wainwright, Constable Cutie, or anybody else about this discovery."

"Solicitor Wainwright said that Mr. Drake reported to the police that things had been stolen over the past year," Tiara reminded her. "He even gave you a list. He said that the castle and its furnishings were yours. Mr. Drake left his money and ephemera to various charities. That's pretty much everything that doesn't have a stuffed cushion or isn't hanging on the walls. And certainly not this," she said, picking out a key ring containing three keys.

Polly snatched the key ring back from Tiara and took a long look at it. "Maybe these go to a safe or a locked box hidden somewhere," she said, her avaricious eyes wide with the thought of even more treasures to be discovered. "Or maybe there's a secret room somewhere with a thousand years' worth of jewels and... *ephemera*."

"Or maybe—" Tiara stopped mid-thought.

Tim finished their maid's thought as he looked at the largest, oldest, and heaviest of the keys. "Maybe one of these goes to the door in the passageway." The trio looked at each other, telepathically relaying the same thought, and then made tracks for the larder.

When they entered the space where, centuries ago, easily spoiled foods were kept for longer-lasting preservation, they were cold and shivering in their cardigans. Polly held the bow of the largest key on the ring at the old door and inserted the blade into the lockbox hole. She held her breath... then turned the shank. The bolt slipped back into its casing.

"Voila!" she exclaimed and stepped aside for Tim to give the door a push.

It was heavier than expected, and when the door was finally open, Tim illuminated the revealed space with the torchlight from his phone.

"Why would someone lock themselves *inside* the passageway?" Polly asked.

Tiara gave Polly a look that suggested the question was dumb.

"No, she's right," Tim said. "We found that stuff in the dungeon cell... on the other side of a locked door!"

After a long moment, Polly stopped to consider the observation. "Whoever stashed the bag of goodies in the dungeon is either still in the passageway... or got out some other way."

"The firewood cabinet in Tim's room!" Tiara said.

"Yeah, I'm definitely not sleeping in there ever again," Tim said, his eyes growing wide with the idea of an uninvited someone sneaking into his room through the wood cabinet to murder him during the night. "Why did we have to inherit a creepy old castle in the first place? I was happy just cruising around Malibu and dating the UCLA football team."

"Think of all the Instagram content you can get from this place, *#CreepyCastle* or *#Zombies*," Polly said. "You'll be dining out on stories of spooky English castles and ghosts for years. Your friends'll eat it up!"

"If zombies from the dungeon don't eat me up first," Tim protested, ducking out of the passageway and back into the larder. "#ImASnowflakeSonOfACelebrityPleaseSaveMyAss!"

~

By the time Tiara had served Polly's first evening bottle of champagne, a dense fog had enveloped the castle. Polly was morose. She sat on the Chesterfield settee, stroking Mr. Boots's black silky fur and listening to the steady rain pelting the windows. She sighed and wondered aloud, "How the hell did Mr. Boots get into the passageway yesterday if the firewood cabinet door was closed and the larder door to the passageway was locked?"

"Maybe Gwellyn went into the passageway when she was here the last night of her life, and Mr. Boots followed her," Tim said. "She came out, locked the door... then died, leaving Mr. Boots trapped."

"But how could Gwellyn have gotten in if the key was in the bag down in the dungeon?" Tiara asked.

The trio tried piecing together different theories, but Polly's frustration was evident. "We literally saw Gwellyn lifeless on the floor. The shelving had concealed the entrance, so it's plausible she wasn't aware the passageway even existed." Polly paused, deep in thought. "Consider this," she began, her voice marked with determination. "Gwellyn wasn't exactly my biggest fan. She might've entered the house to confront me, or worse, hurt me. But what if she had a heart attack just then, as the police think, and passed away? It's possible, I guess."

Tiara quickly chimed in, "Gwellyn was a troublemaker. She wanted to make your life hell. Maybe she came back to the castle to spook us! Then she heard those strange noises, which scared her to death."

Polly considered Tiara's idea for a long moment. "I still don't totally buy the heart-attack scenario. And I suspect she was tough enough to brave a ghost or two. The only things for certain are a dead Gwellyn, a sack full of booty belonging to Mr. Drake, a secret passageway in an ancient castle, and a key to a locked door. Who else smells eau d'Agatha Christie?"

9

Polly burst into Tim's room in the middle of the night, shaking him awake.

Tim shot up in bed, his eyes bulging with panic and confusion. "Wha? What's wrong? If it's the Tooth Fairy, I want a tenner this time!" As Tim regained consciousness, he realized that his mother standing over him wasn't the subject of a dream or nightmare.

"I've had an epiphany!" Polly said triumphantly, sitting on the side of his bed. "Gwellyn didn't come to the house to threaten or spook us. No! She came to collect all the loot, but someone else wanted it too, and she was murdered!"

Tim was now pretty much fully awake. He listened to Polly's prattling about Gwellyn and treasure and murder. "I thought we decided she didn't have a key, so she couldn't have gotten into the dungeon."

"I haven't figured that out yet. Maybe she was good at picking locks. But my gut tells me that Gwellyn was whacked," Polly said. "When she thought I was going to fire her, she came back in the middle of the night to collect her booty. Makes perfect sense!"

"Only to a pirate," Tim huffed. "We established that Gwellyn didn't have a key to the door. It wasn't on the key ring that Lily had. Think about that, and please, let me go back to sleep. I was having a fun dream about Lady Gaga in her meat dress, and there was some weird business about her using a toaster as a microphone."

"I wonder what that even says about your aberrant mind," Polly said dismissively. She retreated into the darkness, back to her bedroom.

Morning arrived, and a strong wind was again pelting rain against the castle.

When Polly entered the breakfast room, she barely acknowledged Tim and Tiara. Then, after buttering a warm croissant, she announced, "Polly has a mystery to solve. Yes, a *murder mystery*, and don't contradict me. It's time to use my star power to ferret out answers from the villagers about Gwellyn and her killer. Yes, *killer*."

"Star power?" Tim said. "I don't think anyone here even knows who you are." His words were not meant to be unkind, but they nevertheless pained the sensitive artist's soul that dwelled in his mother.

"Regardless of my lack of notoriety in Abbots Clover, England, I'm still a larger-than-life presence in any room. People notice me," Polly said, sipping her glass. "If I went down to the pub this very moment, I'd get oodles of attention."

"Because at this very moment, you're in your bathrobe," Tiara pointed out. "And without your COVERGIRL Advanced Radiance foundation, you could easily be mistaken for Ozzy Osbourne. Plus, there's boysenberry jam on your chin."

Polly wiped her chin with a serviette and gave Tiara a withering look. "Well, excuse me for not being a flawless, ageless goddess like yourself. And at least Ozzie is a legend."

Just then, Lily entered the breakfast room. "Mum, I need a new floor mop, and we're almost out of dishwashing liquid, and I don't have any window cleaner. Just so you know."

Do I look like a supply cabinet? Polly wanted to say. However, she checked herself and put on a paper smile. "You like me, don't you, Lily?" she said. "I mean, you don't think I'm a terrible Hollywood diva who goes around harassing people or firing housekeepers willy-nilly, do you?"

Polly glanced at Tim and Tiara for support, then back to Lily. "I've heard Gwellyn was upset because she thought I was going to sack her. But that's so not true at all. What do you really think of me?"

Lily stood mute for a long moment, trying to determine what her employer was getting at and wondering how truthful she should be. Finally, she said, "Gwellyn always said I wasn't paid to have opinions, mum. But she certainly had her own. She said you were... "

"A rich, famous, beloved, and totally down-to-earth international star of stage and screen?" Polly prompted.

"An 'oppressive American capitalist' is how she put it, mum. I don't know what oppressive and capitalist mean, but the way Gwellyn said it, I suspect they aren't very nice words."

While Polly's mouth dropped in dumbfounded shock, Tim and Tiara spat out bits of their croissants.

"It means that Gwellyn was an excellent judge of character," Tiara said, sniggering.

Polly took another fortifying guzzle from her glass, sat straight in her chair, and squared her shoulders. "I'll be damned if I let a dead woman insult me from her grave," she said, then, in a softer tone, continued, "Lily, I saw how Gwellyn treated you, dear. Was she always that unkind? Did she dislike me as much as she disliked you?"

Lily thought about the question. Then, after a sigh of resignation, she said, "Yes, mum, she was pretty much always mean. Very few people liked Gwellyn. A lot of them aren't even sad that she died. She was someone who always seemed to know your weak spots. She had the right words to hurt you at any given moment, if you get what I mean. She had a sixth sense for when I was feeling especially low, and she would use those times to bring me down lower. Like when my dog was dying. Or when my boyfriend decided he liked my brother instead of me. Gwellyn always knew when it was a good time to tell me that she was thinking of letting me go because she said I didn't 'step up to the plate,' even though I'd never step on any plates, and I always cleaned Mr. Drake's plates spotless. Being a Christian woman, I forgave her for being mean. But I don't think Merv is much of a believer, so I doubt he gave her a pass for what she done to him."

"What was it she *done* to him?" Polly asked, genuinely interested. "I mean, other than treat him like a doormat."

"You know how much she hated spiders; she hated Merv just as much. They were even in that. He once told her she was 'a big fat oozing carbuncle seeping onto the pockmarked face of humanity.'"

Polly gagged.

"But Gwellyn didn't need a reason not to like someone," Lily continued. "She sometimes made up her mind without even knowing a person. I know she didn't like Ian Fuller down at the petrol station just because his left eye rolls around all by itself. She said his head reminded her of a pinball machine. She made fun of Arlene in the post office, too. Arlene has a puffy round face, a sort of flat, pushed-in nose, and big nostrils. Gwellyn called her Oinkers, even to her face. 'Hey, Oinkers, gimme a book of stamps, and make it fast,' I heard her say one day in front of other customers. Gwellyn was a snob, too. That's probably why she didn't like me, 'cause I'm not as clever and posh as her."

"But what was it specifically about Merv that she didn't like?" Tiara reiterated, circling back. "He seems like a lovely man."

Lily thought for a moment. "Maybe 'cause he and Mr. Drake got on, and Gwellyn thought they talked about her behind her back. And maybe 'cause he's had such an interesting life. He's been arrested, you know."

"Arrested? Meek Merv?" Polly said, curious about the circumstances.

"What was he in the big house for?" Tiara asked.

"His house is actually pretty small," Lily said. "He was in jail for disrupting traffic while protesting climate change. He called it civil disobedience. I would never be disobedient. Civil or otherwise. But Merv's a very ethical person. He recycles bottles and cardboard. Last winter, he saved Justin Taylor's poodle when it fell through the ice at Crystal Lake. Merv didn't even think twice about how freezing it was and the danger of it all. He just followed his instincts and rescued little Brioche. And he's nice-looking, too. Don't you think? Especially his arms and the way his chest fills out a T-shirt." She looked at Tim as if she suspected he would agree.

Tim grinned. "I get it. Although I'm more of an Idris Elba guy myself."

"Shall we keep the physical objectification to ourselves?" Polly said, amused by Lily's obvious sexual desires. "Did Mr. Drake get on well with Gwellyn? She was with him for a year or so."

"Mr. Drake was always nice to everyone, so it would have been tough for him not to find something to like about Gwellyn," Lily said. "But I think he was sort of afraid of her, too. Toward the end, when he couldn't leave his bed much, I was dusting outside his room one morning and heard him talking to Merv. He sometimes wanted to chat with Merv to fill some time in his day. This time, he asked for advice on how best to take care of Gwellyn. At first, I thought maybe he was talking about his will and what to leave her. Now, I think he meant how to sack her. I couldn't hear much more, but I remember him saying something about not trusting a thief. I don't know what he was talking about, but maybe it had to do with his gold pocket watch that went missing a few days before or a miniature painting that he liked—and I did, too. And some other stuff."

"You need to brush up on your eavesdropping skills if you're going to have a successful career as a maid," Tiara teased. "Do you think Gwellyn may have nicked a few bits and bobs from Mr. Drake?"

"I can't really say. But she was always tight on money and once mentioned needing to sell some stuff to make ends meet."

Polly, Tim, and Tiara looked at each other and simultaneously thought about the bag of loot they'd found, which contained a gold pocket watch and a small oil painting.

"I need my mop and cleaning stuff. I can't work without a mop," Lily finally said, ending the interrogation. Then she left the room.

Polly took another sip from her glass. "Bullies aren't only in casting offices or on movie sets," she said. "They're obviously in castles, too!"

"And TV stars' mansions," Tiara added, giving Polly the eye. "But I promise not to replace your hair gel with Gorilla Glue any time soon."

"Thanks for the mercy," Polly said with a sarcastic edge. "And I promise not to replace your face cream with mayonnaise."

"On that note, it's time for me to shower and dress because I have a date," Tim announced as he pushed back his chair and stood to offer a kiss to his mother's cheek.

"A date?" Polly scoffed. "How'd you manage that since you can't get a Wi-Fi signal for Plunder?"

"Oh, I don't need Plunder anymore," Tim said proudly. "Grayson called and offered to take me on a guided tour of the village!"

"But it's so wet and icky outside, dear," Polly reminded her son. "You should be inside, where it's warm and dry."

"My plan exactly," Tim said with a mischievous grin. "Someplace very warm and dry. And snuggly."

10

The rain had turned to mist, and the castle's inner ward was shrouded in a velvet veil of fog. Except for the distant crowing of a rooster somewhere beyond the walls, silence enveloped the estate. A raven glided through the pallid drizzle and perched atop an oak tree at the far end of the yard on a branch that seemed barely able to support its weight. Even the bird, bobbing like a buoy floating on a gray sea, was reverentially silent toward the tranquility of this bucolic scene. Then Merv came along and disturbed it all.

As Polly watched the gardener stomping around in his Wellington boots, inspecting the muddy puddles in his plant beds, she felt sorry for him working outside in what she considered extreme conditions. And when tea was ready at 11:00, she wrapped her mustard-yellow wool cardigan tightly around her body and opened the door at the back of the house. She called for Merv to join her for a cuppa.

"You'd be better off in California!" she said as Merv came through the doorway, wiping his boots on the doormat. "This weather is for the birds!"

"I'm used to it," Merv said with a smile as he removed his coat and cap and placed them on hooks next to the door. "But I'm glad for the tea."

Rather than usher Merv into the breakfast room, Polly motioned for him to take a seat at the table in the kitchen. It was warmer there, and the stone floors could be easily cleaned of mud from his boots.

Tiara, who only offered Merv a tight smile, placed a teapot, cream jug, sugar bowl, and three mugs on the table, along with a plate of warm scones and an assortment of jams and butter. The threesome sat for a long, uncomfortable moment with only the sound of the rain and wind blowing against the windows.

The awkward verbal silence prompted Polly to say the first thing that popped into her head. "Looks a little wet today." She instantly realized she'd made a stupid remark. "I mean, when will it all end?"

"You know the old saying about the weather in England, mum." Merv smiled. "Rain, followed by showers, followed by occasional dry spells. At least we don't have earthquakes like you do over there in your California. I'll take cloudbursts over them any day."

Merv had a point. Polly had to agree that England was a place where earthquakes, as well as tornados, blizzards, hurricanes, and raging forest fires seldom occurred. And in the UK, one didn't have to apply a thick layer of sunblock before venturing outside. However, with the freezing temperatures and day after day of endlessly bleak skies, she still couldn't see the value of living in such a damp climate full-time.

"Must be a genetic thing," she said. "I guess if one doesn't know any better, England is acceptable."

With that comment, Merv bristled slightly. "I know better, mum, if you'll pardon my impertinence, and Abbots Clover suits me fine," he said, trying not to sound offended by Polly's comment. "I've never been to California, nor even to Wales or Scotland, but I know for a fact that I wouldn't like them places any better than right here."

Polly knew she'd said the wrong thing and quickly reached out and placed her hand on Merv's forearm. "I didn't mean to insult you or anyone who loves living their dreary lives under constantly threatening skies."

"Dreary lives, mum?"

"I only meant that I've been all over the world, and there's no place like home."

"And speaking of home," Tiara said, deftly changing the subject, "we're not wild about people dying in ours. Any idea what Gwellyn Clogg was doing here in the middle of the night on Wednesday?"

Merv reached for his mug of tea and took a tentative sip, testing that it was cool enough to drink. He took a long gulp and said, "I know it's not my place to say, mum, but Gwellyn was a troublemaker. I wouldn't be surprised if she'd come back to confront you about sacking her."

"In the middle of the night?" Tiara scoffed.

"Everybody seems to think I gave her the boot," Polly grumped. "We had a slight argument—I mean an exchange of opinions—and she stormed out in a huff. I didn't see her again until the next day after Lily found her body."

Merv took another long pull from his tea mug. He nodded, then said, "Yeah, that Lily's a clever one, ain't she?"

"Your implication?" Polly said.

"I'll be honest with you, mum. I don't know who disliked Gwellyn more, Lily or me—and I pretty much like everyone— until they give me a good reason not to. Lily and I had good reasons. So did a bunch of other people in the village, like Cheryl Dibbs over at the library and Mark McEwan, the butcher. Mark wouldn't even serve her anymore after Gwellyn said she'd have the health inspector on him fast if he didn't give her a discount on lamb chops. And Cheryl hid behind bookshelves if she saw Gwellyn coming to check out DVDs because they'd argued about what Gwellyn thought were inappropriate titles available to perverts. The list goes on and on. Sorry to say this, but I'll bet there's no one around here who will miss her very much."

Polly considered what Merv had just said and felt a pang of sadness. We all want to think that someone will grieve at least a little when we die, but it seemed that any funeral service for Gwellyn would be absent of true mourners.

"Did you know Gwellyn worked for Lord and Lady Ridgewood-Brimble at Hedgepath Manor before she came here?" Merv continued. "Even them two, who are famous for their generosity, had problems with her. They sacked her after about six months. Some say it was because she was rude and argumentative. Heard a rumor that she tried to blackmail Lord Ridgewood-Brimble for something. Whatever really happened, Mr. Drake didn't know about it when he hired her. She convinced him that the letters of reference she provided were recent and authentic. I liked Mr. Drake a lot. But he was weak and pretty much just accepted her word about her past employment. Lady Ridgewood-Brimble stopped by one day after she'd heard that Gwellyn was working here. She told Mr. Drake what had happened and why Gwellyn was kicked out, but he was spineless and didn't want a confrontation, especially 'cause he was so ill. I think he was intimidated by Gwellyn, too. I get it. I saw how she bullied people. But not me. No way."

"I noticed the first day we met that Gwellyn didn't exactly treat you like a prince," Polly contradicted Merv. "If I worked with someone who talked to me like that, I'd have the union up their bum so fast... "

"I think the only castle with a union is the one at Disney's Magic Kingdom Park," Tiara pointed out.

"What I'm saying is there'd be a price to pay if someone was that nasty to me, especially in public. I brought that pratfalling fool Jerry Lewis up on equity charges after the way he treated me at the Emmy Awards ceremony one year. I refused to accept his insulting behavior, even if he was a big, notoriously insecure star. He was totally gross and made me feel like a cock-a-doodle-doo-doo!"

Merv shrugged. "I usually try to take the high road. I'm here to do my job, not get into workplace politics. But Gwellyn was the type who had to steer the ship and wanted everyone under her thumb. When she wouldn't stop pushing me around, I told her that Mr. Drake was my boss, not her. Then she tried to get me sacked. I talked to Mr. Drake about her, but he didn't want to rock the boat. Gwellyn knew I complained and, afterward, did her best to make my life hell."

"How did you handle that?" Tiara asked.

"Same way I handled other bullies," Merv said. "You gotta give 'em more of what they give to you. Otherwise, they just keep bullying. But I'm not good at confrontations. I never want to hurt anyone or their feelings. Just my nature."

"Not even a good ol' punch in the face?" Polly asked.

"That'd leave marks," Merv said with a grin. "No, I done something better—and more fun." He paused and gave Polly an evil smile, weighing how much to reveal. "I got a rucksack and had EJ down at the chippy fill it with fish guts. Then I hid it in the boot of Gwellyn's car. After a week, it stank so much that she couldn't drive it no more." Merv chuckled as he remembered the prank, and Polly and Tiara joined in as they pictured Gwellyn nearly puking from the smell of fish entrails decomposing in her Honda.

Merv took another sip of tea. "I'm just sayin' that bullies

eventually get what they deserve." He took a dramatic pause, relishing the attention he was receiving. "But that's not even the best part. I also put a few dead prawns in the heating vents. When she turned it on... well, you can imagine."

Polly and Tiara burst out laughing, imagining the horror on Gwellyn's face as the nauseating stench filled the car.

"Merv, you are so deliciously wicked! I never would have suspected you of such divine retribution! But nobody deserves to be murdered," Polly said.

"Murdered?" Merv scoffed. "You think Gwellyn... Nah, that's absurd. She died of a heart attack. Someone in the village would know if it was otherwise. Maybe she died from stinking fish guts rotting in her ugly soul."

Polly shrugged and took a sip from her mug. "I wouldn't be so sure that she died without a wee bit of help."

"As I said, no one liked her very much. I can take care of myself, but most people are like Lily. They're too timid to stand up against tyrants. Regular people don't have the nerve to confront injustice, so if they take revenge, it's done quietly behind their tormentor's back."

"Like you and the dead fish?" Polly asked.

"She knew it was me. Just couldn't prove it," Merv said, looking out the window. "My money's on someone doing something less creative than me to get even with Gwellyn." At that point, Merv decided that he'd warmed up enough to continue his work outside. "Thanks for the tea, mum," he said, standing up from the table. "And just so you know, if Gwellyn died in some unnatural way, we'll probably never know for sure. Here in Abbots Clover, everybody knows everybody else's business. Sometimes, they even know each other's thoughts. But we're good at keeping secrets, too. And protecting each other."

Polly and Tiara watched as Merv slipped his arms into his coat sleeves and placed his gray flannel cap on his head. He looked back and respectfully touched the brim of his cap before walking out the door.

Nodding thoughtfully as Merv's words lingered in the room, Polly sighed and remarked, "Secrets and solidarity, eh? That's Abbots Clover for you. You've got to love this village's knack for hiding skeletons while wearing a wide neighborly smile."

11

———

It was teatime when Tim returned from his afternoon with Constable Jenkins, and he was giddy.

"Grayson's great fun," he raved as he picked up a scone from a plate Tiara had set before him in the reception room. "I can't understand what he's saying half the time because of his accent, but his actions speak louder than words... if you get my drift. Who says that Brits don't know how to show their emotions?" He winked.

"Do tell us *almost* everything." Polly yawned. "Where did you boys go? What did you do for fun? No, forget I asked that."

"His place," Tim said with a wide grin. "Just stuff, like... "

Polly rolled her eyes, and Tim reined himself in. "We had a pint in the pub. He told me about exploring Thistlethorne Lodge as a kid and how he knew almost every inch of the castle grounds. Oh, and he once saw Prince William drive through Abbots Clover on his way to his dad's place at Highgrove. That's in Gloucestershire, you know." Tim didn't think that his mother and their maid could possibly know much about King Charles III or the name of his estate in the Cotswolds. "He said he once saw a real live ghost while exploring here, too."

"We had a shadowy presence of our own today," Tiara said. "Merv joined us for a cuppa this morning."

Tim took a sip of his tea. "Gray says Merv's a great guy, and no one understands why Gwellyn once filed a complaint about him."

Polly looked up from flipping through a glossy magazine with a picture of grazing horses on the cover. "Definitely not a mutual admiration society there," she said. "Merv admitted that he and Gwellyn weren't fans of each other. He stopped just short of saying he was happy that she was dead."

"Not surprising," Tim continued, casually brushing away pieces of a crumbling scone on his lap. "According to Gray, Gwellyn accused him of stealing Mr. Drake's gold pocket watch. She apparently told the police that he took a lot of other valuables, too, but couldn't prove it. And no one believes that, anyway. He may have a bit of a rebellious streak—his political and human rights protests and such—but he's apparently well liked by everyone in the village."

Polly scratched her head. "I keep going back to the mystery of the bag of valuables and who left it in the dungeon along with the key to the door," she said, tossing her magazine aside and pacing the room. "Maybe it was Gwellyn who stole the stuff, hid the bag in the dungeon, then accused Merv of the crime to throw everyone off her scent. But then I'm stuck with one image in my head: dead Gwellyn, neatly laid out on the larder floor, buttoned up in her navy-blue coat, her purse by her side that the police said contained only her car keys, glasses, and a package of breath mints. And then there are the shelves hiding the locked door to the secret passageway. This is utterly infuriating because, although I'm presuming she came back in the middle of the night to reclaim the loot from the dungeon, where's her copy of the key?"

Tim heaved a sigh. "I'm beginning to think that Merv was onto something when he suggested that ghosts were involved."

The trio sat silent for a long moment until Polly huffed, "What about Lily? I don't necessarily buy her Little Miss Innocent act. We know there was no love lost between her and Gwellyn. I'll have a chat with her first thing in the morning."

Tim's phone rang just then, and as Polly and Tiara listened to his side of the conversation, they were soon distracted from thieves, ghosts, and killers. Instead, they tried to imagine what Tim was quietly sniggering about. They quickly decided he was probably in *like* again and making romantic plans with his new beau.

Nighttime came with a depressing cloak of gloom, and the castle seemed even eerier than usual. With rain still raking the windows and the lights flickering in anticipation of a power outage, Polly and her troupe prepared for bed early, ensuring they each had flashlights, candles, and matches and that their cell phones were fully charged. The wind had picked up, and they could hear a whistling sound coming through the chimneys in the upstairs corridor. Although no one spoke of their unease, they felt jittery about going to their respective rooms alone.

"Let's have a slumber party with Tim tonight," Polly suggested when they reached the upstairs corridor. "Safety in numbers and all that."

Tiara smirked, enjoying the idea of her boss being afraid of being alone and the possibility of catching Tim in his PJs again. Although she was like a mother to Tim and had practically raised him to adulthood, she still enjoyed the sight of his sculpted torso. "I'll get another bottle of champagne if Tim comes along to protect me," she said.

"And leave me here all alone?" Polly protested. "What if the ghost wants to snuggle?"

"I'll bring an extra glass," Tim joked as he opened the door to his bedroom, turned on the light, and looked around. "See? Not even a shadow," he said as he scanned the room to ensure there was nothing for his mother to freak out about.

Tim and Tiara left the bedroom as thunder continued to rattle the windows. The storm outside had amplified the haunting atmosphere inside the castle. Polly sat on the edge of the bed, clutching a pillow as a flash of lightning caused the lights to flicker again. The reverberation from the wind, rain, and thunder combined to make her tenser. She was acutely aware of every slight noise. And then she heard something unexpected. Like the night before, it was coming from behind the panel that led to the secret passageway. Polly held her breath to concentrate on listening. Just as she was about to decide it was her imagination, she heard the noise again. She was pretty sure that something was pushing against the door from the inside of the firewood closet. She listened more intently, her mind racing with the possibilities of what could be hiding behind the panel. *Yes, something's trying to get into the room! Something wants to take a bite out of a Hollywood star! Something wants...*

"Brrrraaahh!" Tim roared and giggled as he and Tiara burst through the bedroom door. "It's gonna get you!"

Polly screamed, rolled into a fetal position on the bed, and put her head under the pillow. As Tim and Tiara laughed, Polly cried, "Not funny! There's something in the wood closet again! I heard it! Something's trying to get in!"

"It's just the wind," Tim said, feeling guilty about spooking his mother. "We locked the door to the larder ourselves. Remember? Even Mr. Boots couldn't get in there."

Polly cried, "I swear there's something in that wood store! There definitely is!"

Tim let out a sigh of exasperation. "If it makes you feel any better... " He reached for the knob to the firewood closet and instantly jumped back as if he'd touched a live electrical wire. He heard the sound, too, and instinctively grabbed the iron poker from the fireplace tool set.

As Polly and Tiara looked on in panic, Tim hooked the poker tip around the pull knob and gave it a tentative tug. A loud clap of thunder cracked, the lights flickered, and a black form raced out from the darkness of the wood closet. As Polly, Tim, and Tiara screamed, a drenched and muddy Mr. Boots sat in the middle of the floor, cleaning his coat of wet leaves and twigs.

A half hour later, having finished the bottle of champagne and taking turns petting Mr. Boots (and chastising him, too), the trio were still discussing how the cat could have gotten into the passageway a second time. The firewood cabinet had not even been ajar, let alone open wide enough for access from the bedroom. And the door to the larder had been locked with Mr. Boots most definitely outside.

"There's only one other explanation for a wet cat," Tim said.

"Another entrance to the passageway." Polly nodded, reading Tim's thoughts.

12

By morning, the storm that had bombarded the castle in the night had passed, but a dense fog still enveloped Thistlethorne Lodge. From the windows in the breakfast room, Polly could see Merv with his wheelbarrow, collecting debris that the wind had strewn around the courtyard.

"He's a hard worker, I'll give him that," she said, admiring the gardener's work ethic. "Now, about the secret passageway." She returned her attention to her glass of Prosecco and the subject on everyone's mind. "We have no choice but to go back in."

Tim looked up from his phone screen and suggested they bring along his new policeman friend to help find another way into the castle. "After all, he's used to investigating stuff. And he played here a lot as a kid. He said he knew every nook and cranny."

Polly dismissed the idea. "We can't let even one person know what we're up to, or the entire village will know," she said. "These Brits are practically telepathic!"

As Tiara refilled Polly's glass with bubbly, her peripheral vision caught the silhouette of something furtively moving in the hallway beyond the dining room. She looked up just in time to see a shadow and realized Lily was probably dusting—and perhaps taking the career-advancement advice about snooping on one's employers. "What time do you want to start your mission?" she asked Polly. "I need to get into the village to stock up on candles, batteries, and extra-strength Roundup zombie spray."

"I'm going up to change right now," Polly said, taking a long pull from her glass. "I have to look my best in case we get trapped and emergency workers bring a photographer to document their rescue of an American icon."

"You're reading my thoughts, Mother," Tim said. "It's freezing down there, but I think I'll wear a tank in case Gray has to come to our rescue. But then maybe not, as I haven't been to the gym since we got here, and my arms have shrunk to matchsticks!"

It was nearly 11:00 a.m. when Polly and her troupe assembled in the larder. Tim unlocked the heavy wooden door and signaled Tiara to nudge the cat into the passageway—their guide to another entrance/exit. With a short meow, Mr. Boots dashed ahead and was almost instantly out of reach of the beam of light from Tim's phone.

"Seems to know where he's going," he said, slowly descending the steps, with Polly tentatively following.

The ancient stone corridor seemed narrower than they remembered, and their footsteps generated louder-than-expected echoes. When Tim's flashlight beam revealed more rodent droppings, he realized that the evidence of mice or rats was proof that there was indeed another way into the passageway. When they reached the dungeon cells, he scanned the vaulted chamber with his light.

"I feel like we're being watched," he said, shivering in the cold, damp chamber.

"Shhh!" Polly nervously demanded. "I heard something!

Over there!" She pointed her smartphone light to a dark corridor. "There is something... I think I can see it! For crying out loud, it's huge! It's coming this way!" Polly gasped and took a step back. "It's getting bigger! It's—" In that instant, she realized she was seeing her own shadow cast by Tim's light shining behind her. "I swear this place is scarier than a restaurant with Jeffrey Dahmer in the kitchen!"

Tim wasted only a moment regaining his composure. Catching his breath, he moved toward the connecting corridor. He'd only gone a short distance when he noticed what appeared to be a pin spot of light in the distance. Moving forward, their phones' light beams showed that lichen was spreading onto the stone walls and ceiling, a sure sign that fresh air and dampness were getting in. When they came to the dead end of the corridor, Polly and Tim found themselves standing in an alcove that reminded them of the apse in a church. The concave wall meant they were probably in the base of the tower at the back of the castle. They were facing a narrow opening in the stone wall, and a cold breeze wafted past a jungle of ivy and other foliage creeping in from the outside.

"This is how Mr. Boots got in!" Polly said triumphantly. "I knew it! Another entrance to the castle! Although a narrow one."

"Now, the secret passageway totally makes more sense!" Tim said. "Maybe it was an escape route for a king. Or maybe it was even used by the castle's courtesans!"

Polly knew when her son's imagination was running hither and yon. "Those courtesans would have to be less than a 28AA bust size to squeeze through," Polly retorted. Still, for once, she, too, was fascinated by the possible connection to long-ago clandestine events at the castle.

Tim squeezed through the narrow gap as Polly was picturing

knights and ladies scurrying through the hallway or prisoners in the dungeon being rescued through this secret tunnel.

"If my pecs were any larger, I wouldn't make it either," he said. When he'd pushed past the vegetation, he knew exactly his location on the property. He could even see the village of Abbots Clover below and the church's steeple. "It's so overgrown I don't think anyone could find it from the outside. But the cat... oh, and I can see Hedgepath Manor from here. It's a gorgeous house! Not quite Downton Abbey, but bigger than this place," he reported.

Although Tim was bug-eyed with excitement and wanted to yelp at the thrill of it all, his intuition told him there was a good reason for the entrance to be a secret. So he remained quiet.

At Tim's reference to Hedgepath Manor, Polly recalled Merv mentioning that Gwellyn had worked there for a short while. And as they made their way back through the passageway, she decided to pay a friendly visit to the lord and lady of the manor.

13

Hedgepath Manor, the ancestral home of Lord and Lady Ridgewood-Brimble, was a seventeenth-century, five-hundred-acre estate snuggled in a wooded parkland of green hills and slopes with sweeping countryside vistas. Owned for over four hundred years by succeeding generations of the Ridgewood-Brimble family, the manor was a picturesque Baroque English country house.

Polly had arranged a visit and taxied there with Tiara to investigate Merv's suggestion that dead Gwellyn Clogg had done something nefarious enough that resulted in her being sacked from her pre-Thistlethorne Lodge employment. The more Polly could learn about Gwellyn, the closer she might come to learning who Gwellyn Clogg was in life and whether her theory was correct that she was murdered.

As their car approached the house from a long avenue lined with tall, bare English oak trees, Polly instantly recognized the manor as the exterior location set of one of her all-time favorite movies, *The Rose of Shaftesbury*, a period British costume drama that had introduced her friend Mercedes Ford to audiences around the world—she and Mercedes weren't exactly buddy-buddy, but they were on each other's Christmas-card lists.

"Anyone in that role would have gotten the Oscar," Polly griped, dismissing Mercedes's talent and nursing a long-held grudge that she hadn't even been considered by the director for the part of the beautiful, young peasant girl who fell in unrequited love with a wealthy, one-armed naval hero. "I can cry on cue just as well as Mercedes, for crying out loud."

"You were about twenty-five years too old, your overbite made you look like a chipmunk had stuffed his cheeks with acorns, and the production couldn't afford the prosthetic makeup to give you a chin," Tiara retorted, explaining the many reasons Polly had been wrong for that part. "Plus, the role required an elegant English accent. You sound like Gilbert Gottfried reciting obituaries."

Polly scowled. "It's all about versatility, my dear. I can do an English accent, a Southern drawl, and even a fake orgasm that would make Meg Ryan envious."

The taxi stopped at the front portico, and as Polly and Tiara stepped from the car, they smiled at each other. They silently agreed that although they'd been to plenty of ritzy houses in Beverly Hills, by comparison, this one made all the others look like lean-to shelters for indigents. They stood for a long moment, admiring the façade and the Doric columns the size of redwood trees on either side of the front entryway. Tiara nudged Polly and pointed to a family coat of arms above the enormous wooden front door. The motto read *In Vino Veritas!*

"That's what I always say." Polly grinned, agreeing that *in wine, there is truth.*

A short moment after rapping the enormous iron ring door-knocker, a stern-looking woman wearing a plain black cotton uniform with a white ruffled apron and matching linen cap over severely combed-back hair opened the door. Apparently expecting the visitors, she didn't speak and merely gave a slight curtsy before stepping aside for them to enter. And what an entryway it was! There was no use in Polly and Tiara trying to put on a blasé attitude; both were as impressed as slack-jawed tourists ogling the excesses of Versailles.

"Their lordships will be with you presently," said the maid in what Polly thought was a rather condescending tone.

"Is it my imagination, or do maids in this country have an attitude problem?" Tiara whispered.

"Pot, kettle, black?" Polly shot back with a raised eyebrow.

The foyer reeked of hereditary aristocracy. A giant tapestry and a portrait of King George V hung on walls opposite each other. Gothic hand-carved dragon chairs bookended an ornately carved marble-top console table. Polly, immersed in examining a large oil canvas, was admiring the artist's intricate detail of a woman's shiny blue satin dress when the homeowners arrived.

"Your Majesties." Polly fumbled for words. "I mean, Your Sires. Or is it Highnesses? It's lovely to meet you."

If Polly had been disappointed with how Solicitor Wainwright had dressed and how his too-modern London law office was decorated, Lord and Lady Ridgewood-Brimble and their home took first prize for looking *exactly* as Polly had imagined and hoped they would: ancient.

Someone obviously got the memo from central casting, Tiara silently agreed with what she knew Polly was thinking.

Lady Ridgewood-Brimble looked like a scrawny, human-size chicken, and she sort of bobbed her head like one, too. Her age had to be in the eighties, and she dressed in a fancy style from a far-off era. No modern threads for this traditionalist. A lace shawl draped over her shoulders, and she was otherwise covered in a long-out-of-style, multilayered burgundy dress that touched the floor and seemed way too heavy for her small, fragile frame. She relied on a cane for balance. Thick lenses in round gold-rimmed frames sat on the bridge of her beak-like nose and magnified her fault-finding eyes.

Lord Ridgewood-Brimble also appeared stuck in a fashion time warp. He was dressed in a beige tailcoat with a brown velvet collar, and a gold pocket watch chain was drooped in front of his waistcoat. He looked like an actor about to step onstage to perform in an amateur production of *The Importance of Being Earnest*. He, too, was rail thin and required a walking stick to steady his balance.

After formal introductions, during which Polly and Tiara got the distinct impression that, as Americans, they were being judged as unfit to be in the presence of the British upper crust, Lady Ridgewood-Brimble ordered that they move through to what she called the "Garden Room."

At a tortoise's pace, Lady and Lord Ridgewood-Brimble led their charges over polished parquet wood floors through molded mahogany archways, past faded tapestries and antique porcelain vases set in scalloped alcoves. When they finally arrived in the long and narrow Garden Room, Polly and Tiara continued to be impressed by their surroundings.

The room looked like it had probably once been the estate's orangery or a greenhouse. The walls and roof of multipaned windows brought in plenty of light, and even though the outside sky was pewter gray and the January temperatures cold, inside, it was warm. Tall ferns in large terracotta pots stood on either side of several French doors. Ivy climbed white lattice trellises attached to the stone wall that the room shared with the main house. A sculpted cherub, fat, naked, uncircumcised, grinned mischievously while urinating into a shallow rectangular pool filled with koi. And while the faint sound of harp music issued through speakers hidden behind a couple of potted ficus trees, a parrot shackled to an open perch bounced from one foot to the other, nattering to itself like a crazy person.

"Sit," Lady Ridgewood-Brimble ordered Polly and Tiara in a more forceful tone than one might expect from such an otherwise fragile-looking relic.

The guests obediently parked themselves next to each other on a thick, silk-cushioned settee.

Lord Ridgewood-Brimble, who had yet to say a single word, gazed around the room as if the space were completely unfamiliar to him, or maybe he was determining which exit to take should a delegate from the Save the Royal Corgis movement come knocking.

"Mildred will serve tea presently," the lady of the manor affirmed and sat opposite Polly and Tiara in a leather wingback chair identical to the one her husband occupied.

"I regret to tell you I only agreed to this meeting because my solicitor phoned and said you harassed him into ringing me," Lady Ridgewood-Brimble stated. "He mentioned something about you being a celebrity of sorts... from California." She sniffed and made a dismissive pitying sound, accompanied by a spray of spittle that misted the air. "Minor royalty in America or some equally silly idea. You Americans have a stupid social hierarchy if trivial entertainment people are so highly regarded. Now, what do you want? I'm told it's something about that dreadful creature who used to work here."

Polly's smile at being compared to royalty instantly faded at the suggestion that her showbiz career had been trivial. It was, in fact, considered epic by many, including the Museum of Television and Radio. *And how many times have you been a clue in the* New York Times *crossword puzzle?* She desperately wanted to counter Lady Ridgewood-Brimble's insult. Instead, she cleared her throat and squared her shoulders, trying not to incite eviction before gathering more clues to her mystery investigation.

"I'm sure you've heard the tragic news about your previous housekeeper, Gwellyn Clogg."

"That name is not spoken in this house!" Lady Ridgewood-Brimble spat, holding up her veined, bony, nearly translucent hands. "Tragic? Hardly! She was a disaster!"

"Well, the thing is, she died at Thistlethorne Lodge... "

"Yes. In the middle of the night." Lady Ridgewood-Brimble recited what others had already told her. "And you don't know what she was doing there at that early hour. The whole village knows that story. There's nothing more for me to add."

Polly was taken aback by the fact that in only a few days, everyone in Abbots Clover knew all about Gwellyn and the circumstances of her death. "It's the opinion of some that she suffered a heart attack. But I'm not completely convinced."

"Not convinced of what? That she possessed a heart?"

Polly shrugged. "I knew her for less than a day, but I did get the flavor of her character. A bit of a troublemaker, it seems. I was hoping you could tell me more about her. To fill me in, so to speak."

During an uncomfortably long silent moment, Polly's gaze drifted from Lady Ridgewood-Brimble to Lord Ridgewood-Brimble, who was completely detached from the conversation and continued to look around the room, plucking at invisible specks of God-knows-what from the air.

Lady Ridgewood-Brimble leaned over and blotted strands of drool from his mouth with a linen handkerchief. "She wasn't here very long. That woman, I mean," she finally said evasively. "It was more than a year ago. I don't remember much about her."

"Why did she leave you to work for Mr. Drake?" Tiara interjected, trying to move the interrogation along. She suspected that Lord Ridgewood-Brimble might keel over and die at any moment, causing Lady Ridgewood-Brimble to halt the interview.

After another long moment of only the sounds of harps,

the peeing cherub, and the parrot's nattering filling the room, Lady Ridgewood-Brimble snapped, "That woman was a miserable... I really don't know you well enough to reveal the sordid facts."

Lady Ridgewood-Brimble could not have known that Polly Pepper lived for salacious gossip. The more sordid, the better. She devoured the Hollywood rags and TV entertainment news programs. And it seemed that Lady Ridgewood-Brimble might be holding a whopper of a revelation. Polly was almost drooling like Lord Ridgewood-Brimble in anticipation.

"Hey, the woman's dead. She can't sue for defamation of character if that's what you're concerned about." Polly encouraged Lady Ridgewood-Brimble to spill the tea. "Plus, this is just between us girls. I'm the farthest thing from a gossip."

Tiara's eyes rolled as she recalled the countless instances when Polly's loose lips and scandal-seeking antics had plunged her into hot water. Oh, how she longed to remind her dear boss of the not-so-distant past when a nosy reporter from the *National Intruder* reached out to confirm Polly's claim that Emmy Award-winning actor Stanley Kingsman bore such a striking resemblance to Marlon Brando that he must have been the result of a secret Hollywood cloning scheme, thus putting her again in the limelight for all the wrong reasons. The incident had garnered her a prime spot in the tabloid's Hall of Fame of Bizarro Celeb Conspiracy Theories.

After another long moment, Lady Ridgewood-Brimble sighed again, as if surrendering her willpower. "I suppose you have somewhat of a vested interest," she said. "This has more to do with—"

At that very moment, the French doors leading into the main house opened, and Mildred, the maid, entered, pushing a trolley carrying a silver teapot, bone china cups and saucers, and a selection of cakes.

"Perfect timing," Polly groused under her breath, but loud enough for Tiara to hear and agree.

Lord Ridgewood-Brimble merely offered a guttural noise that sounded like he was giggling.

Polly and Tiara faked yummy sounds as the maid served cups of Earl Grey and offered slices of frosted lemon pound cake on small plates. After a minute of sips and bites—Lord Ridgewood-Brimble ignored his tea and continued admiring the room as if he hadn't been there thousands of times—Polly circled back to their conversation before the interruption.

"You were about to tell us why your housekeeper chose to leave you to work for Mr. Drake."

"I threw her out!" Lady Ridgewood-Brimble spat the short answer. "She couldn't prepare so much as beans on toast, let alone an adequate tea. She was lazy. She complained about her accommodation. She resented us for being rich. But the final straw was when a valuable ruby and emerald brooch—my favorite piece—went missing from my jewelry box, and she accused one of the other maids of stealing it. I foolishly believed Gwellyn. I still don't know why, since she had beady, dishonest eyes. I fired the maid. Then the police found my brooch in a pawnshop. That witless Gwellyn Clogg—yes, I'll speak her name—was too stupid to know that pawnshops report everything they buy to a police database. And I was equally stupid for not pressing charges. I regret that now. I was more concerned about the light of adverse publicity shining on our respectable house rather than doing the right thing. The poor innocent maid I fired had begged me not to send her away because she had nowhere to go. I heartlessly told her that wasn't my problem."

Lady Ridgewood-Brimble sat in quiet self-reflection for a long moment. Eventually, she said, "Yes, I'm a self-absorbed old lady. I understand that. I never learned sensitivity. I lack patience. My social status has made me unable to empathize with those less fortunate."

Polly and Tiara were silent. What could they say? It would have sounded disingenuous if they'd tried to console Lady Ridgewood-Brimble and argue against her self-assessment. They both knew from personal experience that those living in privileged classes were usually much distanced from the disadvantaged and, thus, often couldn't understand the misery of those on the lower rung of the social ladder. *They should pull themselves up by their bootstraps the way I did!* Polly could hear more than one of her rich friends saying. *It's because they're lazy! My success came from determination and hard work!* another had said. Polly knew those same people had been born into middle-class families and had better education and more opportunities than those they disparaged. Polly believed that she herself couldn't possibly be as insensitive as Lady Ridgewood-Brimble. But then she had Tiara and Tim to keep her grounded, reminding her often enough that she was once a destitute little girl, living in a one-room apartment with her mother, studying movie-star fan magazines, and daydreaming of being a rich and famous actress one day. She was one of the few lucky ones whose dreams had come true.

After another long moment of silent contemplation, Lady Ridgewood-Brimble said, "Gwellyn Clogg was responsible for that maid losing her job. And I abetted her. Maybe the girl landed on her feet. I don't know. But she told me through tears that she was all alone and unqualified for any other type of work. And Lord knows there aren't many full-time live-in domestic positions available around here anymore. When I later discovered that Gwellyn was working at Thistlethorne Lodge, I tried to right the wrong I'd done. I went to discuss the situation with Alistair Drake. I wanted Gwellyn sacked. But Alistair was too old and infirm to do much of anything. He was confined to his bed much of the time and needed Gwellyn's help in his house. He assured me he'd keep an eye on her and act accordingly if she behaved inappropriately. But I knew he'd never do anything about the fact that she'd withheld past employment information from him. There wasn't anything more I could do.

"However, before I left Thistlethorne that day, I confronted Gwellyn. I told her what I truly thought of her. She looked at me with high-handed vileness and told me I was just a rich old woman with a limited number of breaths left in my body and that I'd better 'keep my trap shut' about her arrest. She said it would be ever so easy to have something accidentally tragic happen to Lord Ridgewood-Brimble or me. She reminded me about broken hips among the elderly and the steep staircase here at Hedgepath Manor. She was three times my size, but I wasn't afraid of her attempt at intimidation. Lord Ridgewood-Brimble was, but that's another story. I just wanted to say my piece and clear my conscience of the terrible thing I'd done."

For more than a few uncomfortable seconds, the only sounds in the room were the peeing cherub, Lord Ridgewood-Brimble's wheezing, and the parrot mimicking the short, catchy jingle that identified BBC Radio 2.

Then Polly nodded in agreement. "Gwellyn threatened me, too. Not as viciously as she did to you, but I got her message. And she lied to people in the village about me sacking her. If it makes you feel any better, I'm told that quite a few people disliked her, so she probably had a lonely life. I mean, who'd want to spend their free time with someone so disagreeable?"

"Apparently, someone did. She had a gentleman caller who visited regularly," Lady Ridgewood-Brimble said, to the surprise of the room. "He collected her on Wednesdays and Sundays, her days off."

"Well, that's news! Who was he? What was his name?" Polly asked.

Lady Ridgewood-Brimble shrugged.

"Can you describe him?" Tiara pushed.

"Not as repulsive as King William III in that portrait hanging in the drawing room, but not as pretty as King Charles III. If you get my drift."

"Hell, I can't even get a Boy Scout to walk me across the street, let alone someone who looks like royalty, inbred or otherwise!" Polly said of her own barren dating prospects.

Lady Ridgewood-Brimble nodded in understanding. "It wasn't any of my business, but I did get the impression that they were possibly intimate. She was flirtatious around him. As a matter of fact, he came calling for her a couple of days after she'd been dismissed. But maybe they weren't so close after all, because she apparently hadn't relayed that bit of news about her change in employment status and accommodation. Surprised she wasn't here, he demanded to know where she'd gone. I didn't know or care. I nearly had to call the police because he tried to force himself into the house to search for her. It was extremely upsetting for me and Lord Ridgewood-Brimble. The day maids hadn't arrived yet, and we were all alone because we hadn't yet replaced Gwellyn. I thought maybe Gwellyn had something that belonged to him, or she had made a promise of some sort. I don't know, but there was something fishy about both of them. I felt it."

Polly looked at Tiara and made a face that suggested she was adding another potential suspect to her short list. "Do you remember anything more about the guy?" Polly asked, turning back to Lady Ridgewood-Brimble, who shook her head emphatically. "Maybe the type of car he drove?"

"You can't expect me... That was more than a year ago," Lady Ridgewood-Brimble said, as if she'd been asked a dumb question. "But I do remember he always wore blue jeans. Horrid. Like a common laborer. And he didn't have discernible, shall we say, buttocks? Even at my age, I notice such things. And he drove something large and economically depressing—to be polite about his clunker of a vehicle. It was red and had a silly Mickey Mouse ball on the aerial. I recall that detail because I thought it was pathetically common. He, and Gwellyn too, looked like the types who would think that a Disney holiday was posh."

It wasn't lost on Polly and Tiara that Lady Ridgewood-Brimble, after having declared only a moment ago that she wasn't a snobbish old rich lady, basically admitted that she really was. Or at least a pretentious one.

"Would you recognize the man if you saw him again?" Polly asked, imagining a police line-up of ex-cons holding numbered plates in their mugshots.

"I don't ever want to see him again!" Lady Ridgewood-Brimble said. "It's in the past. Leave it there and leave me out of it."

At that moment, Lord Ridgewood-Brimble, who had been dozing off and slowly listing to the side, tilted forward. Polly reacted in the nick of time, just as the lord of the manor nearly slumped out of his seat. He snapped back to consciousness and gurgled like a baby.

"It's time for Alfie's nap," Lady Ridgewood-Brimble said, reaching for a small bell on the tea trolley. A moment later, Mildred returned to the room, coaxed her employer up from his seat, and guided him back into the main house.

"Bless his heart," Polly said without any sincerity, and Lady Ridgewood-Brimble used the uprooting of her husband as an excuse to end the meeting.

Polly thanked her again for her time and trouble and offered to reciprocate her hospitality at Thistlethorne in the nebulous "sometime soon."

However, Lady Ridgewood-Brimble wanted no part in ever seeing Polly Pepper again. "I watched you on Graham Norton once," she said. "I thought you were supposed to be a funny person. You drank too much of Mr. Norton's wine. You insulted Dame Judi—a national and cultural treasure. You think you're at the very top of the pecking order, don't you? I don't see any discernible reason."

At that moment, as Polly was about to offer a verbal backhand to the wretched old woman, the nattering parrot squawked, "Polly has a pecking order!" Then a different, white-aproned maid entered the room to announce that a taxi had arrived. Apparently, the meeting with their lordships had been timed to precisely half an hour, and it was time for the visitors to leave.

Seated in the back of the taxi and looking through rain-streaked windows as Hedgepath Manor faded into the distance, Polly said, "Graham Norton? Judi Dench? Such a little old fibber! She knew exactly who I was all along! No doubt a closeted fan!"

14

———

By the time Polly and Tiara returned to Thistlethorne Lodge, the rain had stopped, and the weak, late afternoon sun was making a valiant but unsuccessful effort to break through the heavy sky. As they entered the castle courtyard, Merv, who was again filling his wheelbarrow with garden detritus—*Does he just push that darn thing around all day?* Polly wondered—smiled and touched the brim of his flat cap in salutation.

Lily greeted the duo in the vestibule and pointed to an envelope placed on the entryway table. "A message from the village vicar," she said. "He stopped by and said to say he was sorry."

"A vicar? We have a village vicar!" Polly trilled with enthusiasm and snatched up the envelope addressed to Miss Polly Pepper.

"What was he sorry about?" Tiara asked Lily. "That we're unrepentant Hollywood heathens?"

"Maybe," Lily said. "Or probably sorry 'cause you weren't here."

"What exactly is a vicar, anyway?" Polly said as she opened the note. "I know they pop up in Miss Marple stories."

"Anglican clergy, for heaven's sake," Tiara said. "You've seen them, musty old geezers, like Father Brown on BritBox. But you never know. Remember that dishy one on *Keeping Up Appearances*—the cute guy constantly trying to wriggle away from Hyacinth and her candlelight suppers? He certainly rocked his frock. Maybe ours will, too."

"Guess he's not afraid to come here anymore... now that Gwellyn's gone," Lily said as she began retreating to the kitchen.

"Mmm," Polly uttered dismissively as she concentrated on the handwritten note scrawled on St. Clematis Church letter-head stationery.

"He sure is nice to listen to, his voice, I mean." Lily seemed to be talking to herself as she slowly wandered out of the room. "And nice to look at, too. I'll bet he's been to a dental hygienist. Gwellyn didn't appreciate him. Oil and water, I guess."

"Mr. Vicar's got the penmanship of a triple-espresso addict," Polly complained and handed the paper to Tiara to decipher. "They obviously don't teach cursive in seminary."

Tiara, too, squinted at the tiny spasmodic scrawl and began reading haltingly:

Dear Miss Pepper, Welcome to Abbots Clover. Please accept my sincere apologies for taking so long to extend my good wishes to you and your family. I would be honored to receive tea if you would be gracious enough to invite me in the very near future. I am eager that we become acquainted.

    Your humble servant, Wallace Aylsworth, Vicar.

"I like the *humble servant* part," Polly said. "Major brownie points. But I think Mr. Vicar should invite *us* to tea. We're the new kids on the block. It's his place to offer the grand gesture. I'm happy to drop a small donation on his collection plate, but I draw the line at baptism."

"You're beyond salvation," Tiara cracked. "And I doubt he's seeking your conversion. Once he gets to know you, I promise he'll exchange his dog collar for a garland of garlic."

Polly sat on the Chesterfield settee facing the fireplace, contemplating Vicar Aylsworth. "I suppose it takes all sorts of virtues and upstandingness to be a man of the cloth," she mused. "Maybe that's why I've never met a vicar in real life. They don't exist in Hollywood. Clergy need a lot of moral character and things like scruples and integrity."

"They need Hollywood-size egos, too," Tiara countered. "Don't tell me they aren't screaming, 'Pay attention to me! I'm a star! I have the power to save your wicked souls!' when they preach from the pulpit."

"Do you suppose they perform exorcisms?" Polly said as she thought of how she might have an immediate purpose in utilizing the village vicar. "If the guy is as seductive as that priest on *Fleabag*, I'll happily go to confession," she said while reading the phone number on the letterhead of the note and tapping the digits onto the keypad of her smartphone. "Just my luck, he'll be more Tim's type than mine," she said before suddenly transforming into her artificial Polly Pepper character and trilling an exaggerated version of her famous (and loud) *Booo-whaaa!* greeting into the phone.

As Tiara sidled up close to Polly, she hung on every syllable of the one-sided conversation. There were the superficial agreements that, yes, Thistlethorne Lodge was indeed a romantic and historic place to live. And yes, the weather in England was completely different from California. But no, it wasn't terribly uncomfortable. And yes, it was a shame that the housekeeper had died suddenly, but they were coping as well as could be expected, considering the tragic circumstances. Tiara pictured Vicar Aylsworth seated at a desk in a vicarage study, surrounded by books and notes for Sunday service sermons, and having no clue about what he was about to encounter in the form of Hollywood diva Polly Pepper. No layman could be adequately prepared for that!

A few minutes later—after she had forced a lot of phony laughter from her lungs—Polly offered an exuberant, "Yes! Lovely. Cheers to you too, your Vicar-ness! Ta!" and disconnected the call. "Tomorrow is Clergy Appreciation Day," she announced. "Eleven o'clock. His Eminence is visiting, and a Mrs. Vicar is tagging along. I guess he's not required to do the celibacy thing. And we don't have to worry about Tim's transubstantiation."

"Trans... what?" Tiara blanched, thinking for a moment that maybe there was something new in the ever-evolving LGBTQ+ politically correct lexicon that perhaps hadn't filtered down to her. And God knows she never wanted to inadvertently insult Tim, one of her life's most meaningful loves.

Polly shrugged. "Transubstantiation. Tom Lehrer sings about it in his religious hymn, 'The Vatican Rag.' Oh, I'm so excited! Our first real house guests at Thistlethorne! I hope he's a nonjudgmental religious man... someone not too nitpicky about my life's choices. It's so hard to explain three or four ex-husbands to someone who isn't in show business."

"He's showbiz adjacent," Tiara said, suggesting that a modern vicar might have more secular views on some of the old-fashioned hot-button social issues.

As the afternoon wore on and darkness began to settle over the castle, Polly's thoughts returned to her afternoon tea with the Lords Ridgewood-Brimble and the small revelations that Lady Ridgewood-Brimble had provided about Gwellyn. Of course, Polly's own interaction with the impudent Gwellyn had given her an up close and personal introduction to the kind of woman she'd been in life. And somehow, Gwellyn nicking a jeweled brooch didn't surprise Polly in the least. However, what did surprise her was the account of Gwellyn's so-called "gentleman caller," and she wanted to know more about him.

Who was the paramour with a red car? Polly thought, imagining a reptilian creature in baggy blue jeans. But then again, in a small village like Abbots Clover, the pickings for eligible partners were probably fairly lean, and one couldn't necessarily separate the wheat from the chaff without tossing out potential mates. One had to take what one could get. Was he a sleepover buddy or just a companion with whom Gwellyn could go to a village fete on her days off from service? If Gwellyn had been someone's girlfriend, surely she would have sought emotional comfort from them after being arrested for stealing and being sacked from her job.

However, the guy in question had apparently been surprised by the news of Gwellyn's dismissal. Polly thought that the man's fit of rage, as described by Lady Ridgewood-Brimble, was in keeping with the response of a guy who'd unexpectedly had his sure-thing rumpy-pumpy taken away. But maybe he wasn't just upset that Gwellyn wasn't available for canoodling. Maybe he was mad because he was an accomplice in her crime, and she had been found out... and he could be next. Perhaps he was in on Gwellyn's scheme to steal the brooch and other valuables from her employer. Polly's famously out-of-control imagination was working overtime and running wilder than usual.

It was now a little after 5:00 p.m., and Polly was settling in with her first glass of fizzy, keen to embrace the evening indulgence. As Tim remained absent, off gallivanting with Constable Jenkins, Polly found herself in need of entertainment. With a mischievous glint in her eye, she turned her attention to Lily, who now stood before her and Tiara like a nervous squirrel on a caffeine high.

Eager to satisfy her curiosity, Polly couldn't help but blurt out, "So, Lily, spill the tea! Did Gwellyn have a secret lover? Any juicy romances hidden behind that surly façade?"

The question caught Lily and Tiara off guard, their expressions frozen in a comical mix of surprise and anticipation.

Lily looked confused. She gave Polly a quizzical look and a noncommittal shrug. "Me and her weren't close. She always told me to mind my business if I asked if she had a nice day off. So I don't know anything about her private parallel parking, if that's what you mean."

Polly and Tiara exchanged amused smiles that conveyed their thoughts that maybe Lily was smarter than she looked. Her taking Polly's question to another level was a sign of critical thinking—although they seriously didn't want to envision the physical intimacy that Lily had inadvertently conjured in their minds' eyes.

"I just want to know if she was sweet on anyone. Or if she had admirers?" Polly said.

"Admirers?" Lily burst into involuntary laughter, then instantly bit her lip to regain her composure and wondered what she should say next.

"There are no right or wrong answers," Polly said. But Lily suspected this was a trick, and Polly already knew the answer and was simply seeking corroboration. After a long internal debate, she shrugged again, but remained mute.

"We have it on good authority that Gwellyn was dating a man with a *red* car," Polly exaggerated the information she'd received from Lady Ridgewood-Brimble. "We're just trying to find out who he is. He needs to know about Gwellyn's death. He may want a reserved front-row seat at the funeral. Or is it a cremation? We thought maybe you would know him."

Lily shook her head slowly and twisted her mouth, trying to recall if she had ever seen Gwellyn show interest in a man or interest in dating generally. "There's Oliver, the milkman," she said hesitantly. "He has broad shoulders and a friendly smile and straight teeth. Gwellyn wrote notes to him. But I think they were probably more like, 'Please leave butter and a dozen eggs.' He drives a white truck. But it does have *red* letters on it. It says M-I-L-K."

"Appropriate," Polly mocked, taking back her previous thought that Lily might have a brain hiding under her page-boy haircut.

"There's the bin collector, too," Lily continued. "He comes on Fridays, but I don't know his name. He looks rough—but maybe Gwellyn liked bad boys," she said with a faraway look of lust. "He never speaks to anyone except when he's expecting the £20 Christmas bonus that Mr. Drake used to give him. His lorry is green, I think."

As Lily tried to identify other men in the village and the color of their vehicles, she stopped when her mental checklist landed on another name. "Once—a while ago—I saw Gwellyn and Christopher Bradshaw together. He's the village chiropractor. He has a Volvo. It's sort of red, or maybe more burgundy. Maybe you mean him? I saw Gwellyn and him having a pint at the Twin Harts over in Warmanshire, the next village before Barnesfield. I was there to have my weekly cream tea with my mum. I know Gwellyn saw me but pretended she didn't. Like she hoped that I hadn't seen her either. But I did."

"Gwellyn didn't drink alcohol except on New Year's Eve." Tiara rebutted the idea that Gwellyn had enjoyed a pint in a pub. "She was pretty adamant about that."

"That's what she said." Lily smiled wryly. "Mr. Drake had a massive stash in his wine cellar when Gwellyn came here. Have you taken an inventory? No. Because there's nothing left to count. It's all gone."

The revelation stunned Polly and Tiara into bug-eyed silence, and they exchanged looks of disbelief. The petty crimes of Gwellyn Clogg were a continuing source of surprise, and Polly was furious that Gwellyn had perhaps cheated her out of inheriting what might have been a valuable collection of vintage vino.

"How many bottles are we talking about?" Polly asked. "Was she ever drunk on the job? Please don't tell me there was a bottle of Domaine de la Romanée-Conti 1945! I'll kill her! Again!"

"I never smelled her breath," Lily said, "but then, I stayed out of her way as best I could, so I honestly don't know. I sort of think she took the wine home—one bottle at a time. She never acted tipsy. Mr. Drake would have been distraught if she'd been under the influence at work. He didn't drink much himself, only one glass of red wine with his dinner. And when he got really unwell, he abstained altogether. Doctor's orders."

Polly processed this information, and the new picture of Gwellyn forming in her mind was even less flattering than the one previously etched there. In only one day, the dead maid had morphed from a poor murdered dear, whose lousy attitude Polly had forgiven because surely her bad behavior had sprung from the fear and anxiety of possibly losing her job and becoming destitute. But now, Gwellyn's moral character was proving to be even lower than originally believed.

Polly suddenly remembered Lily's previous comment in the vestibule about Gwellyn and the vicar disliking each other. "What did you mean before when you said the vicar was afraid to come here... but not now, since Gwellyn's dead?"

Lily stood, making a face and uttering low-decibel, nonverbal noises as though the synapses of her brain were firing but not necessarily engaging all the cylinders, and she was digging deep to remember what she might have said about the vicar versus Gwellyn. Then the cogs clicked into place.

"Right," she said. "About a month before Mr. Drake died, I heard a loud knock on the entryway door when I was cleaning in the upstairs hallway. Then I overheard Gwellyn having a terrible row with someone. I crept closer to the stairs to find out what the fuss was about. I heard Vicar Aylsworth's voice. I knew it was him because of his Scottish accent, and he used to come over to visit Mr. Drake and cheer him up. He was always so nice and even-tempered. But not that day."

"Do tell." Polly listened with fascination, hoping for a juicy scandal.

"I remember he yelled something about Gwellyn not understanding something about something she'd said or done, and the price she was going to have to pay for it was high. I don't think he meant the price of petrol or a pound of broad beans at the village market, either. That's how upset he was. I was afraid their shouting would wake up Mr. Drake. After that, the vicar never came back to visit, not even when Mr. Drake asked Gwellyn to ring for him. I was scared for Gwellyn because I didn't think it was wise to make trouble with a vicar, especially if you want him to pray you a character reference to Jesus for a place in heaven. I hope she didn't spoil her chance for eternity in paradise. But she probably did. Maybe that's good. I won't run into her there."

As Polly and Tiara stared at Lily for a long moment of disbelief, they both thought that tomorrow's tea with Mr. and Mrs. Vicar would come with a great big serving of Perry Mason.

15

____

It was a little after 9:00 the next morning when the sound of rain lashing the windows slowly stirred Tim into consciousness. Semi-awake, he lay in the fetal position, clutching his pillow, not wanting to move an inch from where his body had warmed the sheets. His thoughts were divided between wishing he were on a beach in Malibu, instead of being a human ice cube in this ancient stone castle, and thinking about the fun he'd had the day before with Grayson. Although he couldn't remember how the previous evening had ended—perhaps he'd had too many pints in the pub—or why he'd even bothered to come home, Tim knew he'd had enormous fun with his new chum.

Then a tap on the door was followed by Tiara's loud whisper. "Timmy, dear, are you awake?" She opened the door before he could answer.

Tim grumbled something incoherent as he turned over onto his back, dragging the duvet up to his neck and wanting nothing more in life than to snuggle back into his cocoon.

Tiara smiled at Tim's attempt at modesty. "Be glad the good

Lord gave you what you've got." She sniggered. "I'm glad He gave me the eyes to see it!"

Tim teased her with a quick flash of flesh.

"No need to be shy around me," she said, picking up a pair of socks off the floor and standing beside his bed. "I've seen it all. Don't forget, I cleaned your bottom when you were a baby. And speaking of butts, are the folks in this castle ever going to get their respective rusty dusties in gear today? Your mother's still in the sack, and visitors are coming. Tea with the village vicar and his missus."

Now Tim was wide awake with curiosity, but feeling slightly resentful that he'd probably have to play co-host for a boring tea party instead of hanging out with Grayson.

"How did this happen?" he asked. "There was a Bingo game at the church, and Polly won a hamper of assorted cheeses and crackers and an audience with the pope. Right?"

"Something like that," Tiara agreed. "You missed all the fun yesterday." Then she recapped the events that had taken place while he was entertaining Grayson. "The vicar paid a visit while we were over at Hedgepath Manor. Oh, you'd have loved Lord and Lady Ridgewood-Brimble's house! Makes this place look like a shack for hillbillies! The vicar called in while we were away, so Her Highness is playing Lady Bountiful and giving him tea today. I've baked fresh scones and sent Lily into the village to get a Victoria sponge. Now, take a shower, make yourself look pretty, and come down and lend a hand."

By the time Tim had completed his ablutions and wandered downstairs, most of the preparation work for tea had been completed. In the main reception room, Tiara and Lily rearranged the Chesterfield settees into a conversation pod in front of the fireplace. The coffee table was decorated with a small cut-glass vase centerpiece of colorful winter heather and cyclamen that Merv had collected from the greenhouse. On a wooden trolley, delicate cups and saucers, dessert plates, and a shiny silver teapot had been set on antique crocheted lace doilies.

"How can I help?" Tim said, happy to see that he'd perfectly timed his arrival to avoid doing any real work. "I'm a little nervous about this. How does one even talk to a vicar? I don't want to say something wrong. I haven't been in a church for ages. It's not that I don't believe in a higher power, but my mind wanders whenever I close my eyes to pray. I think about what the minister is wearing under his robe. What do I even call him? Is it Father? Your Eminence? Your Holiness? What if I inadvertently call him *dude*? Would he be offended?"

"Try Wallace. That's his name," Tiara said and looked at her watch.

"When are they due?" Tim asked just as the loud, dull thud of the doorknocker reverberated into the house.

"One guess," Tiara sniped with a look of panic. "And, as usual, your mother's still not ready!"

"Polly Pepper always has to make a grand theatrical entrance when she meets new people," Tim reminded her. "If she could have confetti and trumpets following her around all day, you know she would!"

"Everything'll be fine," Tiara predicted as she took one last frantic look around the room to make sure that nothing was out of place, and pushed Tim out.

"As long as she reins in her tongue and uses substitute words like 'bullspit, monkey feathers, and holy guacamole!' we'll survive," Tim agreed as he walked to the vestibule. Then, with a wide and genuine smile, he released the lock and opened the door.

"I'm Wallace Aylsworth, and this is my wife, Joan," said the smiling vicar as he entered the hallway and wiped his wet shoes on the coir-fiber mat. "Do we need to remove them?"

"No worries. That's what maids are for," Tim joked, immediately feeling at ease with the couple. He guessed they were probably in their mid-forties and seemed to complement each other physically and socially as they profusely thanked him for inviting them to tea (although he had nothing to do with it). They, in turn, saw Tim as a charming young man with a movie-star-handsome face and sparkling sapphire-blue eyes and whose posture hinted at a body well-conditioned by rigorous exercise under his shirt and sweater.

They seem cool, Tim said to himself, his trepidation slipping away as he led them through to the main reception room, where Mr. Boots had claimed sleeping territory on one of the settees. Tiara was standing with a broad smile beside the fireplace.

"The famous Polly Pepper!" Joan Aylsworth enthused as she reached out to shake Tiara's hand. "My mother loves you so much! She often talks about seeing you in person at the London Palladium years ago. The queen was there too. It's an honor to have you in our little village!"

"I hate to disappoint you or your mother, but I'm merely Polly's personal maid and *consœur*," Tiara said affably and introduced herself. "But it's a simple mistake to make, as you'll see if her diva-ness ever gets her fan... er, tush... er, self... down here. Let me see what's keeping her. Please have a seat. Tim will serve tea."

In a very short while, everyone's attention was simultaneously seized into silence and expectation when Lily pulled open the pocket doors that separated the reception room from the dining room. The star had arrived! In a floral, midnight-blue, knee-length dress and white high-heeled shoes, Polly Pepper stood for a pregnant beat as if waiting for an ovation to subside.

Then she regally strolled into the room, looking every inch like the Hollywood celebrity that she was. Although it was way too early in the day to wear a short-sleeved cocktail dress, and the fabric was too sheer for this icy time of year, it somehow worked for Polly. She masterfully played the role of a goddess coming down from her mountaintop temple to wander among mere mortals.

Of course, Tim and Tiara saw right through her act. But they'd had so many years of being fellow co-conspirators in Polly's one-woman show that they instantly fell into lockstep and took part in the charade.

"I'm so sorry to have kept you all waiting." Polly trilled a faux apology. "I had to take an important Zoom call from my agent in California."

Tiara quickly did the time-zone math in her head and hoped that the vicar didn't realize that it was 3:00 in the morning on the West Coast of North America and that at that hour celebrities' agents were deep in the land of dreaming about contract negotiations and 15% paychecks.

"You're very understanding," Polly purred to her audience as Tiara handed her a glass of champagne.

And, indeed, they were understanding, and they didn't think there was anything in the least bit odd that they had been offered tea while the hostess had bubbly. They even felt as though they were in on a bit of backstage show-business intrigue—a star taking a meeting with her Hollywood agent. What might that conversation have produced that they could later look back on and tell friends they were in Polly Pepper's house with her when the call came in, resulting in some important new movie role or personal appearance somewhere?

Vicar Aylsworth and his wife were instantly charmed by Polly. They'd done their homework the night before, googling *Polly Pepper*. They discovered she had become a musical-comedy star when she first stepped onto a Broadway stage. The success of her long-running hit television variety series had further burnished her name. It hardly registered to them that Polly's incandescence had diminished to a flicker lately, and she had been reduced to taking roles in independent low-budget horror films like *Crawling Eyeballs II: The Vision Returns*. But they were still impressed. Years of pandering to her fans and the press gave Polly the tools she needed to dazzle any audience—even a vicar and his wife.

In a very short while, all apprehensions from both sides of the showbiz/church aisle were wholly allayed. Polly and her troupe were enjoying themselves, happy that the vicar was the farthest thing they could imagine from an overly zealous good-time killjoy. The Aylsworths, too, found their hosts utterly endearing. As the moments moved on, Polly became less pretentious. Even if she often dropped names of the stars she'd worked with or had met during her career, the guests didn't think she was bragging. Cher, Barbra, and Bette were apparently her chums. The anecdotes she shared about them were organically and masterfully woven into the conversation. Joan Aylsworth, especially, hung on Polly's every word. She was mesmerized and never stopped smiling and nodding like a bobblehead toy as she imagined what it must be like to have fans and famous friends.

Although the vicar and his wife had the best time of their lives listening to Polly prattle on, Tim knew it was important to include them equally in the gabfest. Their lives couldn't possibly be as interesting as Polly's, but a good host shares the stage, and he waited for a break in his mother's stories about what it was like giving interviews and winning Emmy Awards.

Finally, Tim found a wedge of conversation space. "Mom's a star in her world, but you are in your realm, too. It must be personally fulfilling to be someone everyone in the village looks up to. Tell us what it's like to be a vicar."

"Not everyone looks up to me. Ask our sixteen-year-old." Vicar Aylsworth chuckled at the old joke along with his wife. Then, for the next ten minutes, he rambled on about his God-ordained responsibilities and commitments to the people of Abbots Clover. "I do a bit of spiritual guidance and counseling, of course," he said. "I coach the youth football, too. Then there's charity work. We've been ministering here for the past three years and truly believe we make a positive difference." He included his wife to make it seem like his work was a team effort. "I'm pleased to say that we know pretty much everyone in the area. If you need a seamstress, make an appointment to see Sylvia Postin—as long as she hasn't stopped taking her bipolar meds. The best barber is Sam Kingsman—but not on Tuesdays because he'll still be hungover from his Saturday-to-Monday-night binge. Margaret Jackson's a helpful pharmacist, but if you've got a particularly gross medical condition, expect everyone else to know what's seeping or oozing. Emma Tunsing is our local fortune teller. She's good at generalities, but I've never known her to pick the EuroMillions jackpot numbers, if you get what I mean. Even if they don't all come to church, we still think of the villagers as our spiritual family and love them all. Our door is always open for spiritual support in this life and sympathy when a loved one moves on to their next plane of existence."

Although Polly's interest had noticeably begun to wane—she really didn't care about the finer details of anyone's job unless they were famous—she did her best to make it at least appear that she was curious about how the vicar tended his flock.

"When you stop and think about it, I'll bet the people we'll meet here in our new village aren't all that different from the ones who live in my Hollywood neck of the woods," she said, unconsciously making herself the subject of the conversation again. "No matter where I go around the globe, I always find a divine Julie Andrews type or a loveable Tom Hanks clone. Of course, I've come across a couple of Harvey Weinstein monsters, too." She laughed and made a fake shudder. "I think we naturally attract the same variety of people everywhere we go. Don't you agree?"

Joan Aylsworth nodded and said, "You've just named my favorite celebrities. Oh, not Harvey, of course! But Julie and Tom, for sure. Did you ever meet them? Or Meryl Streep? I'd kill to meet Meryl Streep. Oh, and Chris Hemsworth, too. What is he like in real life?"

"Big cities are really just a collection of small villages bound together by an assortment of citizens." The vicar sided with Polly. "When we lived in London and Birmingham, the neighborhoods comprised many individual ethnic communities. Oh, and we have our very own Julie Andrews right here in Abbots Clover," he said with pride. "Mae Billings. She sings in our choir and last year starred in St. Clematis's original musical production of *Cats on a Hot Tin Roof*."

"She's less Mary Poppins and more Victor/Victoria if you get what I mean," Joan Aylsworth stage-whispered behind the back of her hand, letting Polly and the others know she wasn't as impressed with Mae Billings and St. Clematis's stupid musical show that ripped off Tennessee Williams's play title and Andrew Lloyd Webber's songs.

The last person on earth that Polly wanted to meet was an amateur performer from what was basically the UK version of Hooterville. But she pretended to be fascinated by the vicar's description of the local entertainer, whom he claimed was equally adept at baking a blackberry crumble as she was at coaxing the celestial choir down from heaven to sing backup on "Supercalifragilisticexpialidocious."

Polly took another fortifying sip of her champers. "She

sounds fascinating." Polly silently advised herself to be careful not to say anything that might encourage the vicar to suggest introducing her to whoever the local version of Taylor Swift was.

Then she deftly shifted gears to steer the conversation toward the potential crime she was investigating. "If Mae Billings is your Julie Andrews, I'll bet ol' Gwellyn Clogg was Harvey W." She laughed at what she thought was a funny comparison and expected universal agreement. But the room suddenly turned quiet. "What a character Gwellyn was. Am I right? The more I learn about her, the more I think it's not so bad that she was hauled back to the big dustbin in the sky. Did you know—I guess everybody around here does—that she died in this house? It's nerve-racking enough to find a dead mouse in the larder. But a dead housekeeper? Oh my!"

At the mention of Gwellyn's name, the jovial smiles on the vicar's and his wife's faces vanished like a magician's rabbit, leaving behind an awkward silence. It was as if a gust of wind had blown out the candles on a birthday cake, extinguishing all the joy in the room. But Polly remained oblivious, her tongue continuing its acrobatics, flinging barbs like a slingshot. Yet Tim and Tiara felt the sudden chill of walking into a freezer on a scorching hot beach day. They exchanged puzzled glances, desperately searching for clues, wondering if they had unintentionally stepped on some invisible social landmine. Had they unknowingly offended the vicar? Was gossiping about a dead person a scriptural no-no? Sure, Polly's blabbering wasn't exactly hurting anyone, especially not a departed maid with a less-than-gleaming reputation, but something was amiss, and they had to figure out how to unravel the mystery of the suddenly icy atmosphere.

After a moment that felt longer than a snail race, Tim cleared his throat, mustering his best attempt at reviving the stifled atmosphere. "Bless her soul," he said, his voice dripping with forced politeness. "We didn't have the pleasure of truly knowing Gwellyn. Perhaps our initial judgments were a tad hasty. I, for one, am suspending my judgment indefinitely." He shot his mother a comically exaggerated look, crossing his eyes and raising his eyebrows as if hoping to deliver a message of respect via telepathy. "As a member of Mr. Drake's household, Gwellyn must have had some redeeming qualities. I mean, she didn't abandon him during tough times, right?"

"Fiddlesticks!" Polly exclaimed, waving her hand dismissively. "She was after his money. Your eternal optimism sometimes blinds you to the obvious. Let's not forget that she had a rap sheet longer than a giraffe's neck. She got arrested for pinching Lady Ridgewood-Brimble's brooch. She tried to extort an inheritance from me. She lied about being sacked. And let's not overlook her audacity in breaking into the castle in the dead of night, only to end up a murder victim."

"Murder?" the vicar harrumphed, sitting up straighter and adjusting his clerical collar. He glanced around the room as if searching for hidden cameras. "You're not suggesting... What gave you that... Not in Abbots Clover! This is a community of tea and scones, not crime and chaos."

"Oh, I know nothing, really," Polly countered with an innocent smile and tapped the side of her empty glass to attract Tiara's attention. "That's just a theory from someone I know who has a nose for news. But it does give one pause. And a murder can happen even in the most picturesque villages."

"Gwellyn Clogg died from a congenital heart condition," Joan said in support of her husband's objection and defending the general morality of the village. "It said so in the *Abbots Clover Overview*. Sad."

The vicar, too, deflected the notion of criminality with a wave of his hand. "Evidence, my dear friends. Is there any evidence? I'd trust the newspaper before putting any stock in grapevine hearsay. We must have a solid foundation of truth before we build our house of suspicions."

"I read a newspaper article once that said squirrels have developed a secret society and are plotting to take over the world, one acorn at a time," Tim said, trying to lighten the mood with levity. "So the next time you see a squirrel staring at you with those beady eyes, remember they might be hatching their diabolical plan for world domination."

The vicar gave him an incredulous look. "You've become rather popular with Constable Jenkins. He hasn't said anything to you about a crime, has he? I'd ignore the busybody who made such a comment about Gwellyn Clogg's death."

Holy moly, everyone really does know everyone else's business in this small village! Tim screamed to himself, wondering if the specific intimate details of his friendship with Grayson were common knowledge among the locals, too. *And was the vicar's tone just a tad condescending?* He took a deep breath and shrugged. "I think Grayson—Constable Jenkins, that is—has the same elevated ethics you do. You don't reveal the secrets that your parishioners share with you, and he doesn't talk about his police investigations." Tim wanted to add *we have far more interesting things to do with our time together, wink-wink,* but he stopped himself. "You said yourself that everything that happens in big cities also happens in small villages. Maybe Polly has a point about there being more than meets the eye to Gwellyn's death."

"No, Vicar Aylsworth is right," Polly said, trying to maintain the appearance of trusting the clergyman and his analytical thought processes. "Conspiracy theories are the devil's playground. Princess Diana's death was an inside job. The moon landing was faked on a soundstage. And the Earth is as flat as a pancake to a bunch of numbnuts who flunked General Science 101. Some people can't accept simple, obvious, black-

and-white explanations for what they think are inexplicable events."

Tiara chimed in, "On the other hand, from personal experience, even stories in the *National Intruder* have a kernel of truth to support their celebrity muckraking. Your toes are only slightly webbed, not the big ol' Donald Duck feet they claimed."

"Who are these *some people*?" Joan asked, suggesting Polly elaborate on the credentials of the Nosey Nancy who suggested an alternative cause of Gwellyn Clogg's death. She glanced sideways at her husband. "Surely, those *some people* aren't from around here. We would have heard about this. We know almost everything that goes on in Abbots Clover. Not that Gwellyn would have won any Miss Congeniality awards, but no one in our tranquil village would actually kill her... or anyone else."

The teacup and saucer Joan Aylsworth held on her lap quivered ever so slightly. Polly noticed it and wondered if it was the caffeine in the Earl Grey, or was she just edgy at the thought that someone in her beloved village had committed a mortal sin? The vicar also noticed the twitch, reached over, removed the fragile porcelain pieces from his wife's hand, and placed them on the serving trolley.

"We live in an oh-so-charming village," Joan continued. "It's one of the main reasons we asked to be assigned here; we wanted to live somewhere idyllic, our very own *Escape to the Country*, somewhere with less stress and drama. Occasional disagreements between friends and neighbors are bound to happen no matter where you live, but we know everyone for miles around, and they're all decent people."

"They are indeed," the vicar heartily agreed and offered a faint patronizing smile to Polly. "It would be terrible to spoil the village's reputation if there was a whisper of anything menacing going on here."

"You'll not hear another murmur about it from me," Polly

said brightly, pretending that she concurred with the vicar's disbelief in any monkey business and insinuating that she would not fan the flames of gossip. End of subject. But she did think it was rather curious that the vicar and his wife had quickly dismissed the idea of a potential dirty deed occurring in their midst and labeled it false. Most people, she thought, would have been wide-eyed with intense interest and wanted to hear more details about how a dead body came to be before coming to definitive conclusions. Murder fascinates most people—if only to be grateful that it didn't happen to them.

And why did Mr. and Mrs. Vicar seem so defensive? Maybe they didn't want to hear anything negative about their little slice of heaven. But the needle on Polly's intuition meter was pulsating, and she began subtly addressing the vicar with questions that she hoped would offer a glimpse into how well he had known Gwellyn.

"As a man of the cloth and one who gives free advice, it must make you a bit exasperated when someone like Gwellyn, who probably could have used a bit of spiritual support, doesn't take advantage of your professional services," she said. "If you were a shrink in Beverly Hills, you'd be raking in three hundred fifty dollars an hour! No doubt your sermons are uplifting, too; she would have been inspired. Did Gwellyn volunteer at the food bank? Was she part of a friendship group that visits shut-ins or the elderly? Was she on a quiz team at the Fox & Hare?"

"I wouldn't know. I think she mainly kept to herself," the vicar said, shaking his head before taking a sip from his teacup. "I imagine she was too exhausted by the end of the day to do much more than pour a glass of wine and put her feet up."

"I can't really blame her for not wanting to spend her free time doing a lot of churchy charity chores," Polly said. "I'm the same. I have my own version of philanthropy called 'avoiding the wretchedness of the world's disasters.' It's how I keep my sanity. And speaking of disasters, I'd rather read dissertations on the intricacies of knitting with spaghetti than any headline about Meghan Markle."

Tiara, who was always plugged into whatever was going on in Polly's head, now surreptitiously piggybacked on her boss's line of questioning, trying to make it appear that this interrogation was merely a casual conversation. "Lily tells us you used to visit with Mr. Drake every week," she said. "What a good man you are. Even if it was part of your job, it's still above and beyond the call for most people."

The vicar smiled bashfully but was obviously drinking in the kudos because he seemed to swell like a sponge sucking up gallons of flattery.

"I hope Gwellyn took advantage of your kind ear while you were paying your weekly visits," Tiara continued, trying to draw secrets from the vicar. "Did she ever discuss her challenges—there must have been many. Or any personal problems she might have been having? Maybe she was still coping with grief after her brother died last year. Or maybe something else was going on, like breaking up with somebody? We heard that she might have been seeing someone, and maybe it hadn't ended well. I hope she didn't feel entirely alone in life. Your thoughts?"

The vicar shook his head and shrugged. "None, really. I mean, yes, I would have been delighted to help her if I could have, but she hardly ever spoke to me except a curt hello when she answered the door. She usually sent Lily to Mr. Drake's room with tea and a couple of biscuits, but otherwise, we never interacted much. Familiarity breeds contempt," the vicar said cautiously. "She didn't know me well enough to find fault, I guess." He was suddenly guarded and hyperalert to the surveillance he felt coming from his hosts. What had begun as a convivial meet and greet with superficial questions about family, work, and celebrity gossip had turned into what now seemed more than a passing inquiry into his relationship with the recently deceased Gwellyn Clogg.

"As I've said, Joan and I hardly knew Gwellyn. Not to sound elitist—we're the farthest things from fancy pants—but Gwellyn was from a different class, if you get my meaning. Not that we see labels of any kind on people. Absolutely not. And working in service isn't anything to be ashamed about. We love our cleaners and clerks. We depend on them. They perform important tasks. Any able-bodied person who has work and isn't on public benefits is to be highly commended. However, since Gwellyn wasn't a member of the church or a participant in community activities, or even a close neighbor, we had little reason to associate with her."

The vicar and his wife might not have been conspicuous snobs. Polly Pepper definitely was—although she'd never in a gazillion years have enough self-awareness to recognize it—and she completely understood what the vicar was saying about not mixing with second-fiddle players. But she wasn't buying his declaration that he didn't know much about Gwellyn Clogg and her personal life and activities. After all, he seemed to have a dossier on everyone else in the village: Sylvia Postin was bananas without her psych drugs, Sam Kingsman was a sloppy drunk, Margaret Jackson had ditched her pharmacist's oath to protect customers' health information, and Emma Tunsing was a charlatan clairvoyant. He probably also knew who farted in their pew on Sunday morning. And yet, suspiciously, he couldn't summon any relevant information about Gwellyn other than to say she wasn't in a social class sufficiently elevated to interact with him and his wife. Polly wasn't buying it, but she didn't want to risk overtly pointing out that she thought he and the missus were full-on fibbers. She had to be furtive.

Polly was a master manipulator. To those uninitiated in her wily ways—which obviously included the vicar and his wife—it now seemed that she was merely changing topics to take a less controversial conversation path when she suddenly started asking about the Aylsworths' son.

"I'll bet he's adorable," Polly convincingly squealed as Joan eagerly opened the photos app on her phone and shared a dozen pictures of bucktoothed Sebastian, who needed an operation to pin his ears back and wore eyeglass lenses thick enough to magnify paramecia.

During all the years she spent working on *The Polly Pepper Playhouse*, her iconic television show, she was able to rule the roost while still maintaining her goody-goody image by having others do her bidding. If she found something lacking in a stagehand, makeup girl, or dancer in the Polly Pepper Prancers, her resident company of hoofers, a quick, confidential word to the director or producer took care of the good-for-nothing slacker. Then she could take a bouquet of flowers and a $100 gift card for Trader Joe's to the poor son of a gun, who believed her when she insisted she had personally fought like the devil to keep them employed, but that because of silly union rules, her hands were tied in the matter. There were a lot of idiots who believed her when she said that even though she was the star of the show and her name was literally the program's title, she was helpless.

But as she now tried to maneuver her guests similarly, they weren't cooperating. So she tried another strategy: Lily. Polly hoped Lily might help refresh the vicar's memory of Gwellyn's personal life. As she prattled on about the challenges of raising children and how you never know if your kids will turn out like Hugh Jackman or Kanye West, she wandered over to the servant's bellpull and gave it a tug. A moment later, Lily stood in the reception room, her apron a splattered mess and her eyes as wide as a meerkat's.

Was it just Polly's imagination, or did Lily cast a quick, nervous eye over the vicar when she was introduced to the guests? Of course, the little scamp was always nervous. Everything from expiration dates on milk cartons to news on the internet that the Second Coming was back on the calendar this week made her anxious. So who could tell?

"I already know the vicar from when he used to visit Mr. Drake," Lily said, offering him a shy smile and slight curtsy.

"Delighted to see you again, Lily!" the vicar said with genuine enthusiasm. He seemed pleased to see her and politely asked how she was getting on without Gwellyn by her side and how much fun she must be having working for a celebrity. "You're looking well, and I miss our little chats."

"Yes, please, and thank you," Lily said, not knowing if his comments required answers. As for her work being fun, she almost laughed out loud. She hated working for anyone and considered herself little more than a wage-earning slave. She resented every boss she'd ever had, famous or otherwise. But she caught herself just before that truth slipped past her klutzy tongue. Instead, she said, "I think of Gwellyn a lot, but no, I don't miss her very much. Do you think she knew she was going down there? To h-e-l-l, I mean? Because she told me once that she and the devil would see each other in person before you ever darkened the doorway of Thistlethorne Lodge again."

At that statement, even Mr. Boots sat up and gave a loud, bitchy, "Meow."

Then Lily looked at Polly and said, "By the way, I dropped the Victoria sponge."

16

The tea party had been an epic disaster. Not only was the Victoria sponge a wasted mess all over the kitchen floor, but the vicar had felt insulted and essentially accused of lying and misrepresenting himself and his association with Gwellyn Clogg.

"You know nothing about me, our village, or the people who live here, Miss Polly Pepper!" he hissed as he raced for the exit with his wife. "You're a loo-loo from La La Land who's waltzed into our community—uninvited, I might add—and decided, without a scintilla of evidence, that there's been a murder of one of our citizens, and you think that you're the one who can prove it. Yes, we read about you online and found an interesting article in *Daily Variety* that quoted your old TV co-star, Frank Merchant. He said you've been booted out of Hollywood because you think you have a talent for sniffing out stiffs. Even though you did help the Beverly Hills Police Department a couple of times."

"Frank's a mean-spirited hack I discovered in a dive stand-up comedy club in Phoenix, Arizona. I should have left him there to bake among the rattlesnakes and scorpions in the summer heat," Polly said, trying to cut through the diatribe. "He would never have amounted to anything more than a cut-rate version of Dana Carvey. He was never nominated for an Emmy and resented my winning twelve of those babies."

The vicar talked over Polly, reminding her she was a foreigner who had come to Abbots Clover only a few days earlier, so she couldn't possibly know what the customs and traditions were, let alone who the people were and what they were or were not capable of doing. "As a Christian, I'm not going to publicly stir the pot—I'll leave that to others—but I'm also not going to be a party to your idiotic attempt to turn Abbots Clover into a game of *The Traitors* for your personal entertainment. And don't be surprised if people come to their own conclusions and start treating you in a way that will make you wish you'd stayed in California."

He took a short breath and continued the character assassination. "We're a lovely and hospitable village, and we give everyone the benefit of the doubt when inviting new people into our lives. But it's a two-way street. Newcomers must prove their worthiness, and so far, you've failed miserably. The next thing we'll hear is that you think everyone in the village has collectively conspired to cover up the real cause of Gwellyn Clogg's death! Keep your plastic, surgically sculpted nose out of places where noses have no business sniffing around!"

And then he huffed out of the house with Mrs. Vicar in tow and not so much as a "thanks for the scones."

"Boy, am I glad I met Grayson before today," Tim said sarcastically as he followed his mother and Tiara back to the reception room. "I'd have never stood a chance of making friends with him once word gets out about what just happened and our weird family."

Polly had slipped into a daze and didn't hear her son's comment or Tiara agreeing with him. All she could hear was the vicar saying she'd been laughed out of Hollywood. That was a stinging slap in the face. She'd never really thought about it like that, but maybe the fact that she now only worked sporadically was a consequence of what she'd previously thought of as a fun hobby: linking killers to murdered dead bodies. *What's wrong with using my brains and celebrity clout to solve a murder mystery or two? But maybe people really are laughing at me instead of with me.* That thought made her deeply depressed. *I obviously don't belong in Abbots Clover. Maybe I don't belong in Hollywood anymore, either,* she thought as she idly picked up Mr. Boots, sat down glumly on the settee, and began stroking the cat on her lap.

If there was one thing that Polly detested, it was being told she was wrong about anything. She'd even memorized the Trivial Pursuit deck of answer cards so she'd never be wrong while playing the board game with family and friends. Some would have called that cheating. Polly considered it being prepared. Her entire life had been spent proving she was right when others rejected her and her abilities. *"No, you don't have any talent! No, you'll never become a star! No, the most handsome producer in Hollywood will never marry you; look in the mirror."* But Polly Pepper could see Polly Pepper more clearly than anyone else, and now she had a project nearly equal to the task of becoming a living legend. She had to prove that she was right about her theory that Gwellyn Clogg was a victim of murder.

In an instant, her downcast face changed to a yellow smiling emoji, and she set the cat aside. "Kiddies," she sang out, "get your coats and scarves. We're going stalking!"

Tim raised his hands as if to shield himself from the magnetic beams his mother was famous for casting like tentacles to rope others into her plans and schemes. "Not me, thank you. I'm meeting Grayson for lunch." He tried to sidestep her rally cry. "He's promised to show me how to escape from handcuffs."

"And I've got to supervise Lily in the cleanup of that sticky Victoria sponge." Tiara added her own excuse. "I don't know how it could possibly have gotten on the ceiling, and I know how you feel about mice in the kitchen!"

Polly stepped out of her high heels and whined, "You heard what the vicar said. He wants us to find Gwellyn's killer!"

Tim and Tiara exchanged open-mouthed looks of astonishment that Polly could have misread the vicar so utterly and completely. "He literally called you a loony from La La Land!" Tim said.

"He said 'loo-loo,' not 'loony,'" Polly corrected. "He said a lot of things that sounded unkind on the surface, but I think he was basically challenging me to prove myself by investigating Gwellyn's death."

"Prove yourself as what? The village idiot?" Tim protested.

"And how in God's name do you get 'Keep your plastic, surgically sculpted nose out of places where noses have no business sniffing around!' as a call to arms?" Tiara exclaimed.

"He also said that newcomers to the village have to prove their worth," Polly countered. "The vicar's basically goading us to find evidence that Gwellyn was murdered! He can't do it himself because that would be like insider trading or something. He lives here and can't risk alarming people or calling one of his flock a killer."

"Oh, brother!" Tim cried, shaking his head and putting his hands over his ears. "He was telling you to mind your business and get out of Dodge!"

"Even if that's what he said, he didn't mean it the way it came out," Polly countered. "My mother was the same way. She told me I'd never amount to anything. That I didn't have a drop of talent. That I was ugly and stupid and a hopeless dreamer and that nobody would pay for a ticket to see me do anything. But those words only made me more determined to succeed. After I became famous, she called what she'd said and done 'tough love,' as though she had been intentionally unkind to prepare me for a callous business and see how serious I was about making it. I still don't think it was very nice, but that's what energized me to keep going—to prove her wrong. That's what Vicar Aylsworth is doing. He researched me and knows how persistent I can be. He's goading me to push forward."

Tim and Tiara continued to shake their heads and make cockeyed faces of disbelief that Polly could be so totally removed from reality. But, on the other hand, they knew she was right about forcing down barriers with her single-mindedness.

They knew from Hollywood lore and firsthand experience that Polly Pepper had faced nearly insurmountable odds to achieve her success, and it was primarily due to her extraordinary self-determination and trust in an inner voice that told her she was special enough to confront naysaying agents and producers who told her that she was too different from everyone else to ever be successful in a profession that values physical attractiveness and mediocrity over originality and talent.

"What's your plan?" Tim finally asked, sounding defeated and knowing full well that it was a lost cause to try to get out of joining forces with his mother on whatever crusade she was embarking on. It was best to surrender early to whatever scheme Polly was concocting because she'd win in the end anyway, and this way, there would be fewer casualties.

Tiara, too, knew that it was futile to stop a tsunami. Her boss was a force of nature, and there would be less bloodletting if the weaker of the two just gave in without a struggle.

"Who's the US ambassador to England?" she asked. "We'd better put his name and number on our speed-dial list because I smell an international incident brewing," she said while asking herself how she keeps being drawn into Polly's cockamamie schemes.

Polly made the face of someone contemplating the answer to a riddle. "You know me, I don't blueprint anything," she said. "I set a goal and then let the universe guide me. It works every time! The vicar gave us a few clues to follow."

Tim and Tiara couldn't remember one thing that the vicar had said that could remotely be considered a clue to a murder mystery. Unless he was offering up Emma Tunsing's psychic abilities, there was nothing in what he'd said that anyone with common sense could interpret as an invitation to turn the village upside down and rummage around in other people's closets. Or was there?

Polly seemed to be keeping her cards close to her vest when she exclaimed, "Don't look at the big picture. It'll appear too overwhelming. One baby step at a time." Then she quickly flew out of the room, leaving Tim and Tiara staring at one another and telepathically agreeing that Polly was probably losing her marbles faster than they'd previously suspected.

Tim and Tiara followed Polly through the castle courtyard and waved to a smiling Merv as they exited the ancient fortified walls. Without questioning their Pied Piper, they trundled the half mile to the village high street. Up the small incline of a narrow, cobbled lane, they arrived at Polly's destination: Bound to Read mystery and romance book and coffee shop, which had been featured in a tourist's guide to Abbots Clover that Solicitor Wainwright had added to the raft of pamphlets he'd included with the key to Thistlethorne.

The book/coffee shop faced opposite St. Andrew's Church, which was a dark-gray stone, fifteenth-century house of prayer whose bells had pealed every hour on the hour since before King Henry VIII destroyed the monasteries and convents in the 1500s. According to the brochure, Bound to Read was *the* place for locals to meet for a cuppa.

"I've heard that they have a divine loganberry tart," Polly said as an explanation for their visit as she opened the door. They were instantly met with the scent of freshly brewed coffee, the sound of a hissing espresso machine, and what appeared to be convivial conversations all around.

It was a cozy space of exposed-brick walls on which hung framed, famous front-page newspaper headlines announcing "World Mourns Diana," "Aliens Abduct Politicians, Replace With Intelligent Life," and "Big Foot Spotted at Local Starbucks: Orders Mocha Frappuccino." The ceiling was low, with wide wooden beams showing the place's centuries-old age. A purple velvet settee fit snugly against the front wall under a large multi-paned window. Eight tables gathered within touching distance of each other were occupied by various villagers, many of whom had their dogs lying calmly at their feet.

Polly spotted one available table that still had takeaway coffee cups, wooden stirring sticks, and torn packets of sugar scattered on top and directed Tim and Tiara to grab it before anyone else came along.

The bookstore portion of the shop began just beyond the café section and two steps down on the left side of a balustrade. Polly and her troupe could see display tables draped with tartan cloths and stacks of new and used books. Signs announced Staff Recommendations. Shelves against the walls were labeled by reading genre and lined with colorful book spines.

The café's menu blackboard was above the front counter. Although Tim and Tiara couldn't remember Polly ever standing in a queue for anything other than a stall in the ladies' restroom, she volunteered to buy the snacks.

"I want the locals to see for themselves that I'm just like everybody else and not the harridan diva that Vicar Aylsworth is probably making me out to be at this very moment."

The smiling young barista behind the counter—her name badge read Sarah—was probably in her mid-twenties and had the ideal attitude for anyone in a front-of-house service position. She was perky, good-natured, and accommodating to her customers, the type of staff who made patrons want to continue handing over their money to a local small business.

"Medium-sized cappuccino with one pump of caramel syrup, one pump of vanilla, a dollop of whole milk, extra whipped cream, and a sprinkle of cinnamon. Of course! You got it!" she said to one customer.

Then, to another, "Oh, go ahead, Mrs. Cuttler, you deserve something as sweet as you are," she said, removing a chocolate brownie from the display case and easily persuading one of her loyal patrons to indulge.

To still another, she said, "This chocolate cinnamon twist is seriously yummy, Mrs. Simson. I mean *seriously* yummy!" Her emphasis on "seriously" made Mrs. Simson's mouth water. Although she could afford to lose about fifty pounds, she simply couldn't resist agreeing that her day would not be complete without the tasty snack accompanying her cup of tea.

By the time Polly reached the front of the queue, Sarah had already recognized her and greeted her by name. "We've heard that we have a celebrity living in Abbots Clover. You don't look much like Brad Pitt, so you must be Polly Pepper!" she cooed in a manner that was more witty than obsequious.

"Oh, call me Polly!" the star crooned graciously. "And you're far too young to know who I am! But please don't insult me by saying your great-grandmother was a fan of my old show. I'm getting pretty darn tired of people reminding me that I've been around longer than the pyramids and that I sign my autograph with hieroglyphics."

"Okay, how 'bout my grandmother's the ardent admirer?" Sarah laughed. "I saw her the other day, and she was so excited to hear that you're living at Thistlethorne. She told me she saw you in a Royal Variety Performance when she was pregnant with my mother."

"Grandmother! I'm leaving your shop this very instant!" Polly deadpanned.

Sarah already felt like a potential friend. She was young, intelligent, droll, and apparently not obnoxiously starstruck. When Polly finished placing her order and held out her bank debit card, Sarah brushed it away. "On the house. My way of saying welcome to Abbots Clover."

Polly beamed. "I never get freebies! People think I'm rich. They see my face and see an ATM on my forehead. You won't get in trouble with the boss?"

"I've got that she-devil wrapped around my baby finger."

"In other words, you're the boss," Polly correctly guessed, laughing along with Sarah. Then she looked around, *oohed*, and *ahhed* about how quaint and typically English she thought the place looked. "It's so... Renaissance!" she said approvingly. "How do you handle a coffee bar and a bookshop? You can't be in both places at once!"

"I've got Josh," she said, pointing to a young man ringing up a purchase at the cash register in the bookstore section of the shop.

As Polly observed Josh placing a book into a paper bag, she instinctively turned to look at Tim, who had already set his approving eyes on Josh. And who could blame him? Josh was probably in his early twenties and had broad shoulders, light beard stubble on a milky white complexion, green eyes, dimples, and a mop of curly black hair. He was the kind of walking advertisement for the shop that money couldn't buy.

"Don't introduce him to my son," Polly said, grinning. "They may disappear together."

"I'd do almost anything to keep him here," Sarah said, with obvious disappointment. "Unfortunately, he's just handed in his notice. In six weeks, he's moving up to Scotland to start working on his girlfriend's father's sheep farm. I'll never find anyone who's as good a worker. He's always on time and doesn't complain if I ask him to stay an extra hour when we're busy. And I won't find anyone who brings in a lot of giggling schoolgirls who could just as easily buy their coffees from Mrs. Smith at the bakery."

"Good," Polly said. "Oh, not good that you're losing a gem of an employee, but Tim, my son, shouldn't be distracted just yet. He's got his eyes on someone else. Someone whom I think I could like. I'm not saying it's anything serious at this stage, but I'm sort of crossing my fingers."

"Constable Jenkins?" Sarah smiled and nodded knowingly.

Polly twisted her mouth in amusement at the broadband speed of the village grapevine. "Does everybody around here know?"

"Pretty much," Sarah agreed. "There's not a lot to do in Abbots Clover other than gossip about each other. There's reading, of course, which I try to encourage. But other than crafts groups like the Bitch and Stitch Quilting Queens and the Deep Roots Garden Club, it's fairly monotonous, especially in winter. I think it gives some people a sense of power when they think they know others' secrets. It breaks up their routine lives. You know the adage, 'If you haven't got anything nice to say about someone… come sit by me.'" She laughed. "But we're all fairly harmless."

"Let me guess, a psychology major?" Polly said, addressing

Sarah's obvious advanced education and knowledge of human behavior. She also reluctantly recognized her own social failures in what the barista had just said. How many times had Polly herself eagerly telephoned a friend to share tittle-tattles that she'd heard—or made up—about the Sussexes, Jennifer Lopez, or Victoria Beckham?

"Philosophy degree, actually," Sarah explained. "But I had a very interesting class in personality science," she added, then quickly excused herself to help another customer.

Polly, carrying a tray with cups of Frappuccino, black tea, and a flat white, as well as plates of loganberry crumble, rejoined Tim and Tiara.

"She's divine!" Polly trilled in praise of Sarah. "I think I've made an honest-to-goodness new friend. She gave us all these yummies for free!"

"Did she say anything about the other yummy... Mr. Bookseller down there?" Tim said, cocking his head toward the guy in the bookstore.

"She said he has a date with sheep and to leave it at that! I say stick with the semi-sure thing in uniform, sweetums. Change of subject, lovies: I've invited the delightful Sarah—that's her name, isn't it sweet?—to Thistlethorne for dinner. We need someone in the village who's on our side and can counter all the nasties."

17

As Polly and company retraced their steps back to Thistlethorne Lodge, "God Save the King" suddenly blared out from Tim's phone. As he only knew one person in the UK, the caller had to be Constable Jenkins.

"Isn't puppy love disgusting?" Tiara said with a silly smirk. "It's never taken Timmy very long to give a new crush a special ringtone, but this time, he's broken his own speed record."

"In the last six months, we've lived through 'Love Me Tender,' 'Crazy for You,' and 'I Honestly Love You,'" Polly joked sotto voce. "What's next? 'Total Eclipse of the Heart'?"

"Then, inevitably, 'You Don't Bring Me Flowers.'"

As Tim tapped *accept* on his screen, all ears were on high alert to eavesdrop on what they hoped would be an intriguing and lascivious conversation. With pathetically intermittent love lives of their own, Polly and Tiara got their jollies from living vicariously through Tim, who was young and filled with all the stupid optimism of an innocent. But it had been ages since the light of their lives had been in anything more than *like*. Yes, he *liked* the gym trainer, but the guy turned out to be mainly interested in access to Polly's outrageous costume wardrobe. He *liked* the television soap star who was famous for his dark, hypnotic eyes and seemed, at first, to have long-term potential. But when he started making dates based on his astrological forecast, it was only a matter of time—and the stars—before he got the heave-ho. And he *liked* the waiter from the Ivy, the one nicknamed Fuzzy Wuzzy. But Fuzzy Wuzzy turned out to be a furry and spent his free time dressed in a squirrel costume and attending FurFest conventions.

Like his mother, Tim claimed to have high standards (although you couldn't tell from the men they attracted). And after only a few frenzied outings with the same person, his romances inevitably fizzled like a damp firecracker. If Tim began dating someone at Thanksgiving, it was bound to be over by the time carolers started singing "Run, Rudolph, Run" at Christmas tree-lighting ceremonies. It was a sad fact of his otherwise charmed life.

Now, aside from Tim's low-decibel sniggering and a couple of "me toos" and an occasional "you're so funny," the only perceptible sounds came from a pair of squabbling magpies and a flock of bleating sheep looking miserable standing in a cold, soggy field.

Tim finally giggled, "Same here," and disconnected the call. He was in a daze as deep as a coma. He wore a self-satisfied grin, and his faraway look was obviously seeing something—something other than the muddy, rain-filled pothole on the side of the road that he stepped into and that snatched him back to reality.

Finally, to the inquisitive eyes staring at him, he said, "Grayson." As if Polly and Tiara were too dense to figure out on their own whom he'd been flirting with on the phone. "We're meeting up at 6:00. Just for a pint. Maybe a game of darts. Maybe a meal. Maybe... "

Maybe a *maybe*, Polly wanted to say but held her tongue,

glad that Tim had found someone to hang out with in Abbots Clover. She'd had her concerns about him being bored in rural England. Other than playing tourist, there was so little to do here for a young man from Southern California, where the opportunities for fun and games had been unlimited around the clock. Tim was about as interested in reading as a cow in deciphering the nutrition facts on a milk carton. He loved rom-coms, but watching Hugh Grant woo Julia Roberts was out of the question with the internet slower than a sloth on sleeping pills. And sports? Forget about it. The only time he found athletics even remotely interesting was during the men's diving competitions, and that was because the divers' swim trunks left little to the imagination. Unfortunately, here in Abbots Clover, you needed a serious hobby if you weren't fascinated by tractors or farm animals that required herding, shearing, or plucking. So, at least for the time being, Constable Jenkins would be Tim's main leisure activity.

Grayson Jenkins lived in a small one-bedroom flat above the Sherwood Florist flower shop on the far end of Abbots Clover's high street. When Tim arrived, he saw it was kind of a hoarder's paradise. A laundry basket was tipped over on the settee, spilling out wrinkled clothes. The kitchen counter was littered with boxes of breakfast cereals, half-eaten bags of potato chips, and stacks of mail, leaving little space available. A television monitor hung slightly lopsided on the sitting room wall. A puny, dried-up Christmas tree that had yet to be discarded after the holidays sat in a corner like a tinsel-draped dunce.

"Nice place," Tim lied, not really caring a bit about the condition of the flat. All that mattered was Grayson's smiling face. "You ride?" he asked, looking at a mountain bike leaning against a wall. "Maybe you can teach me. I never learned. Grew up with four wheels and an engine."

"Oh, you Americans." Grayson sniggered, trying to fathom the life of anyone who had never had their own bicycle. "Is it true that walking in Los Angeles is illegal?" He laughed, shaking his head. He was serious; he'd heard that somewhere. Then he grabbed his jacket and scarf. "I've booked us in at the Blue Swan," he said, quickly ushering Tim out the door again.

A dense fog had enveloped the village, and they walked along the wet, cobbled street, adjusting their scarves to shield their throats and chins from the bitter cold. They passed a children's charity shop, a men's clothing store, a bakery, and a shoe store. Tim was struck by how delightfully old-fashioned the shops all seemed, especially the men's clothing store with its front window exhibiting headless mannequins wearing dress jackets over Oxford cloth shirts above a scattered display of neckties and even an elegant walking stick. It looked to Tim like what most Americans would imagine a British men's shop to look like, and he loved the yesteryear atmosphere. They passed another shop, and he chuckled at the sign: Family Butcher.

"It sounds like they're serial killers." He laughed.

It was close to 7:00 p.m., so the shops were long closed, and the street was nearly empty. Fog swirled around the streetlights, and other than the sound of their shoes on the cobblestones and the small talk they exchanged, the village was eerily quiet. And then they arrived at the pub.

The Blue Swan was a quintessential English pub/restaurant, complete with rustic wooden beams and walls adorned with framed portraits of hunting dogs, taxidermied animal heads, and football clubs' faded pennants. A stuffed pheasant stood on the mantel above the fireplace while the aroma of comfort foods like fish and chips, shepherd's pie, and bangers and mash floated through the air. The jukebox played a selection of classic rock hits from the Beatles and the Rolling Stones. At the same time, a group of elderly men huddled around a table, playing cards. At the bar, colorful beer taps for Guinness, Stella Artois, Carlsberg, and Strongbow stood at attention as a chap in an unbuttoned black vest pulled the levers to fill tall pint glasses. On the restaurant side, a blazing fireplace was surrounded by dining tables and a half-dozen people eating meals.

Tim and Grayson ordered beers, and the bartender told them to take any available table and to come back to the bar when they were ready to order their food.

As they studied their menus, sipped beer, and absorbed the ambiance, Tim couldn't tell who was having more fun: him or Grayson. Tim ordered fish and chips, while Grayson had mac and cheese. They talked and laughed and told stories of their respective lives. Grayson was proud of his achievement of breaking up a sheep-rustling ring last year and how he'd found himself in the middle of a dispute about the height of a hedge between two neighboring farmers. As the moments lapsed, each believed the other lived in a more interesting world.

Grayson was intrigued by what it must have been like to have Hollywood movie-star friends and asked questions that made Tim laugh out loud.

"Yes, it's not unheard of for them to take their private jet and fly to their beachfront mansions in the South Pacific or to hire personal masseuses for their dogs," Tim said.

"Who's the nicest celebrity you've met? Who's the worst? Did you ever want to be an actor? You're better looking than a lot of the ones I see on telly."

Tim chuckled, equally happy for the flattery and to answer Grayson's questions. He talked about how actors were mostly a nuisance to him. Yes, he knew a lot of famous ones, but he really couldn't care less that they were celebrities.

"They're all aging in the same direction as you and me," he

said. "The nicest ones are the ones you'd expect, like Carol Burnett, Keanu Reeves, and Sandra Bullock. As for the worst ones, you can probably guess who they are, too. They're the Jekyll-and-Hyde types who make news for throwing tantrums at restaurant servers, assaulting their makeup person, or having a hissy fit because there's no unsalted designer butter at the craft services table for their gluten-free bagels in the morning. Need I say more? And no, I wouldn't want to be an actor. It's too hard. You have to be really smart to be a star—unless maybe you just get lucky—like Will Ferrell. I'm sorta glad I don't have any talents."

Grayson said that he'd wanted to be a rock and roll star when he was growing up, and laughed along with Tim when he confessed that he couldn't sing or play any musical instrument, which was sort of a requirement of that job. He said that he became a policeman because the position became available.

"I thought it would be fun to run around arresting people and saying things like, 'You do not have to say anything. But it may harm your defense if you do not mention when questioned something which you later rely on in court.' I basically just wanted to be David Tennant in *Broadchurch*."

He confessed that he'd thought that being a policeman might give him a bit of prestige in the village, too. "But I'm not sure I'm getting the hang of the job. It's actually pretty boring most of the time. I mainly respond to calls about missing cows or sheep or someone accidentally taking in their neighbor's rubbish bins. I hardly ever get to see dead bodies like the one at your place. That was cool. Oh, not cool because your house-keeper died, of course! What I mean is, it had unexpected bene-fits... " With a lascivious smirk, he winked and added, "If you get what I mean."

Although Tim hadn't brought up the subject and hadn't even anticipated talking about Gwellyn Clogg's dead body and how she got that way, he took advantage of the change in topic. He was still annoyed by what Vicar Aylsworth had said that morning when he'd basically called Tim a liar and shouted that Polly was crazy. He'd adamantly dismissed the idea of Gwellyn's death being anything other than a heart attack. Tim was also still unnerved by the vicar's insinuation that everyone in the village knew about his budding relationship with the constable.

"Let me ask you something," Tim finally said, folding his hands on the table and looking into Grayson's eyes. "Do you think Gwellyn died the way Constable Towers said? Is there any possibility that it was something else?"

Grayson made a pouty face with his lips and set down his cutlery. He looked at Tim and shrugged. "Something else? Gwellyn was overweight. She was no spring chicken. And she was under a lot of stress on account of being made redundant by your mum. Which I've since heard wasn't true. But all things considered, yeah, her time was probably up. Why? Do you think—"

Tim shrugged and assured Grayson that he personally didn't really think anything one way or another about it, but that his mother had ideas. "We had Vicar Aylsworth and his wife to tea this morning. A disaster!" Tim began to explain the root of his question. "Things got a little testy when Polly suggested that Gwellyn might have died another way, and the vicar wasn't interested in hearing about it."

"Died another way?" Grayson repeated. "What other way? What did your mother say?"

It was a long story, but Tim began recounting the whole nauseating episode and the resulting explosion of tempers when Polly suggested to the vicar the possibility of murder. "Yeah, my mom has a wild imagination," he said, trying to distance himself from Polly's speculation, in case Grayson thought it was totally nuts.

On hearing the word "murder," Grayson made the same facial expression that the vicar had: suspicion and doubt. Then, in only a moment, his look changed, as if he'd carefully considered the counterpoint of a political debate.

"I sort of have to tell you something," Grayson said, looking around for eavesdroppers. Staring directly into Tim's eyes, he said, "It's weird, but ever since we were called out to Thistlethorne, something's been nagging me, and I'm not sure why. I mean, as I said, Gwellyn Clogg wasn't exactly a physically fit person. It seemed totally plausible when my partner suspected that she'd had a heart attack. Like 'Nothing to see here, folks. Please move along.' There wasn't any blood or discernible blunt-force trauma. She was just sort of... dead. But Ella told me your mum was being contrary and wondering why the body was so neatly laid out—and that got me thinking."

Tim nodded and described the strange noises they'd heard at the castle in the middle of the night that Gwellyn had died. "We were sure it was a haunting—maybe the ghost you told me you saw years ago. But later, we came to the conclusion that the sounds had maybe come from Gwellyn getting herself killed."

"For as long as I can remember, even way before I was a policeman, Gwellyn Clogg was a character in the village," Grayson said. "A lot of people disliked her. My mum, who's a saint and never has a mean thing to say about anybody, says that Gwellyn gave off negative vibrations. Mum was sort of a Glastonbury hippie in her day, which may explain why she gets vibes about people. But often, she's totally right. Gwellyn had all sorts of disagreements with people about everything from the parish counsel's plans to honor a Teacher of the Year whom she didn't like, to authorizing community garden allotments, and even opposing some books in the library and the ones that Sarah Rogers carries in her very own bookshop, for crying out loud. She was basically a nasty person who enjoyed stirring things up and being contrary. Not that anyone would kill her just because she was a pain in the neck. That would be dumb. But she had enemies, that's for sure.

"I did a bit of a background search on her and found out a few things," Grayson continued. "For one, she'd been arrested a couple of times for thefts in places where she worked as a housekeeper. But, for some reason, the charges were always dropped. She had a few disorderly conducts against her, too, and even a restraining order from a guy over in Whitcombe. None of that adds up to very much, I guess, but her cause of death hasn't sat well with me. We'll have a better idea when her autopsy report comes in—which could take ages. There's a backlog in Bristol."

Grayson took a sip from his beer glass and looked sheepishly at Tim. "Don't take this the wrong way," he cautioned, "but wouldn't it be sort of amazing if it *was* murder? I mean, imagine the excitement in the village! Talk about something to help us all escape from the drudgery of everyday life here! People love to speculate about the who, what, where, why, and how of missing lambs—it's usually a fox. Imagine a real-life murder!"

Tim felt guilty smiling as he did, but part of him agreed, if only because of the novelty of such a monstrous crime in a sleepy English village.

"Polly's going to love you for agreeing that there might be some merit to her murder theory," he said. "You probably don't know this, and it's the one thing she doesn't boast about, but she's solved a few murder mysteries in Hollywood. She's like a cadaver search dog that sniffs out human remains. Other than a deviated septum, her nose works pretty well in these things. It's sorta freaky. Like a superpower."

For the first time that evening, there was silence between the two men. Each contemplated dead Gwellyn Clogg and alive Polly Pepper and how the two were now forever interconnected.

In life, neither woman would ever have become significant to the other. Gwellyn was someone whom Polly would have identified as NOCD—*not our class, dear*—and pretentiously avoided being around her. And apparently, Gwellyn resented rich people. But fate had other plans for them. Now, in a manner of speaking, it could be said that they were inseparable. In fact, Tim and Grayson simultaneously came to the same conclusion: they were indebted to Gwellyn in a way. They'd probably never have met if she hadn't had the cursed luck to die at Thistlethorne Lodge.

Tim smiled at that thought and raised his glass. "To the Mystery of the Maniacal Maid!" he said, clinking Grayson's glass.

"Maybe not a mystery for long if the power of a TV star's nose is in good sniffing condition." Then he added, "It's getting late... if you still want me to take you in for interrogation... "

18

It was after midnight when Tim returned home. He was surprised to find Polly still awake in the reception room. Wearing silk jammies and a bathrobe, she was sitting with her slippered feet outstretched on the Chesterfield settee, staring at the last of the embers in the fireplace, sipping the remnants of her champagne, and scratching Mr. Boots behind his ears. Tim had tried to slip quietly into the house, but with the maddening sounds from creaking door hinges, loose floorboards, and his wet shoes making squeaking noises as he crept through from the vestibule, that proved impossible.

"I can't sleep in this big old spooky place until all my chicks are safely tucked into their Laura Ashley Homeware Collection nests," Polly said in salutation, explaining why she was still awake and playing mother hen. "Tiara's a turncoat. She gave up on me hours ago. Said the events of the day had sucked the life force out of her like an alien vampire and that I should be in bed too and not worry about you because you're an adult and in good hands. The *hands* part is what kept me awake."

With a mischievous grin, Tim gave a lustful growl and said, "Talented hands." Then he picked up what was probably Tiara's half-empty glass of champagne and knocked it back. "But, hey, good news! You'll be happy to know that your Gwellyn murder theory has an advocate, a *professional* one. Grayson said he wouldn't be surprised if we discovered that someone really did kill the old bird. He's not saying he totally buys into it a hundred percent, but he's had his doubts about the cause of death from day one."

Polly didn't show the excitement that Tim expected. She simply nodded as if it were a natural conclusion that someone had finally come to their senses and paid attention to her theory. "I don't cry wolf," she added.

"Except for that time on *The Tonight Show* when you had too much wine and insisted that the Weight Watchers portion-control regimen made you *gain* weight," Tim reminded her. "What you didn't say was that *you* couldn't control your portion control. Like Bud Light, the company's stock still hasn't recovered."

"They'll get over it," Polly said dismissively. "By the by, Sarah from Bound to Read called this evening. The annual village Hedgehog and Ferret Festival is the weekend after next, and she asked if I'd help with her bookstall. At least she was up front about her greedy motive: a celebrity would draw attention to her business."

"I love hedgehogs! They're so cute! It could be fun," Tim squealed, looking around and hoping to find a few drops left in another champagne flute. No luck. "It's another way for you to meet the locals. I know we're only here for a short time, but venturing into the community might counter any negative rumors that the vicar, or anyone else, spreads. Let people see the real—but not too real—Polly Pepper up close and personal and give them some fun memories."

Polly groaned. "I don't want to go into retail at this stage in my career. I mean, can you imagine Katharine Hepburn running a lemonade stand? And don't get me started on the cow pies in the fields. If I wanted to step into something smelly, I'd try on Melania's pumps."

"It might be good practice, in case you're ever washed up and selling autographs on a street corner—like Mickey Rooney had to do," Tim said.

"This is why I hate sweet people. It's so hard to say no to their little, innocent, puppy-dog faces!"

"You had no trouble saying no to that sweet little orphan girl who wanted to present you with her stuffed teddy bear at last year's Little Annie Award banquet."

"You saw that ratty thing! The teddy, I mean," Polly exclaimed. "The fur was matted with her lonely tears and drool and Lord knows what other bodily fluids. She'll need a cuddly companion in the gloomy years of neglect ahead."

After a long moment of contemplation, Polly sighed and agreed that it couldn't hurt to participate in the upcoming village fete. She'd heard that Bound to Read was apparently a great place to hear gossip. If Polly was going to insinuate herself into the local population and poke about for evidence to prove that Gwellyn had been a victim of murder, she was going to have to at least pretend to be interested in village affairs in order to fit in. It was too early in her relationship with Sarah to risk rejecting what was surely meant to be a gracious invitation. Lots of other people would have jumped at the chance to stand behind a table and peddle copies of used paperbacks by Stephen King, John Grisham, and Hannah Dennison.

"It's only for one day," Polly conceded. "If I get bored, I can always fake meningitis."

For Polly Pepper, hosting a dinner party in Los Angeles had always been easy-peasy. All she had to do was be herself and look like the star she was: glamorous. With very little notice, she could get Fernando at Catherine the Great Caterer to deliver spicy tuna tartare, duck potstickers, roasted bass, or braised short ribs to a table full of friends. If she wanted something faster, she simply handed Tiara the platinum American Express credit card. A visit to the mega-pricy Lawson's Farms store on Doheny Drive in Beverly Hills yielded all the ingredients necessary to rip off one of Jamie Oliver's delicious recipes. Voila! Happy hostess, happy guests.

But here in Abbots Clover, not only were caterers an unheard-of profession, but Polly and her team had yet to see any artisanal food shops in the village. Polly wanted to present Sarah with a meal that would make an extra-special good impression. Lobster thermidor or *faisan sous cloche* came to mind. But as the morning bled into early afternoon, and a long back-and-forth rant of indecision between mistress and maid persisted, it was decided that Tiara would prepare a tasty—if unexciting—truffle chicken and potato au gratin.

"As long as Sarah doesn't have any food allergies, she won't give a fig about what you serve," Tim reassured his mother, who was already fidgeting with the silver cutlery that Tiara had laid out at each place setting. "She'll be impressed with the castle and grateful for the invitation. She won't even know if the dessert forks and spoons are facing in the right direction, so there is no need to fear the etiquette police. Just don't talk with your mouth full. Which you do."

"I want this to be a special evening!" Polly explained. "It's important that we make a good impression. Especially me. I'm representing Hollywood. I wouldn't want her to think of us as Homer and Marge."

"The Simpsons?" Tim and Tiara howled in unison. "I know

you're a cartoon character, but are you suggesting that I behave like Bart?" Tim bawled with terror and insult.

Tiara added, "Come to think of it, you and Marge both have weirdly colored hair and wear pearls. And if you don't stop drinking so much, you'll have yellow skin like her, too."

As sunset settled over the castle, Lily was sent on reconnaissance throughout the house with the task of flushing toilets, lighting scented candles, and collecting stray champagne bottles from under or behind the settees in the reception room. Tim assumed his usual dinner-party role as a combination DJ, bartender, and emotional support pet for Polly. He selected music by Sinatra, Streisand, Mozart, and Karen Carpenter from Mr. Drake's collection and placed the discs on the CD carousel of the central music source in the library. Tiara was in charge of the kitchen, and Polly's domain was Polly—making herself look dazzling. At 7:00 p.m. sharp, they all heard a loud thud at the main door. Sarah had arrived.

"Everyone knows that when I say 7:00, I mean 7:15," Polly groused from her bedroom.

Sarah Rogers, wearing a long-sleeve, burgundy tunic dress accented with a silver layered necklace with blue glass stones, handed her raincoat and umbrella to Tim, then followed him through to the reception room. "You'll have to ignore the longer-than-average tongue lolling out of my mouth," she said, looking around with obvious awe at the antique paintings and furnishings. "Mr. Boots!" she exclaimed and bent down to pet the cat as he meowed a friendly greeting.

"You know the little scoundrel?" Tim asked.

"The whole village knows Mr. Boots!" Sarah said in a tone that suggested Tim should know by now that everybody, including pets, was familiar to the Abbots Clover citizenry. "I've admired this castle all my life," she continued, quickly forgetting about the cat. "This place is magnificent! So many secrets—or so I imagine."

"It's sometimes hard to believe that we actually get to live here," Tim agreed. "We're not just in a foreign country visiting a friend or staying in a swell hotel that's made to look medieval. If only we could transport it back to sunny California. I'm not a fan of the cold and rain. And I'm homesick for blue skies and bougainvillea."

"You've got the best of both worlds!" Sarah exclaimed. "Spend the summers here in historic England and the winters in fabulous California. Just follow the sun. That's what I would do!"

As Tim agreed that Sarah had a good plan, Tiara wandered into the room, drying her hands on a dish towel. "Just a quick hello before I skedaddle back to the salt mine," she said, shaking hands with Sarah. "Polly should be along presently. Maybe. Hopefully. An extra hour in front of the makeup mirror won't magically wipe away twenty years, but don't tell her I said that." Then she turned to Tim. "Perhaps a splash of champers while we wait for Her Ladyship?" It wasn't so much a question as a rebuke that he was failing in his co-hosting duties.

When Tim and Sarah were again alone in the room, sipping champagne, admiring the ancient ceiling beams and the stone fireplace, Sarah pointed to the portrait of an English nobleman hanging over the mantelpiece. "Men have certainly become more attractive over the centuries," she said, sniggering at the portrait subject's round face, pasty complexion, red lips, long hair, and dour expression. "I had an art history class at university, but other than the Greek and Roman sculptures we studied, I don't think the guys back then hit the gym much." She chuckled.

"Yeah, the Duke of Droitwich up there probably had plenty of attendants, coachmen, and valets to do all the strenuous stuff that required muscles. Those nobles would have been a disaster as serfs or galley slaves! Apparently, there's some legend about his dog, Loki, perpetually passing wind and the duke blaming the stink on other guests rather than offending the dog. Can dogs even be offended?"

In the instant before Sarah could offer a laugh, the protons and electrons in the room noticeably changed, and there was a subtle sense that, like an opening night on Broadway, something momentous was about to happen. Then, as if she had intentionally timed her entrance (she had), Polly Pepper strolled with purpose into the reception room just as Karen Carpenter was singing "Superstar" over the music system speakers. Wearing the same cocktail dress in which she'd entertained the vicar the day before, Polly took center stage, opened her arms as if to embrace the world, and grandly insisted that Sarah and Tim remain seated (they hadn't thought to rise in the first place).

With faux generosity, she declared, "Welcome to our wee castle! We've been looking forward to this evening for ages. In fact, I didn't sleep a wink last night."

Chewing the scenery, a tad like a woodchipper, Tim wanted to say, as his mother got carried away with her pretentious greeting. Instead, he handed her a flute of champagne, which was almost as effective as giving a baby a pacifier.

"But seriously, you're our very first dinner guest, so I'm a tad nervous," Polly said, sipping champagne and selling half-truths. Yes, Sarah was the first person in Abbots Clover to wangle an invitation to dinner at Thistlethorne, but when it came to playing hostess with the mostest, Polly was never more than slightly apprehensive. A total pro with every nuance choreographed and rehearsed, she could win grand prizes if she were in a party-hosting competition. She was always as cool as a minty breeze in the starring role of Lady Bountiful. From the doyennes of Doheny to the barons of Benedict Canyon, the upper crust in Hollywood couldn't wait for a Polly Pepper soiree at Pepper Plantation. Years after her famous Scottish Highlander party, people still talked about the Loch Ness Monster in Polly's swimming pool.

"I'm easily entertained," Sarah insisted, allaying Polly's faux fears and reminding her that Abbotts Clover was a place where sheep and foxes outnumbered humans two to one, so being invited to Thistlethorne Lodge was probably going to be a highlight of her life. "I won't say it's always boring here in the village," Sarah added. "Once in a while, there's a news headline —like when a certain celebrity moved into the castle on the hill —but aside from that, there's not a lot going on except running my business."

For the next half hour, Polly bubbled with stories about her life and career—basically to prove that Sarah was right that her own life was indeed pretty darn boring in comparison. But, of course, Sarah was mesmerized by Polly and her career.

When Tiara finally appeared in the doorway, she dinged a little tea bell and, with a fake English accent, announced, "Dinner, as they say, is served."

Entering the formal dining room was almost overwhelming for Sarah. "My goodness, I'm at Downton Abbey," she said, absorbed in the ambiance of the candlelit room. The polished mahogany table, with seating for twelve, was set for four at one end. Mr. Drake's Royal Doulton rose-pattern dinner plates sat on sheer lace embroidered placemats accompanied by Waterford cut-crystal glasses and antique silverware. Two five-arm silver candelabras buffed to a high sheen with tall, tapered candles dominated the center of the table.

"I'm afraid Mr. Carson has the night off," Tiara joked, playing on Sarah's *Downton Abbey* reference, as she gallantly pulled out Polly's chair at the head of the table and instructed the others to be seated.

The music had shuffled to Mozart, and as Tiara served the meal, Tim masterfully directed the conversation away from the horrors of Hollywood to Sarah's café and bookshop.

"We're about the same age, and you've already got your own business. That's so cool," he said as everyone *oohed* and *ahhed* over Tiara's culinary presentation. "It must be great to be your own boss."

"My customers are my bosses." Sarah downplayed the joys of self-employment. "I love it, but it's more work than fun, believe me. Each morning, I'd better have Mr. Taylor's gluten-free raspberry almond scones when he arrives, or else I'm dead. And Natalie Clark will pitch a hissy fit if her caramel macchiato cupcakes with cream cheese frosting aren't in the cake display case when she arrives. But I feel lucky. Especially in the early mornings when the customers begin to dribble in. They're usually full of eager anticipation for what the day might bring. Even the older folks, whose days are pretty much all the same, seem to think that maybe, somehow, today will be different. Anything will be possible. A clean slate. But I'm passionate about books, so running that part of the business is what's really fulfilling. I don't make much money, of course, but I feel like I'm part of the community, and people love to hang out in the book nooks to read or in the café to gossip. No matter what business you're in, there's always a troublemaker or two, but most of mine are harmless."

"Most are harmless?" Tim teased. "What could be more benign than coffee and Capote?"

Sarah nodded enthusiastically. "You'd think so, right? Although there are a lot of incendiary books out there, too. But shouldn't a warm cuppa with a slice of carrot cake on a frosty morning make you feel all fuzzy and contented? Apparently, it has the opposite effect on some people. Your deceased housekeeper, for instance. Oh, I hope I'm not being insensitive."

At the reference to dead Gwellyn, Polly stopped mid-sip of her champagne and sat up straighter in her chair. "Not insensitive at all, dear. But I didn't take her for a coffee- or tea-drinking gal. Maybe a martini with a splash of battery acid."

"You're not far off." Sarah laughed as she held her knife and fork over her truffle chicken. "She definitely had opinions. Ask anyone. I was lacerated by her tongue more than a few times. She didn't approve of some of the books I carried or displayed in the windows—as if it were any of her business. She objected to anything with romance and sexuality. She took issue with violence, such as thrillers and real-life police procedurals. Gwellyn once went on a rampage in the shop, tearing down a poster of Stephen King's *It*, claiming it was too disturbing. Anything that didn't fit into her narrow view of what was acceptable was fair game for criticism. If she'd been upset by *One Flew Over the Cuckoo's Nest*, I might have understood because she basically was the village cuckoo and thought everyone was conspiring against her."

Sarah laughed at her own joke and explained that Gwellyn was bonkers and sort of reminded her of Nurse Ratched, the psychopathic character in the Ken Kesey novel. "She even accused Mary Radcliff of making her a character in *Lust Among the Bluebells*. Oh, that's Mary Radcliff's self-published romance novel," she explained. "Yeah, we have a local Barbara Cartland wannabe right here in Abbots Clover. I'd navigate around her if I were you. I love to promote local writers. And I probably deserve a medal for reading her so-called 'work of fiction,' but it was so ponderous I couldn't finish it. And a case could be made that she'd actually written about some of the locals and included them in her book. For instance, it wasn't much of a stretch to figure out that Prysm Garfield, *the server with a secret*—as Mary described the character—had to be Crimson Wakefield over at the Fox & Hare. And it's probably fair to say that the character

Helen Wood was actually Gwellyn Clogg. Their first names rhyme, and there are other similarities, too. I stocked the book and even hosted a book launch because Mary kept hounding me to do it."

In only a moment, with the story of Gwellyn believing that she was immortalized in the pages of a tawdry self-published novel, Sarah had taken the top prize away from Polly for the most engrossing urban legend of the evening. Her hosts stared open-mouthed, their knives and forks suspended over their plates as they listened to Sara describe the night Gwellyn had stormed into Bound to Read. It was during the book signing event for *Lust Among the Bluebells*. What was supposed to be a joyous celebration for the author's milestone achievement of writing and publishing a novel turned out to be memorable in a way completely opposite to what she had planned and dreamed about.

Recalling the evening to her hosts, Sarah described the bell on the shop door tinkling and nothing less than a tornado in a black raincoat sweeping in, making a beeline directly for Mary Radcliff, who was seated at a card table, reading aloud from a chapter in her book. En route, Gwellyn overturned not only a stack of Mary's books on a display table but collaterally obliterated an exhibit of the latest popular mysteries from Peter Boon, Richard Osman, and Lauren Elliott before setting her sights on Mary herself. With a dozen eyewitnesses watching in disbelief, Gwellyn flipped Mary's table over and, only inches from her face, threatened to sue her for libel, defamation, slander, and a bunch of other legal-sounding things that she probably didn't know the meaning of and could never succeed in litigating. Sarah and her assistant, Josh, only barely kept Gwellyn from physically attacking Mary.

Mary Radcliff's lifelong dream event had been utterly ruined. She was heartbroken and sobbing and raging with fury.

Gwellyn was forcefully ejected from the shop and told never to return, not even for a cappuccino or a cheesy scone. Sarah called Constable Jenkins, but only to file a report. She didn't want to make a criminal complaint because, although Gwellyn had been disruptive and threatening, there wasn't any real property damage, nor had anyone been more than emotionally wounded. She also didn't want negative publicity attached to the shop.

In an unexpected twist, Gwellyn's stunt, like the so-called "Streisand effect," did the opposite of her goal of suppressing the book. Probably only a few of those who were present that night would have purchased a copy of *Lust Among the Bluebells*—they were really only there for a night out and free doughnuts—but by the end, they all wanted to know what was so explosive within the pages that it made Gwellyn lash out as she had. Word of mouth spread and resulted in Mary selling twenty-five copies of her book, which was about twenty more than predicted. Even the Abbots Clover Public Library bought a copy. It was a lemons-to-lemonade moment, and a local best-seller was born.

Sarah ended her story remembering that before leaving Bound to Read that night, Mary was snarling and growled that Gwellyn was a monster who should have been put out of everyone's misery long ago and was destined to have a shorter-than-average lifespan.

"She's a better psychic than writer because that forecast of a shorter life for Gwellyn actually came true," Sarah said, returning to the moment and her meal.

Polly gasped. "She actually said Gwellyn was 'destined to have a shorter-than-average lifespan'? It sounds more like a threat than a psychic prediction!"

For a moment, Sarah looked confused. "Gwellyn's death was just a coincidence," she said, twisting her mouth and looking to Polly for further clarification. "A heart attack, right? Are you suggesting something different?"

Polly shrugged. "Retribution can be fun and rewarding. And if I'd read that bookshop scene in a script, especially with Mary's cheeky prophecy of death, I'd grab the role in a heartbeat! There are so many plot possibilities! I can see myself in a Netflix movie, playing a popular author of best-selling novels being threatened by would-be-censors and book burners, defending my literary integrity and the world of popular literature in general. Of course, the Mary Radcliff character would have to be rewritten as massively talented and critically acclaimed. Unlike the Mary you describe."

"I'd watch that movie in a heartbeat." Sarah smiled. Then she looked at Polly and said, "I'm remembering something else. There was a bit of idle talk in the shop about Mary vowing to get even with Gwellyn for ruining her big night. She never said anything like that to me, but I overheard Shandy O'Connor—she's on the village council and one of Mary's best friends—say that Mary had been seething for days and vowing to even the score between her and Gwellyn. I thought little about it because, although Mary has a big ego and can be pushy, especially when it comes to thrusting her book on everyone she meets, she fancies herself as a meek and introspective author. She pretends to be the antithesis of one who might seek retribution. *The pen is mightier than the sword* sort of thing."

As the evening ticked away and the after-meal brandy snifters were set aside, Polly had more questions about Gwellyn than Sarah could answer, and the tribe eventually said their goodbyes at the castle's main gate.

Polly cooed about seeing Sarah again soon, adding, "In fact, we'll drop by the shop tomorrow. I'm in the mood for a trashy novel. Especially one with a tasty title like *Lust Among the Bluebells.*"

In the reception room, Polly kicked off her heels, tossed a resentful Mr. Boots onto the opposite-facing Chesterfield, and plopped herself down. Tiara decided to save the kitchen cleanup for Lily to tackle in the morning and joined her boss. Tim wandered in with another brandy and poked at the embers in the fireplace.

"A pretty successful evening, if I do say so myself," Polly said, sipping another bubbly. "I knew I'd like Sarah. She's clever and has a good sense of humor. Too smart to get married at such a young age, too. I admire that."

Tim and Tiara agreed that Sarah seemed to have an elevated work ethic, a clever head on her shoulders, and was someone they were happy to have as a new friend.

"Her stories about finding guys to date around here were hilarious," Tim said. "Especially the one about dinner with the dude who got drunk and kept putting his elbows in his spaghetti Bolognese. Sounds like the date I had with the guy I had to put in an Uber because he was too drunk on espresso martinis to find his car! I heard he spent days afterward looking for it!"

Tiara piped in, changing the subject, "Is it just me, or does this Gwellyn person get more despicable by the day? The picture I get is that of a schoolyard bully who picks on weaklings who can't fight back. We haven't met one person who's had anything good to say about her. And people almost always say nice things about someone after they die."

"It's a social obligation," Polly agreed. "People tend to forgive others and focus on the positive. I wonder if Mary Radcliff is praising the dearly departed for the bump in book sales after the launch party. I intend to find out!"

19

——————

Bound to Read was super busy when Polly and Tiara strolled in the next morning and joined the queue for a coffee. They remembered salivating over Sarah's description of a caramel macchiato with cream-cheese-frosting cupcakes and were dying to try one.

In her green apron with the Bound to Read logo of a book sitting inside a heart-shaped coffee cup, Sarah worked behind the counter, smiling effortlessly as she filled orders and made small talk with her patrons. She seemed to be enjoying herself, but after what she'd revealed the night before, Polly and Tiara knew she was putting on an act.

"That scarf you're wearing really complements the rest of your outfit, Maggie," Sarah said to one older woman. "How about a slice of frosted banana walnut bread? It's fresh," she said to another customer as she set a cup and saucer on a tray and insisted that Maggie have a wonderful day. She referred to another patron as "my lovely" and asked if their nan was feeling any better. Apparently, Nan was still at death's door. And when the woman changed her order to a large mocha after Sarah had already prepared her Americano, it didn't seem to bother the barista one iota, and she cheerfully dumped out the cup and started over.

And on it went until Polly and Tiara were at the front of the line, facing a beaming smile and lips that reiterated words of appreciation for the previous evening's fun.

"I hardly know how to reciprocate," Sarah said. "I'll find a way. But there's no way I'd even attempt to cook you a meal after Tiara's brilliant one! Oh, and I've set aside the book you wanted. I can't leave the counter for a while, but tell Josh it's next to the computer on my desk in the office."

When Polly and Tiara finished their coffees and cupcakes (they were as yummy as they'd hoped), they wandered down the two steps into the bookshop section of the café. They realized they were in the very spot where Mary Radcliff had been accosted by Gwellyn Clogg the night of the book launch and could visualize the entire altercation and imagine the shock of the author and the readers who'd come out for free doughnuts and wound up with a juicy story of their own to tell.

While Josh was assisting another customer, they wandered around, looking at books and pointing out book-themed novelty items.

"Your birthday's coming up," Tiara wisecracked as she held up a miniature book titled *How to Speak Cat*. Then she pointed to a deck of cards printed with bawdy lines from Shakespeare. "Oh, now this is perfect," she said, picking up a wineglass etched with the quote:

> "She has many rare and charming qualities, but sobriety isn't one of them."
>
> — JANE AUSTEN

"The possibilities are endless," Polly deadpanned and gave

Tiara a withering look. Then she realized that Josh's customer had left, and he was now arranging books on one of the display tables. They sidled up to him... and nearly fell in love.

Charming and apparently unaware of how seductive he was, Josh had a genuinely radiant smile and was beguilingly gangly. His blue Oxford cloth shirtsleeves were rolled up to his elbows, and Polly was distracted by the blue veins that ran up and down his thick forearms. Maintaining eye contact with him was a challenge, but imperative. They couldn't risk giving themselves away as two women of a certain age with an immodest impulse for a man who was probably young enough to be their grandson. Polly broke the spell and introduced herself, telling Josh that Sarah had set aside a book for her, and they'd come to retrieve it.

When Josh slipped away, Polly stage-whispered to Tiara, "I envy the sheep in Scotland." In only a moment, Josh returned, making Polly almost weak in the knees and with a desperate wish to be twenty-one years old again. *Thank God we didn't meet forty years ago, or I might have tossed my career plans aside*, Polly thought as she pulled herself together.

Josh handed her the copy of *Lust Among the Bluebells*, with its cover of a young woman embraced by a shirtless hunk, rolling on a lilac-colored carpet of bluebells in the woods.

"Looks intriguing. Have you read it?" Polly asked.

"Just the fun bits." Josh chuckled sweetly and blushed. "Like the part where Prysm Garfield—who's really Crimson Wakefield over at the Fox & Hare—sends flirty text messages to Lance Blade, who's really Fergus Vole, who runs the bicycle shop in the book—and in real life too. We all know it's Fergus because Mary Radcliff describes him as short and paunchy, with eyelids like a turtle's, basically stupid, hypersensitive, and combs what little is left of his hair in a way that makes it look like there's a small dead animal on his head. I memorized that from the book. It's Fergus to a T."

"Dreamy," Tiara said vacantly.

"I'm enthralled. With the cover of the book, I mean," Polly said. "By the by, I heard there was quite a ruckus in here over this little potboiler."

Josh nodded with a smirk and unconsciously finger-combed the floppy mane of hair that fell over his eyes. "That was a wild night, for sure. Ms. Clogg accused Ms. Radcliff of writing about her in the book. Everyone knows Ms. Clogg was sweet on Fergus Vole once—the book's real-life Lance Blade character. Or maybe she was angry because Ms. Radcliff had written a character so blatantly like Fergus. Don't know."

Polly twisted her mouth as she contemplated how Gwellyn could have known in advance of the big night that she was represented in the novel. "It was a self-published book, and there aren't any other bookstores in the village, so how did she get an advance copy?"

Josh shrugged and guessed that she'd probably purchased it online. "Ms. Radcliff's book was a print-on-demand title. It was available at least a whole week before the launch party."

But who would have tipped her off? Polly wondered, fanning the book's pages and making a show of inhaling the scent of ink and paper. "Intoxicating!" she gushed and ran a hand over the sultry cover. "When I was a young girl in school, my favorite thing in the world was to be chosen to open the box when the extracurricular reading books we ordered came in. I savored the aroma. My other favorite thing is meeting famous authors. I have oodles of signed books at home in California. Everyone from Truman Capote to Tom Wolfe to Michelle Obama. I even have an autographed first edition of *To Kill a Mockingbird*." She didn't say that the only reason she had any books at all—autographed or otherwise—was because they were presents from friends. Somehow, the falsehood had gotten around that Polly collected books inscribed by their authors. So that became her default birthday and Christmas presents. "I must meet Mary Radcliff and get her to sign this!"

Josh made a nonverbal gesture that politely suggested *"Whatever floats your boat,"* but provided Mary's address, anyway. "She lives at Wishing Well Cottage, over by Duck Lake," he said. "She'll probably flip when she hears that someone took the time to read her book. But don't mention that you didn't buy it. Authors hate it when someone says they borrowed a copy of a writer's book or checked it out of the library. They don't make any money. We've actually sold some copies, but no one's proclaiming it's the second coming of Jacqueline Susann."

Josh noticed a customer waiting to pay for a book and excused himself. Polly and Tiara watched as he charmed the buyer into also purchasing a hand-painted mug that had *Books are more loyal than husbands* written on it.

"He could charm an illiterate into joining the Book of the Month Club," Polly said wistfully.

When they were finally back at Thistlethorne, Polly sequestered herself in the library, sat down on the leather Chesterfield, and turned to the first page of *Lust Among the Bluebells*.

Prysm Garfield was a home-wrecker! And when they found her brutally murdered body buried in a shallow grave in her very own garden, no one was very surprised. Many were glad she was dead and no longer around to cause trouble!

The story started out with a bang, and Polly quickly found herself immersed in a tale of adultery, unrequited love, and murder in a tiny English village. Cliché after cliché. But Polly quickly found herself absorbed in the soap-opera-like lives of the main characters. She'd been prepared to roll her eyes at ridiculous situations and scoff at cringe-inducing dialogue—and there was plenty of that. But although she'd seen these unoriginal characters before in old movie melodramas and perhaps even in the pages of other romance novels, Mary Radcliff had a knack for keeping up a brisk pace. By six o'clock, when Tiara came into the library to serve the first of the evening's champagne, Polly was three-quarters of the way through the book.

"It was so quiet in here I expected to find you passed out or hanging from the chandelier with a rope around your neck," Tiara said as Polly stood up to stretch and take a fortifying sip of bubbly. "Your eyes aren't bleeding, and it doesn't appear that you're ready to murder the writer for the wasted hours that you'll never get back. What gives?"

Polly held up the book and waved it at Tiara's face. "I think I want to buy the film rights," she declared.

Tiara blanched. "You're pulling my leg! Everyone says it's a steaming pile of caca."

"It is a steaming pile, at least from a literary standpoint," Polly agreed. "Not that I know anything about literature. But I do know good stories! No, this isn't at all original, and we've seen the plot a squillion times: a naïve young widow with a teenage son falls in love with a rich married man who promises to leave his wife but never does. When her son finds out about the affair, he confronts his mother, who insists that the guy really does love her and wants to take care of her, but the lover has reasons why he can't leave his wife just yet. Son goes bananas and confronts the cad, who tells him he's too young to understand adult things and to take a hike. Skunk is found dead, and the angry son is arrested because someone overheard him threaten the dude. Blah, blah, blah."

"Blah is right! That's basically the story arc for every season of *Days of Our Lives, General Hospital*, and *The Young and the Restless*. I already know how it ends," Tiara lamented.

Polly agreed that she probably knew the ending too, but that Mary Radcliff had given her characters more heart than expected. "There are some good ancillary characters with interesting B-stories, too. There's something real about these people. The only difference between the book's protagonist, Helen Wood, who must be Gwellyn Clogg, who lives in the village of Decons Dell—the fictional name Mary gave Abbots Clover—and our very own Shirley Minton in Beverly Hills is their accents. The tawdry sex scandal is the same. I'll finish reading it in bed tonight, and then tomorrow, we're paying a visit to dear Mary Radcliff. She needs to tell her side of the story of why Gwellyn attacked her. And I need to nab my next TV or film project before she realizes its potential... or has to sell the rights to someone else to pay her legal fees after I pin Gwellyn's murder on her! Our dear Gwellyn Clogg's becoming a win-win for me!"

When Polly arrived in the breakfast room the next morning, she wore one of Mr. Drake's brown tweed herringbone suits. A *Remembrance Day* poppy pin sprouted from the jacket lapel, and a matching necktie and pocket square of yellow, orange, and petrol blue completed the classic look.

"Let me guess," Tim said, mid-sip of his tea and stifling a laugh, "you're transitioning. Which pronouns do you want us to use?"

Tiara tsk-tsked and shook her head as she examined Polly's eccentric wardrobe. "Jeeves and Wooster motoring off to the countryside for a lakeside picnic is my bet," she said. "You're only missing a briar pipe between your lips and an open shotgun resting over your arm."

"We're paying a call on Mary Radcliff this morning, and I want to look literary. Authors wear tweed," Polly said with annoyance and sat down at her usual place at the table.

"You're not an author," Tim reminded her.

"I'm getting into character."

"You're an actress who smells a good role and is ready to shamelessly exploit the unwitting creator of the source material," Tiara added.

"I hope Mary knows what happened to Tolstoy," Tim said.

"What happened to Tolstoy?" Polly asked.

"Nothing, because Hollywood didn't exist then. But I'm sure if it did, they would have ruined *War and Peace*."

"Stephen King's done pretty well with Hollywood," Polly grumped. Then, after a heated discussion in which she defended her motive for meeting with Mary Radcliff and insisted that in any potential business transaction, Mary would be the greater beneficiary, she threw up her hands in exasperation. "I'm merely a conduit for Mary to reach a wider audience," Polly insisted in her bid to convince Tim and Tiara that she was embarking on a semi-noble, semi-selfless cause.

Only after Lily entered the room to clear the plates—and mistakenly curtsied at Polly and addressed her as "Your Lordship, sir"—did Polly agree to ditch the wool pants and necktie and wear a blouse under the jacket. Then she was ready to set out on her mission.

The journey to Duck Lake was a pretty one. Tim had become more adept at driving the standard-transmission rented Honda and confidently maneuvered through the narrow serpentine lanes bordered by stone walls and rolling fields. Although the sight of grazing animals still made him giddy with excitement, he no longer shouted, "Sheepies! Sheepies!" whenever he spied a flock of lambs and their mothers. He, Polly, and Tiara were starting to take rural living in their stride.

Wishing Well Cottage was at the far end of Abbots Clover and a longer distance from Thistlethorne than Polly and her team had been led to believe. When they arrived, they found a charming thatched-roof stone house adorned with trellises that would be hosting colorful climbing roses and wisteria, framing the door and windows in the spring and summer. A chimney jutted up through the center. The trio made nonverbal sounds that translated into thoughts that if they didn't already have a very cool castle, this wee residence could do quite well for short-term accommodation, thank you very much.

Tim parked the Honda behind a dark blue Mercedes SUV in the gravel driveway, and together, they entered the front garden through a rustic split-hazel gate. The slate stone walkway leading to the oak front door was splotched with gray-green lichen and bordered by tall stems of winter-dormant lavender, which they imagined was an abundant, vibrant purple color in the summer.

Polly took a deep, fortifying breath and rapped the door-knocker. In only a moment, a smiling Mary Radcliff opened the door.

"I'd heard through the all-knowing grapevine that Polly Pepper might pay me a visit," she almost squealed. "Do come on in!"

Of course she knew we were coming. Everyone in this village is connected telepathically, Polly reminded herself as she stepped through the doorway into a tiny boot room, profusely apologizing for not calling ahead of time. "We were in the neighborhood, so to speak," she insisted. Mary graciously affirmed that she was thrilled that the "visiting Hollywood celebrity" and her troupe had dropped in and welcomed them into her cozy sitting room.

The cottage's interior was as quaint as the exterior and boasted restored wood plank floors and low beamed ceilings. The snug sitting room was painted magnolia, and bookshelves along one wall were stuffed with paperback and hardcover volumes. A two-seat settee upholstered in a brown plaid fabric and garnished with casual throw pillows sat against another wall, flanked by two mismatched wingback chairs and a rustic French oak coffee table. Dominating the room was an ancient inglenook fireplace with an iron wood burner set into the mouth of the space and cut wood stacked on either side. An old cocker spaniel was curled beside a grandfather clock on a soft, flannel-covered dog bed. Mary insisted the trio make themselves comfy while she put the kettle on to boil.

In a short while, they were all seated together, sipping tea and nibbling on biscuits. And soon, Mary began sniffling and dabbing away tears of joy as Polly talked about how much she had enjoyed reading *Lust Among the Bluebells*.

"It was a labor-of-love book," Mary explained. "Oh, how I'd wanted to be a writer as far back as I can remember. I had a rather limited education, but I read all the time as a little girl. I loved the classics: Jackie Collins, Jacqueline Susann, and Judith Krantz. I worked on writing *Lust Among the Bluebells* for years. Whenever I had a free moment or two, I added a sentence here and a paragraph there. Over time, the pages added up like coins in a piggy bank. Of course, my beloved rescue dogs took up pretty much all my time. Bless their angelic souls. And our little girl—she's not so little anymore, she's the size of an orca—has a lot of social anxieties, so I need to support her until she's well enough to find a job. But she's not as bad as my poor son,

Douglas, who has to remain in an assisted-living facility for the rest of his life."

Tim and Tiara sat listening to one of the saddest stories they'd ever heard and obliquely glanced at Polly, whom they hoped felt miserably rotten about her plan to take advantage of this poor woman in a potentially lucrative book-to-film deal.

"Of course, I didn't dare tell anyone except my late husband, Carl, about my writing and dream of one day publishing a book," Mary continued. "Friends and family would have thought I was crazy to think I could write a novel. There were times when I thought I was crazy, too. Then when I decided that the book was finished, and that it was the best I could do, I tried finding a publisher. You can't imagine how hard it is to get an agent. I spent years looking for one. No one wanted me. I almost gave up.

"It was Carl, may he rest in peace, who, one night when I was very depressed because I believed in the book and nobody else did, yelled and said, 'If they don't want you, you don't want them! Publish the damned thing yourself!' I think he was just tired of hearing me complain. But he was right. Even if I never write another sentence, I've fulfilled my dream. I've published a book! Although I was hoping that I could make enough money to put Douglas into a better home. Thankfully, the doctors don't think he knows too much about what's happening around him. Please, dear Lord, don't ever make me have to live in a place like that. But if I do, please let me be like Douglas so I don't understand the depressing atmosphere and miserable conditions. Of course, I now know that very few writers make any money at all on their work. God knows I'm no Laura Levine!"

Then Mary abruptly stopped her gloomy monologue and cheerfully announced, "Enough about me! You've read my book and liked it! That means the world to me!" The conversation was still about her but now disguised in a smokescreen of starry-eyed wonder that someone as important as Polly Pepper would take the time to read an obscure self-published fiction writer's work. "I'm sure you have so many other more important things to do."

Nothing's as important as a potential job, Polly thought as she considered a resurgence of her acting career. Over the next few minutes, Polly continued to praise Mary for the realistic characters in her novel and said that she could even visualize the book being made into a movie.

"A movie?" Mary squealed. "Only if you star in it!"

Polly laughed. "Me? Play one of your delightful characters in a film adaptation of *Lust Among the Bluebells*? Heavens no!" she said dismissively. "That's flattering, but the only part I might be vaguely right for is Mrs. Porter, the owner of the Harvest Orchard boardinghouse."

Mary giggled in agreement. "She's only the main character and my favorite one in the book, so of course that's the role you should have! I'll insist they cast you!" Mary was already envisioning herself walking down a red carpet in Hollywood, posing for paparazzi, and signing autographs at the film's world premiere.

"Of course, it's a million-to-one shot that movies without superhero bats and crime-fighting mutant spiders get made at all these days," Polly said pessimistically. Like a fish on a hook, she was reeling Mary in and taunting her catch. To drive home her point, she reminisced about a writer friend whose novel had been optioned by Sissy Spacek. The Oscar-winning actress had loved the book and wanted its screen adaptation to be her directorial debut. But the low-budget film had yet to get off the ground a decade after commissioning a screenplay. Polly's author friend had died broken-hearted because it had been her dream to see her name in the credits of a movie.

"If someone with a big movie-star name and clout like Sissy

Spacek can't get the story to the screen, it's probably impossible for anyone who isn't Steven Spielberg or Christopher Nolan to make it either," she said. "'Many are called, but few are chosen,' as we say in the biz. But it's fun to dream about."

By now, Polly was getting tired of playing sycophant to a nobody. A barely stifled yawn wasn't lost on Tim and Tiara, and probably not on Mary, either. But Polly had been waiting for the right moment to organically interject a question about Mary's connection with Gwellyn.

Finally, in a split second between Mary explaining the symbolism of the badger that appeared in each chapter of her book and whatever other tedious bit of self-praise was on the tip of her tongue, Polly tossed in a non sequitur. "Speaking of badgers... I imagine the real people from Abbots Clover who appear in the book are pretty excited to be made famous by you. Crimson, over at the Fox & Hare, and Fergus at the bike shop especially, must be over the moon. They take up so many of your delicious pages!"

Suddenly, the room was quiet enough to hear the old dog snoring on his bed.

Mary shifted uncomfortably in her wingback chair and set her teacup and saucer on the coffee table. "There's a disclaimer in the beginning about persons living or dead being fictional," she said guardedly.

"Of course. But we know all writers use bits and pieces from real-life experiences," Polly said evasively. "Actors do, too. I had a crazy yoga instructor when I first moved to Hollywood, and I created a character based on her for one of my show's most popular comedy sketches. Remember Bendy Wendy?" She fake-laughed to Tim and Tiara, reminding them of the audience-favorite character. "Lord, she was a caution! Of course, I exaggerated everything, from her incessant gum chewing to her shag-cut bleached hair and the ubiquitous bottle of water she carried.

And her speech pattern, too. That was one of her most quirky and obnoxious traits. She talked in word salads and peppered her sentences with phrases like 'As if!' and 'He's a totally rad dude!' or 'Take a chill pill and call me a cab!' She was totally ripe for caricature." Polly imitated herself imitating Wendy. "But she somehow recognized herself on my show one night and sent a legally threatening letter to the network. I was in so much doo-doo! I imagine it's possible that Gwellyn Clogg might have been just a tad peeved that you used her as a character, too."

Bingo! Tim and Tiara suddenly got a second rejuvenating wind of interest.

"Gwellyn Clogg?" Mary asked, perplexed. "What does she have to do with. . . " Mary's eyes narrowed as she looked at Polly, then Tim and Tiara. "Gwellyn Clogg was your housekeeper at Thistlethorne Lodge, wasn't she? You sacked her, and then she died of a heart attack in your house. Odd."

Polly barely resisted rolling her eyes at the erroneously prevalent rumor that she'd fired Gwellyn. "Yes. Odd. It's never much fun finding a dead body anywhere, but especially in the place where you're supposed to be all cozy and safe," Polly said. "As for a bum ticker, there seems to be some uncertainty about how she died."

"As in natural causes versus mysterious circumstances?" Mary asked.

Polly shrugged. "Gwellyn herself was a mystery to me. She didn't give us much time to know her. I have to rely on third-party sources, and, so far, there doesn't seem to be a lot of love lost for her."

"She was a paranoid sociopath. That's all you need to know," Mary said, defiantly folding her arms. "Gwellyn disliked me for the same reasons that she disliked a lot of people—which is to say I don't know why, and nobody else does either. I assure you it wasn't because of my book. For some reason, she had a boulder-size chip on her shoulder and took her self-loathing out on everyone around her. She was unkind and vicious."

Although Polly was walking a razor-thin line and was desperate not to scare away a possible career-making meal ticket and possessor of potentially important investigative information, she sensed the author was on the verge of ending the meeting. But Polly hadn't schlepped all this way just to endure tepid tea and sob stories about the hardships of someone's otherwise dull life. Polly wanted at least to advance her theory of murder, so she plowed ahead. "In your book, you write that Crimson Wakefield and Fergus Vole were plotting with Helen Wood—who is clearly Gwellyn Clogg—to poison the owner of the Wolf & Rabbit—which I imagine is the Fox & Hare pub—where they work. What have Crimson and Fergus said about you making them local celebrities?"

"Those two illiterates couldn't read alphabet soup, let alone a book," Mary said, dismissing any idea that the two were aware of their infamy. "Anyway, I used artistic license. Isn't that what they call it? That's what I said to that despicable Gwellyn Clogg when she threatened to sue me for defamation of character." Mary caught herself, but it was too late to deny her possible motive for killing her.

Silence again enveloped the room. They all felt nervous energy radiating from Mary.

Then she quietly added, "Gwellyn thought she could make money off me. That's what that whole show in the bookstore was about. I know you've heard about the row; everybody has. She wanted witnesses to her 'emotional distress' from 'injury to her feelings.' Yeah, that's what she actually said: 'injury to her feelings.' That was an ironic laugh and a half considering how she treated everyone she ever came in contact with!"

"Then you basically said, 'boo-hoo, waah-waah,' and told her to join the Sob Sisters Club?" Polly suggested.

"It was about time she got a taste of her own medicine," Mary agreed.

"It's also been reported that you said Gwellyn was destined to have a shorter-than-average lifespan. What did you mean by that?"

Mary's eyes narrowed their focus on Polly again, and she pursed her lips. "Nothing. I mean, I never said that."

Polly shrugged. "Maybe the grapevine is wrong... for once."

Mary thought for a long moment. "It was just a figure of speech," she said, realizing that it was useless to contradict Abbots Clover's perpetually churning rumor mill. "She completely ruined the most important night of my life. I was understandably angry. How would you like it if your Bendy Wendy interrupted one of your Emmy Award acceptance speeches and threatened to ruin your life because they believed you defamed them? It's only because Gwellyn died so soon after I made that comment that you think I might have had something to do with her death."

"Did you have something to do with her death?" Polly asked.

"That's absurd!" Mary shouted. "Why would I—"

Polly shrugged. "There's that scene in the book where Helen Wood—aka Gwellyn Clogg—colludes with Crimson and Fergus in a plot to kill their boss, Daniel Johnson, by putting poison in his pint of ale. The conspiracy is so delectably convoluted. And Daniel's final words in the book: 'No, no! The drink, the drink! I am poisoned.' That sounded familiar." Polly pretended to rack her brain to find the obscure literary reference. "Because it's Gertrude's line in *Hamlet*, act 5, scene 2."

In that *aha* moment, all eyes looked at Mary.

"Obvious plagiarism of Shakespeare," Polly said.

"Artistic license," Mary spat.

"More like artistic laziness. You couldn't be bothered with coming up with your own original death scene. Instead, you took a tired old poisoning plot that's been done to death—pun intended."

Mary's cheeks flushed red with anger as she clenched her fists. "I'll have you know that I worked years on that book. And I have an airtight alibi for the night Gwellyn died."

The tension in the room was palpable as Polly, Tim, and Tiara exchanged nervous glances. If Mary was telling the truth, they were back to square one in their investigation. But if she was lying, they'd gotten one step closer to unraveling the mystery.

20

———————

The *Abbots Clover Overview* was a free monthly paper delivered to all twelve hundred households and businesses in the combined surrounding villages and towns. The publication was basically a community service. Birth and death notices were listed, and there were short feature articles about local farmers' charity fundraisers and students winning environmental awards. Longer pieces about scammers taking advantage of elderly citizens or the disappearance of various species of flora and fauna due to climate change became the subject of intense conversation and debate in pubs and barbershops. In each issue, there were lots of color photographs of smiling sheepshearers holding champion ribbons and silver-plated loving cups. But the most popular feature was a segment titled I Dare Say... !

I Dare Say... ! was a questions-and-answers profile spotlighting minor local celebrities. Usually, it was an obscure actor, a former BBC Radio traffic report presenter, or someone who had worked behind the scenes in television. Anyone who had achieved at least a minor level of success onstage in London or in a soap opera and had moved down to the semi-rural English countryside to spend their final days puttering in their gardens was considered an acceptable subject. The residents in question all had one thing in common: wrinkles. Otherwise, it was a grab bag of personalities.

Each I Dare Say... ! piece began with a thumbnail bio reminding readers who the highlighted person used to be, followed by twenty trivial questions and the pseudo-celebrity's equally superficial answers.

What's your favorite movie?
The Sound of Music. Casablanca. Psycho.

What's your least favorite movie?
Elf. Elf. Elf.

You're on death row. What's on the menu for your last meal?
Chicken marinara with polenta. Broccoli pesto pasta. Pizza.

Do you believe in ghosts?
Yes. No. Yes.

It was a mystery why so many people looked forward to reading this monthly column only to learn about someone's favorite holiday destination or a preferred brand of ice cream. But the paper's editor, Terrence Marks, knew from the number of emails he received each month that I Dare Say... ! had wide appeal. People seemed to enjoy racking their brains to recall where they'd seen or heard the subject's name before. And the never-really-very-famous-in-the-first-place person now living in the *Abbots Clover Overview*'s delivery area was almost always flattered to be asked to answer the insipid questions and pose for a couple of pictures with their pet or sitting in their rocking chair.

Then Terrence Marks called Polly Pepper.

Lily, who had taken the call on the house phone while Polly was trying to interrogate Mary Radcliff, was excited because she, too, loved the I Dare Say... ! segment of each issue. For example, she thought it was fun to know that village midwife Pauline Lawrence, whose claim to fame was that she once appeared as a contestant paired with Cilla Black on the game show *Suite Success*, liked scented bubble baths. Lily did, too. And that Damian Lawrence, who found a modicum of fame in the recurring role of Peter the pompous postman on the short-lived sitcom *White Rabbits, White Rabbits*, was fond of Twiglets snack foods. Lily was, too. Who knew that Reginald Beckwourth had wanted to be a professional ventriloquist before he became Miranda Richardson's podiatrist? Lily had never been to a podiatrist, but she wanted to go to one. Now, she reasoned that since the paper wanted to feature her employer, Polly Pepper had to be a real celebrity. She was suddenly impressed with her status as a maid to someone whose picture and answers to dopey questions would soon appear on everyone's doorstep.

Polly's eyes didn't exactly light up when she arrived home, and Lily excitedly told her about the phone call from Terrence Marks and showed her an old issue of the *Abbots Clover Overview* for reference.

"Brian Forrest, Gardener to DEAD Comedian Dudley Moore," Polly said with a dismissive frown, reading an I Dare Say... ! headline from a year ago and looking at a prune-faced old man who'd obviously spent too many years working outdoors without an SPF lotion. "It's not exactly *Vanity Fair* or *60 Minutes* or even *Parade* magazine," she complained as she dismissed the paper, wandered into the main reception room, kicked off her shoes, and put her feet up on the Chesterfield.

"But it's apparently a popular feature," Tim said. "Judging by the terrible lighting of Dudley Moore's gardener, I doubt they'll send Annie Leibovitz with her camera, so you'd better insist on photo approval."

"It's apparently a local honor to be asked," Tiara added, handing Polly a champagne and championing the idea that Polly should give Terrence Marks an hour or so of her time.

Polly pondered the idea for a moment. "I like salt and pepper on my popcorn." She started answering potential questions. "I detest invitations to destination weddings. And to a make-believe dinner party with three people from history, I'd invite Marie Antoinette, Audrey Hepburn, and Adam from Adam and Eve—to see if he has a belly button."

"Easy-peasy!" Tiara affirmed and raised her own champagne glass to Polly's. "You're ready to get this done and make it fun."

After returning Terrence Mark's call and arranging an interview for the following morning at 10:00, Polly practically skipped around the room, feeling famous again.

"They're on a tight deadline to put the latest issue of the paper to bed." She repeated what Terrence had told her. "Seems that the guy who played Knuckles the Clown on *Blue Peter* had a stroke yesterday, and they need a replacement celebrity."

During the evening meal—served in the kitchen because Tiara said she was too pooped to set the formal dining room table—Polly and company talked about their huge waste-of-time meeting with Mary Radcliff. There were no juicy revelations proving that Mary had taken out Gwellyn in retribution for ruining the biggest night of her life. No film rights were locked down for *Lust Among the Bluebells*, either. And they hadn't even returned with a handwritten inscription in Mary's novel.

As Polly thought about the squandered encounter, she pushed bits of shepherd's pie around her plate and decided that

Mary was a liar. Maybe not a big fat pathological one who goes around murdering people, but at least one who embellishes the truth. *That's what writers do*, she reminded herself, and said she wasn't buying Mary's sob story about her past and family tragedies.

"I'm not feeling it," she said to four wide eyes taken aback by her unfeeling judgment of poor, sad-hearted Mary. "I didn't see one single family picture or photos of her beloved rescue dogs. Everyone on the planet has precious moments scattered around the house."

"Maybe she prefers her tragedies without frames," Tim said. "Constant reminders of a painful past are hard. I can't listen to Whitney Houston because I get sad about her death."

"Why would she lie about her past?" Tiara scoffed, not ready to give in to Polly's uncharitable attitude.

"Perhaps she's hiding her present," Polly said. "Camouflage. Subterfuge. Bait and switch. 'Look over there, not at what's right in front of your eyes.' I think she's guilty as sin... at least for ripping off other people's sins for her novel. She doesn't have an original story idea, so she steals them from real life. Mary has something to hide and wants to throw us off her scent."

"Her *scent*?" Tiara scoffed. "What are we now, a pack of bloodhounds tracking a prison escapee?"

"Maybe a path *to* prison," Polly suggested as she continued to pick on Mary Radcliff and suggest her possible motives for knocking off Gwellyn Clogg. "All I'm saying is that Mary had an obvious grudge against Gwellyn. I'd be pretty cheesed off, too, if I were publicly humiliated and threatened on the biggest night of my life. I reserve the right to at least add Mary to my list of potential suspects!"

～

When Terrence Marks arrived at ten o'clock sharp the following morning, Tiara ushered him into the main reception room. Polly was waiting there, posed on the Chesterfield and petting a contented Mr. Boots. She faked a blithe laugh as if she'd forgotten about their scheduled meeting (she'd been prepping for hours and was wearing her cocktail dress) and held out her hand in greeting. Polly had an instantly positive impression of Terrence. Was it his smile? His brown eyes? His prematurely grayish hair? Polly wasn't sure, but found herself feeling uncharacteristically self-conscious. *Yummy!* her covetous eyes said of her visitor. *Good posture. Healthy complexion. Nice nose. No discernible tummy-tum.*

Terrence was slightly timid, like a teen meeting his girlfriend's father for the first time. But Polly was used to that response from people. His voice was pleasing, too, more like Prince Charles's accent rather, than Lily's West Country.

Obscure though Polly Pepper was in England, it turned out that she was actually one of Terrence Marks's favorite celebrities. His mother was American (which explained his softer accent), and she had often said that comedienne/singer Polly Pepper was her all-time favorite TV star in the States because she seemed "like a real person." His mother had been a devoted follower of *The Polly Pepper Playhouse* when she was younger and had introduced Terrence to clips from the show on YouTube when he was old enough to appreciate them. Polly was by far the most famous of all the people he'd interviewed for the paper.

Tiara served tea and freshly baked chocolate chip cookies before leaving Polly and Terrence alone. In no time, the two were settled into a comfortable camaraderie. They were both charmed by the other and felt at ease making little jokes and observations about the age of the castle, the wet weather in England, and the UK prime minister versus the United States president. Soon, they were giggling like friends at a sleepover. Their conversation organically evolved into the purpose of their meeting, and Terrence eventually got down to business.

"Mind if I record us? My scribbling is pretty lame," he confided. "I don't want to take a chance of getting anything wrong. This is a little different from interviewing Claudia Riser."

"Claudia... " Polly shrugged.

"I'd never heard of her either before we put her in the September issue last year." Terrence chuckled. "She under-studied Paige Bostik in the West End production of *The Lemon Tart* some forty-odd-years ago. Not much happened with her career after that, and now she lives in the area, so she was of interest to the locals. A little up her own bum, if you know what I mean."

Polly didn't know what he meant. She'd never heard that expression. It took hours before she figured it out, and then she laughed at the visual that the phrase conjured up for something as simple as someone being full of themselves.

Then Terrence tapped the voice recording app on his phone and explained again the format of I Dare Say... !

Polly Pepper excelled at interviews. She'd been giving them for the past forty-five years and would surely earn an A+ if she were graded on how she charmed the press with her witty repartee and clever answers to usually frivolous and often down-right stupid questions. If she'd counted how many times someone had asked, "How old were you when you first stepped onto a stage?" the answer would have been exactly three hundred seventy-two times. "Who is your comic idol?" That amounted to seven hundred fifty-seven times. "Who was your favorite guest on your show?" That question clocked in at four hundred twenty-two times. (Official, but not necessarily true, answers: age fifteen. Carol Burnett. Eydie Gormé.)

It was rare for anyone to walk away from an interview with

Polly Pepper without a smile and the feeling that they'd just made a new friend for life. Terrence Marks was feeling that way now. In fact, Polly Pepper was everything he'd ever hoped she would be: gracious, lively, and, above all else, funny. Polly had him happily wrapped around her wee finger. And on this cold winter morning, she was beginning to melt in the palm of his hand, too. She wasn't sure she liked that. It meant she wasn't completely in control—of the interview or herself. And soon, she was listening to Terrence more with her eyes than her ears. She almost didn't hear the next question: "What's your favorite philosophical quote?"

Polly paused for a long moment as she considered which of her many favorites would play well not only to the readers of the *Abbots Clover Overview* but perhaps also to Terrence personally. There was something fascinating about him, but Polly tried her best not to show her interest.

"A quote," she repeated, pondering her potential answer. "Something funny?" she asked. "Perhaps Mae West: 'You only live once, but if you do it right, once is enough,'" she said, imitating Mae's distinctive cadence and rhythm.

"Or something serious? Henry Ford: 'Whether you think you can or think you can't, you're right.'

"Maybe some royal humor from Prince Philip? 'When a man opens a car door for his wife, it's either a new car or a new wife.' That sounds more like Groucho Marx, but I'm pretty sure it was the Duke of Edinburgh." Then she recalled her very favorite literary, movie, and stage character, Auntie Mame—a role she'd performed multiple times to great success: "'Life is a banquet, and most poor suckers are starving to death!' There! That's my all-time favorite quote! It's my personal motto, too. You can print that!"

Terrence laughed, and his laugh made Polly laugh, too.

"That's a great one," he said, transfixed by Polly's wit and hazel-colored eyes, which he tried to avoid looking into too deeply or for more than a fraction of a nanosecond at a time for fear of embarrassing himself—or Polly.

Polly, too, felt a strange self-consciousness pulling at her. Terrence was surprisingly fun and comfortable to be around, but she started panicking slightly. A delirious feeling radiated up from the area around her navel, but she hoped it wasn't showing on her face. Perhaps it was evident because she sensed that Terrence was feeling something good, too. She was eager to know more about him.

Adept at being the interviewee, Polly was equally skilled at surreptitiously turning the tables on her interrogators, and soon, it was Terrence who was being sneakily quizzed about his life. He revealed that he'd grown up in Abbots Clover. He'd gotten a media and communications degree from Cardiff University. He had a passion for news and current events. He loved that his job gave him carte blanche to poke around in other people's lives and activities and expose secrets hidden under various proverbial rocks. But after spending several years working for the *Financial Times* in London and getting married and then quickly divorced, he returned to his childhood home in the Southwest of England and took over as editor of the *Abbots Clover Overview*. It was a career move that his friends in London had said was crazy stupid and that he'd miss the excitement of the capital.

But Terrence knew in his heart that moving back was absolutely the right thing to do. He'd missed the green English countryside and realized he got more pleasure from writing articles about gardens, cheese festivals, and local artists than from reporting about the Bank of England's bleak economic forecasts. Anyway, there were plenty of interesting stories in rural areas to investigate and write about.

"I'm just as busy in Abbots Clover as I ever was in London," he admitted.

Terrence explained that there was always a local nut or two who thought they had a lead to the biggest story since Harold Shipman's days as a serial killer. He sniggered as he recalled that Lucy Lawrence over in Upper Wrythe was sure that Miles Miller, the optometrist in Lower Wrythe, was using special eye drops that enabled him to control her thoughts. And that Willard Storm from the RSPCA charity shop suspected that some of the clothes Marcy Drummond brought in for donation contained DNA samples that would conclusively prove that she was having an affair with Stan Carpenter, who owned the Dusty Attic antique shop. And Rence Williams insisted that the American renting the old Edwards farm was likely to be an MI6 spy because he was aloof, and wouldn't a spy be that way to not call attention to himself?

"That whole mind-controlling eye drops story is marvelous." Polly laughed. "Combine it with an MI6 operative, and it might make a good plot point in a movie."

"And everyone knew that Willard Storm's wife was fooling around with Marcy Drummond's husband anyway, so it was only news to her other lover, Mark Stillman."

With the topic of conspiracy stories and paranoid villagers proposing scenarios about international crime syndicates in sleepy Abbots Clover, Polly decided it might be the perfect opening to ask about real crime in the village.

"Dear me, there's so much going on here it's mind-spinning. You need a scorecard to keep up!" she said, priming Terrence for a direct question. "From my outsider's view looking in, everything seems idyllic here. Well, except for the rumor I keep hearing that my former housekeeper, Gwellyn Clogg, was murdered."

The room suddenly became quiet. Even Mr. Boots's usually loud purr was muted, and he looked up. Polly looked at

Terrence, who looked back at her, and they both grimaced simultaneously.

"A little too farfetched?" she asked.

"As a matter of fact, no. I wouldn't be surprised if she were killed," Terrence said.

Ding, ding, ding! Nail on the head! Go to the head of the class! Polly heard a game show host's voice in her head, combined with the sound of a Vegas casino slot machine making a big cash payout. Polly might have been falling in lust with Terrence since his arrival for the interview, but now she was falling in real *love* and wanted to kiss this very kissable man. *He doesn't think I'm an idiot!*

"Why wouldn't you be surprised?" she asked, following up and trying to maintain her composure.

"She was a pill, to put it nicely," Terrence said. "Most people thought that Gwellyn Clogg belonged in a locked hospital ward. She came into my office a dozen or so times, demanding that I write editorials about things like hedgerows being dangerously overgrown, bin lorries hogging the roads, or various petitions she wanted to circulate. She wasn't being civic-minded; she was just a pathological troublemaker who liked to stir the pot and cause controversy. She accused a couple of the manor houses in the area of closing off public right-of-way paths on their land, which was false. I think Gwellyn just resented anyone who had more than she did. It was obvious that she was bitter about working in service. Of the rumors you've heard, which ones stand out the most? The one about Gwellyn and Stan Carpenter, probably."

Stan Carpenter? If Polly had been excited only a short moment ago when Terrence suggested that her theory about Gwellyn's demise was a distinct possibility, now she was on her way into orbit from another name to add to her list of suspects: Stan Carpenter. Whoever he was.

"Stan Carpenter owned the Dusty Attic antique shop over in Divershim and had been friends with Gwellyn until they had a falling-out," Terrence said. He explained that, apparently, Gwellyn and Stan had a business deal whereby she would nick small items of value from Alistair Drake—and Lord and Lady Ridgewood-Brimble before him—then Stan would sell them in his shop. They'd split the money. But then she wanted more from him. She knew he was earning quite a good income from the business—which was even featured on *Antiques Road Trip*— and wanted him to dump his wife and marry her. That wasn't going to happen. For one thing, compared to Stan's wife, Cindy, Gwellyn was the female equivalent of Quasimodo.

Polly nodded in understanding, recalling Gwellyn's attempt to shake her down for a dip into Mr. Drake's money bag and selling off Mr. Drake's wine collection. It wasn't a stretch to believe that Gwellyn could also have been a wannabe home-wrecker. Nor was Polly at all surprised when Terrence said that Gwellyn had squealed on her partner-in-crime to HM Revenue and Customs for his nonpayment of taxes.

"I was covering his trial for the paper, and as soon as the judge declared him guilty and sentenced him to six months in prison and a £20,000 fine, I heard him say that if he lived to be a thousand years old, he'd make her pay for what she'd done to him. He actually got out of jail last week. I ran into him at the Fox & Hare, and he said he was in the village scouting for a location to open another antique shop. That was the very afternoon before Gwellyn died. Coincidence? Maybe."

Oh, boy! Now, this was what Polly called a hot tip! A reliable source telling her that someone with a definite motive had publicly threatened Gwellyn! The very fun interview had turned into a stunning one. Polly clapped her hands and wanted to reach out and pull Terrence's handsome face to hers and kiss the heck out of it. She could visualize her smooth hands on his rugged face, staring seductively into his brown eyes and her Revlon Really, Really Red lips smooching his equally voluptuous ones. She was more aroused than she'd been in ages.

And then it happened...

No, not that! Tiara walked in.

Really? You couldn't have waited for just a few more intimate minutes? Polly silently seethed and made a face that let Tiara know she was annoyed. But it was one of Tiara's assigned duties; whenever Polly was being interviewed for a specified amount of time, she was to interrupt five minutes before the time was up, offering the phony excuse that Polly had another appointment and should wrap things up. But no, no, no, this time, Polly was peeved by the sham disruption. Polly reluctantly decided that nothing physical would have happened between her and Terrence, anyway. But that wasn't the point. Darn it all!

Tiara had done more than interrupt the interview. She had somehow fractured a fairy-tale spell that had enveloped the entire room. Polly decided that maybe it was a good thing that she came in when she did. After all, it would have been mortifying if what she was sensing as a mutual attraction was only a handsome man doing his job by courting her ego for his newspaper article. After all, she knew there was a symbiotic relationship between celebrities and the press. Still, as she shook his hand goodbye and offered to be available anytime to answer further questions, Polly had a nagging feeling. It was a feeling she liked very much, but one she'd only recently thought she was probably too old ever to have again.

The morning became afternoon, and Polly busied herself reading—but not really reading—one of Mr. Drake's celebrity biographies, *My Heart Belongs*, by Broadway legend Mary

Martin. And by the time Tiara served Polly's six o'clock champagne, the star was noticeably melancholy.

"What's with the little-lost-lamb act?" Tiara asked. "You've been moping around and acting stranger than usual all day. Even Lily's keeping her distance." And then it hit her. "Oh, I get it. Someone who hates window-shopping and only wants the instant gratification that comes with immediately buying any pretty bauble she fancies has found a shiny new toy and is trying to figure out how to get it. A trinket engraved with the name... *Terrence Marks*."

Polly rolled her eyes in derision at Tiara's lame assumption. But then she backpedaled. "I know, I know. It's stupid. But every time I think about him, my heart does this little *skip-to-my-lou* flutter thingy. My body is saying, '*Oui, oui,*' but my brain is screaming, 'Don't be an idiot! You're too old!'"

"Polly," Tiara contradicted, "one is never too old to fall in love. You've heard the saying 'You're as young as the man you feel?'"

"That's not a saying."

"It should be. You're a catch! You're famous. You have a star on the Hollywood Walk of Fame. You still have some of your looks."

"I sound like a carnival prize. Let's be real. I'm not exactly a spring chicken. I mean, I'm sixty-something... "

"You got the 'something' part right! But what I'm saying is age shouldn't be a barrier to falling in love. You clearly know that the most important thing is finding someone who makes you laugh and whom you can have fun with on a daily basis. And hey, maybe Terrence has a thing for cougars."

"Don't be gross. Why do I even have these stupid teenage-girl thoughts at my age? But do you blame me? Terrence is just so... He's rather... He's got... " Polly's voice trailed off, but Tiara knew exactly what her boss was thinking and trying to explain.

Tiara shrugged and raised an eyebrow. "Stats?" she said, playing grand inquisitor.

"Divorced. No kids. Lives with Lionel."

"Boyfriend or husband?"

"Lab retriever."

"Then he appreciates loyalty and a game of go-fetch."

"It might be rather fun to have Terrence throw a tennis ball at me." Polly smiled impishly.

"That settles it. You should absolutely have a night out together. Go on a date, for heaven's sake! You've got to reel him in like a fish. Just pray he doesn't end up a red herring like your other husbands!"

"I can't go on a date! Abbots Clover is more of a fishbowl than Hollywood!" Polly pooh-poohed the idea of exposing herself to the village gossipmongers. But her face suggested she was well ahead of Tiara in the planning stages for another meet-up with delectable Terrence. She wandered over to the coffee table in front of the Chesterfield settee. "He might have to visit our Lost and Found Department," she said mischievously.

"For a kissy-kissy with a certain TV-star lady?" Tiara asked.

Polly made the face of a delinquent child forced to produce the evidence of a stolen cookie. She reached behind the settee and retrieved Terrence's camera case. She made a pouty expression and imitated the innocent voice of Shirley Temple. "We have a very naughty kleptomaniac spirit living in this house!"

21

———

Tim returned to Thistlethorne with Grayson and bounded into the reception room.

"Mummy! Mummy! Look at my hypothermia," he cried and hurried to warm himself by the fireplace. He'd been determined not to complain about the cold and rainy weather all day, not wanting his new friend to think he was a California snowflake who couldn't endure soggy socks and a few frostbitten fingers and toes. Now that he was safely back in the womb, he decided the hours spent hiking around the castle grounds and exploring a nearby Iron Age fort in inclement weather had only served to tempt pneumonia, but he was on the cusp of admitting it was a worthwhile trade-off.

When the two young men were sufficiently thawed and their blue lips were pink again, they took seats on the Chesterfield opposite Polly, and Tiara served them bubbly.

Americans are weird, drinking champagne all the time, Grayson thought. Although he knew Polly wasn't a typical Yank—or typical anything—he still suspected that everyone in the States was probably an alcoholic. Then he looked at Polly.

"Has Tim told you the news?" he said.

Polly looked blankly at Grayson, thinking, *You're definitely cute, but please don't spring wedding plans on me. Not today.*

"CrimeClue called. That's the organization that the public can contact to anonymously report illegal activities," Grayson explained.

"After all these years, they've finally tracked you down, Tiara." Polly sniggered and gave her maid a playful look.

"Someone called in a tip about Gwellyn Clogg," Grayson continued. "I've been summoned up to Bristol for a meeting with the chief inspector tomorrow to discuss it. I got the impression that this is potentially serious."

"Like *murder* serious?" Polly asked. "Like maybe someone finked on someone who killed Gwellyn?"

Grayson shrugged. "CrimeClue is where you go when you want to pass on information about crimes without having to give official witness statements to the police. The calls aren't recorded, and the telephone lines are scrambled, so no one can track the source of a call. It's pretty cool, especially if you're maybe close to the criminal—like a disgruntled spouse—to sidestep dealing with the authorities. The inspector wouldn't say much, but they wanted Gwellyn's file forwarded to them. They asked for a couple of others, too, including Becca Lucas, one of the stylists over at the Clip & Curl, and her boyfriend, Alex Bates, but we don't have anything on either of them. I'm actually sort of surprised that Alex has never been in any serious legal trouble, we were in sixth form together, and he was a mischief-maker of the first order even back then. He always had a gang of lads around him. You know the type—cocksure bullies popular with the girls who like to hang around with bad boys. Alex never bothered me, but he sure had it in for a couple of others, including my best mate, Edward."

Grayson described how Alex Bates and his posse had treated his friend Edward Swindon. It was classic: name-calling, vicious rumors, and dumping yogurt into his backpack. Edward was a smart kid and preferred science and literature to sports. But the persecution he'd received from Alex had sent him into a deep depression, and his grades went down.

"In the end, Edward made it to university and is now a lead environmental marine scientist in Scotland," Grayson said. "And Alex—he can't even afford to fill his tank with petrol. I see him riding his bicycle everywhere. The same bicycle he had in school."

Polly nodded in understanding and recalled her own school days. She could honestly say that she'd never been bullied. Even as a child, she had a larger-than-life personality. She was popular with the student brainiacs, the thespian crowd, and the competitive sports set. However, she acknowledged that she'd been scared to death every single moment of every single day of her high school experience in Edding, Indiana. Her bravado had been a big fake. She'd expertly cultivated that persona. Today, she would probably have been diagnosed with generalized anxiety disorder, but there was no such thing when she was growing up. And if she'd stayed in Edding and not gone into show business, she'd probably have ended up in a mental institution—or burned at the stake as a witch. As Walter Winchell once said, "Hollywood is where they place you under contract instead of under observation."

Polly was excited that the police might be ready to consider an alternative to the original theory regarding Gwellyn's death. But she wasn't prepared to let go of her own investigation just yet. In fact, if the UK police were anything like their Beverly Hills counterparts whom she'd dealt with on several murder cases in the past, she knew they were too busy and underfunded to pay much attention to an insignificant dead maid in an insignificant rural village. They could use her help.

"Darling," she said to Grayson, "I have interesting news, too.

I have it on good authority that someone named Stan Carpenter once threatened to do something nefarious to Gwellyn... and he was seen down at the Fox & Hare the very afternoon before she died. May I suggest you take his file with you to Bristol?"

Grayson nodded. "That is interesting. We were notified that he'd been released from jail. But according to the terms of his parole, he's not supposed to be anywhere near Abbots Clover for the full six months of his probation. Maybe I should have him re-arrested."

"Can you wait a day or two, sweetums?" Polly cooed. "I want to pay him a wee visit tomorrow. I'm told that his wife divorced him while he was in the slammer, and he's now living somewhere in Divershim."

"Rather than an up close and personal visit, just send him a post-prison greeting card," Tim joked. "Something fun that says, 'Be courteous to criminals. Let them finish their sentences.'" He laughed at his own joke but knew it was no use trying to dissuade his mother from fulfilling whatever goal she had in mind. If she was intent on meeting up with a jailbird, that was exactly what she would do. No ifs, ands, or buts.

And although Grayson had only known Polly briefly, from what he'd observed and heard secondhand from Tim, there was no use advising her to stay away from an ex-con. He shook his head apprehensively and said, "I'll text you his registered address when I get home tonight."

Although Tim had invited Grayson to stay for dinner, the constable declined reluctantly and promised to visit the following day after returning from his appointment with the police chief inspector in Bristol.

"By then, I should have more information about CrimeClue

and Gwellyn, and Polly might have something to report from her meet-up with Stan Carpenter," he said as Tim walked Grayson to the main gate. They stood there for a long moment, whispering and agreeing to see each other the next evening.

As Tim wandered back into the house and toward the reception room, Tiara sidled up to him.

"Be extra gentle with your momma tonight," she said. "The interview with Terrence Marks went well... maybe a little too well... but in a different direction than she expected. She's feeling a bit more vulnerable than usual. That's all I'm going to say. You'll know what to do."

Although puzzled by Tiara's comments, Tim rejoined his mother and topped up their respective glasses with Star Lady's fizzy elixir.

"Tiara tells me she's making lasagna for dinner, your favorite comfort food," he said. "That always means one of two things: you've got a job, and there's something to celebrate, or you lost a job and need something to beat away the blues. What's up? I hear the interview went well."

Polly shrugged. Not only did she not want to talk about her meeting with Terrence, but she also hadn't a clue what she could say about her drippy feelings other than maybe she was homesick for California.

"It's just your old mum in a pensive mood, that's all." She half-smiled and sipped her champagne. "It must be this incessant rainy weather."

"Tell me about it," Tim agreed. "I'm never going outside again as long as I live!" After a moment of silence, he said, "Tell me about Terrence Marks and your interview. What was he like? Friendly? Intelligent? Attractive? Do you get a dozen extra copies of the *Abbots Clover Overview* to send to your friends back home?"

Tim had noticed that when he spoke the words "friendly"

and "attractive," Polly had made noncommittal nods. He'd been around long enough to recognize that what his mother really meant was an enthusiastic "yes!" Then, in an *aha* moment, he connected Tiara's comments with Polly's perfunctory responses to his questions about the interview.

"In other words, Terrence is hot. Is that what you're not saying?"

Polly smiled sheepishly and shrugged. "Yeah, I guess. We had a lovely connection. Terrence—don't you love that name?—is smart and has a fun sense of humor. But you know how it is. I'm a celebrity, and I can't trust that he's not just impressed with my fame. Plus, I'm a bit older than him."

Tim was silent for a long moment. It was certainly true that his mother was loved and admired by a lot of people who only wanted to know her because she was famous. But he'd also discovered that Abbots Clover was not like Hollywood, and he reassured her that the people he'd met in their village didn't seem as dazzled by celebrity as Americans often were. He'd met a few locals when he and Grayson were at the Fox & Hare. After telling them where his accent was from and answering a few questions about living in California, they dropped the subject as if it were cool that he knew movie stars, but lame to be all goo-goo for them. In Hollywood, his genetic association with Polly Pepper made him a bit of a celebrity, too, but here in Abbots Clover, he was just another bloke. And he liked that.

Tim reminded Polly of how Sarah at Bound to Read had been more impressed with how much fun Polly was as a person than by her career.

"She even had to be told by her grandmother who you are!" Tim teased. "Sarah just likes you for you. She thought you were witty and amusing. Tell me the name of one person here who has treated you like the diva you are?" Tim challenged with a laugh. "Maybe this guy likes you despite your fame. Invite him over. In fact, text him this very minute. Dinner here tomorrow night, if it's okay with Tiara."

Polly melted. All the negative thoughts and fears she'd been harboring since Terrence left the house that morning began to disappear. She reminded herself that she had always been good at visualizing her future. Sometimes, she was right, such as diving into showbiz at a young age. And sometimes she wasn't so right, like with the three losers to whom she'd said "I do" at the altar before really knowing that her grooms were duds. And in this moment, she sensed that maybe there was a bigger reason for being lured to England beyond simply taking possession of an inherited castle. She didn't want to jinx what she felt by saying "love" out loud, but she was optimistic.

Then she raised her glass in a toast. "To all the fascinating and unexpected fun surprises that life brings!"

"And to CrimeClue," Tim added. "May they arrest your heart with your one true love!"

22

Gwellyn Clogg's alleged estranged paramour, Stan Carpenter, was in his early fifties and had long gone completely bald. Polished bowling ball bald. He was stocky and short—no taller than five feet seven—but had seductive green eyes and a wide, Colgate extra-white toothpaste smile. And when Tim dropped Polly and Tiara off at the Divershim Fabrics shop on the Divershim high street, and they knocked on the door to Stan's one-room flat above, he was in a good mood and happily invited them in.

"I knew you'd get around to me," Stan said, obviously tuned into the radio-waveband-like village grapevine and knowing Polly Pepper was nosing around.

The room looked like it had been furnished by a monk who'd taken a vow of poverty: a burnt-orange, thin-cushioned, charity-shop couch with frayed fabric arms; a coffee table littered with days-old newspapers and Chinese takeaway cartons; a square dining table with two folding chairs; and an unframed, mass-produced painting of a long-hair Scottish Highlands cow (they seem to be ubiquitous these days) staring down from the magnolia-colored wall behind the sofa. He didn't say so, but he'd obviously just moved in. And he also didn't say that his most recent accommodation was hosted by His Majesty's prison service either. But, of course, they knew.

"You're that American TV lady," Stan said in greeting Polly and merely nodded in Tiara's direction. "Have a seat. I'd offer to fetch you a wee bit of tea, but I only have one cup." He was apologetic as he ushered them to the settee and dragged over a chair from the dining table for himself. After only a fraction of a moment, Stan said, "Neither of us has all day, so let's get to the point. You're not here to play US ambassador to Abbots Clover. You want to ask me about Gwellyn Clogg and my relationship with her, right?"

"Not a fan of foreplay," Polly said, half-joking and pleased that she didn't have to sneakily lead Stan to the reason for their visit.

Stan looked straight into Polly's eyes and slowly shook his head. "It isn't anyone's business, but yes, I did hate Gwellyn Clogg as much as you've probably heard. And I publicly wished her dead. I hated her dumb last name, too. *Clogg*. One syllable. The moment it's spoken, it just sort of plops like a stone in mud. *Clogg*. But the name kind of suited her, if you think about it. Like a toilet waste pipe plugged up with gunk. That was Gwellyn Clogg." Stan laughed at the picture in his head. Then he shrugged, implying there was no reason not to be fully forthcoming. "Did you ever notice how some people are so toxic that they seem to pass their toxicity on to everyone they come into contact with? I tried to be nice to Gwellyn at first, like I am to everybody. But her negative energy sort of brushed off on me. Like metal shavings to a magnet. Totally my fault for getting involved with her in the first place."

Polly nodded in understanding, and her memory instantly flashed back to an experience she'd had only a few years earlier in Palm Springs. She'd rented a holiday property from the now-infamously failed entrepreneur Horst Russell (he pretentiously pronounced his last name Ru-SELL). They'd met at a dinner party, and although her inner voice cautioned against getting too chummy, she foolishly ignored the feelings. She somehow agreed to rent his house in the desert for a couple of summer months. Who in their right mind even goes to the desert in the summer, for crying out loud? Upon her departure from the property, Horst had tried to fleece her for far more money than they'd agreed upon for the rental. To Polly's shock, he'd had the temerity to present her with a bill for tens of thousands of additional dollars.

They'd originally agreed on a price of $5,000 per month, plus the cost of utilities. In California, rental utilities consist of water, electricity, and gas, but Horst had insisted on compensation for the gardener, pool man, window washer, pest control, tree trimmer, refuse collector, security alarm system, property insurance, and property taxes, among other items that are the responsibility of the homeowner. But that wasn't the worst part. He tried to blackmail her with the threat of selling a preposterous story to the *National Intruder* about Polly Pepper ransacking his home, holding drug-induced orgies, and letting her dog urinate throughout the house and thus ruining the carpets. Most ludicrous of all, he said she'd left bedbugs behind.

Okay, maybe a visiting friend's pet poodle had had a little tinkle accident, but nothing more than that! Polly had been mortified by Horst's odious treatment of her, but rather than take the man to court, even though she would have surely won her claim against him, she ultimately settled a fraction of the unexpected debt just to be rid of the little pile of human poop. She shuddered at the thought of ever having to deal with Horst again but couldn't help feeling a bit of satisfaction that she had been the one to tip off the FBI that his Salvadoran housekeeper was in the country illegally and, essentially, kept as his slave.

Now, several years on, Polly was still seething over Horst's hubris and thus completely understood Stan's parallel to the toxicity of people like Gwellyn Clogg.

Without prompting, Stan revealed to Polly and Tiara that it was true he'd sold items in his antique shop that Gwellyn had brought to him.

"Were they stolen?" He shrugged a confession. "I didn't ask, but I assumed. Maybe. Probably. She had an uncanny eye for the good stuff, like jewelry and antiques that might not be easily missed by their owner. And she got a crash course in heirloom appraisals from me. I imagine she took that knowledge back to whichever manor house she worked in and did on-site evaluations. Her employers were old and not necessarily *compos mentis*, if you get what I mean.

"She was greedy," Stan continued. "She saw how well my shop was doing and decided she wanted to partner with me—in more ways than one. She wanted to be a supplier of some sort. I soon saw the authentic Gwellyn and shut her out. She promised to get even. By then, I'd inadvertently divulged some information about my, shall we say, 'business practices.' Then the revenue service boys came calling. And yeah, everyone knows I threatened her at the trial because she's the one who called CrimeClue about me. I'll never forget the day of my sentencing. She sat in the gallery, smiling at me smugly and obviously taking a lot of satisfaction from how I was suffering. She had one of those begging-to-be-punched faces. I lost everything, including my wife—which, frankly, in retrospect, wasn't much of a loss. Maybe I should have thanked Gwellyn instead of threatening her."

As Polly and Tiara sat listening to Stan excavate his memory and many reasons for detesting Gwellyn, he finally ran out of steam and said, "But I didn't kill her. She wasn't worth spending the rest of my life in prison. I totally realized that while I was literally spending my life in prison."

"Not a fan of prison porridge?" Polly cracked, then leaned forward to look directly into Stan's eyes. "And yet, you risked being sent back in when you violated the terms of your parole by coming to Abbots Clover only a few hours before Gwellyn was found dead. Why?"

Stan stared back at Polly, starting to show his boredom at having to explain himself after he'd already flatly stated that he hadn't killed Gwellyn Clogg. He took a deep breath. "It was a dumb lapse in judgment," he said. "I had an appointment with an estate agent to discuss letting a place for a new shop, and she took me to Abbots Clover. Then, because I hadn't been to the Fox & Hare since before prison, I wanted to say hi to Garfield and Blade." He laughed. "Those are the names Mary Radcliff gave to her Crimson and Fergus characters in a so-called 'romance' novel she wrote. Have you read it? I'm no English lit expert, but even I understand why she had to self-publish that piece of rubbish. It stank up my cell, too. That's probably why they kicked me out."

Stan laughed at his own joke, but Polly was bewildered about why she liked *Lust Among the Bluebell*s and thought it had potential value, but everybody else thought it was doo-doo. Like Stan, she was no connoisseur of the literary arts, but she wasn't unsophisticated. And she had a decent sense of what the public liked.

"Honestly," Stan continued, "I wouldn't have been looking to find Gwellyn, anyway. I was terrified of running into her. The idea of us coming face-to-face made me shake. I never wanted to see her again as long as I lived."

Polly considered Stan's motive for violating his parole requirements. Then, considering he knew the barkeeps at the

Fox & Hare, she asked the question that had been on her mind since meeting with Mary Radcliff.

"Speaking of Crimson/Prysm and Fergus/Lance, what did they think about being characters in Mary's novel? I don't know if I'd be amused if a writer described me as 'a crumpet with a pint of maple syrup ladled over it,' as Mary did of Crimson. And yes, I've read *Lust Among the Bluebells*. I thought it was… amusing. So shoot me."

Stan sniggered. "As a matter of fact, and as hard as it is to believe, considering the high-speed telepathic broadband of this village, Crimson and Fergus hadn't even heard about the book. At least that's what they said. I know, crazy, right? I suggested they might like to take a look, but neither seemed to care. I guess they're too busy making love when they're not at work. Or maybe they're illiterate. Yeah, that's my best guess. Sex-addicted illiterates."

Then, suddenly changing the subject, Stan said, "Before Gwellyn and I fell out, she talked a lot about retiring. I was pretty sure it was a pipe dream. She was far from old enough for her state pension and wasn't making much money working for Mr. Drake. I just went along with her. Hell, everyone needs a dream. But I eventually suspected that she had a plan for financial independence. Sometimes, when she brought me a ring or antique doodad of one sort or another, she talked about bigger prizes that she couldn't get her paws on just yet. These huge old houses—like Hedgepath Manor and Thistlethorne Lodge—have tons of secrets hidden in them, so I imagine she found something of value and was biding her time."

Hearing the name of their house attached to the word "secrets," Polly and Tiara suddenly became more intrigued and sat up straighter in their seats. They'd already discovered a few secrets of their own at Thistlethorne. But could there be more unrevealed spaces and/or precious booty?

"What secrets?" Polly asked eagerly. "We've got a ghost. Isn't that enough?"

Stan Carpenter said that although Gwellyn had never provided specifics, he'd learned to sense when she was telling the truth, lying, or just withholding something. "She was expecting an inheritance," he said. "Gwellyn said she knew that Mr. Drake didn't have any heirs, so she thought it was reasonable to assume that since she's in his orbit every day, he'd probably think about her when he made his will. She didn't expect a lot, but hopefully enough to give her the financial freedom to move back to Wales. That was another one of the dreams she talked about. She was hoping to buy a small farm near where she was raised. I got the impression—and I have nothing more than a hunch to back it up—that she was just waiting for a windfall from Mr. Drake until she could make the move. When I heard about Mr. Drake's death, I thought the next thing I'd hear was that she'd moved on. I was right. But I didn't expect she'd move on to *The Twilight Zone*. Murdered, right?"

There. Stan had said the M-word out loud. Polly and Tiara were surprised he was so confident that Gwellyn had been dispatched into the afterlife by human hands.

"If I were you, I might start looking for someone who would gain more than just the peace of mind that a real-life Bellatrix Lestrange was no longer around to torment them," Stan suggested. "Someone out there wanted her gone for some reason, a reward far better and longer-lasting than just not having to see her pudgy, beady-eyed face. Or hear her annoying accent. I don't know what someone's reason would be... but when you sit around in a prison cell for six months, you get all sorts of thoughts and ideas."

"About... " Polly pressed.

Stan shrugged.

The trio sat silently for a long while, each unsure of what to say next. Stan wanted to end the meeting and get a Chinese takeaway for lunch. While Polly wanted Stan to name someone, anyone who might want to interfere with a scheme that Gwellyn might have been plotting. But Stan claimed to be completely destitute of names of potential co-conspirators or even anyone whom Gwellyn would have been friendly enough with to have shared a blueprint for her setting up a comfortable retirement for herself.

"I could name plenty of her foes, but no friends. At least not real friends," he said. "But I suspect you might find someone who got to her before she had a chance to get to them. Know what I mean? Someone she thought she could take advantage of, but they turned out to be cleverer than her. That's what I'd like to think happened. It would give me enormous joy to imagine the moment when she realized she was bested by someone more devious than her."

Stan took another deep breath and stood up to signal that it was time for his guests to leave.

"I'm actually feeling rather pleased," he said with a wide smile. "I like to see people get their just deserts—good or bad. I like to think that karma's door hit Gwellyn's big butt on her way out of this lifetime. Sweet. Oh, and if you want an alibi for me on the night of Gwellyn's death, you can talk to Marcy Drummond. She was the one who found this flat for me and stayed from the night I got out of prison until just this morning. We have an understanding, if you get my meaning."

23

Polly and Tiara left Stan Carpenter's flat, and as a soft drizzle sifted from the pewter-colored sky, they walked to the Crown pub to meet Tim for lunch. Polly had agreed he could shop for a new shirt while she and Tiara interviewed Stan, and by the number of bags he carried, it was obvious that he'd made a few shop owners happy—and richer.

"What?" Tim deflected Polly's look of disapproval. "These are just essentials. I only brought American clothes with me to England."

The trio ordered toasted sandwiches, and while waiting for their lunch to arrive, Polly and Tiara babbled about their meeting with Stan and agreed that although they could probably rule him out as a suspect in the murder of Gwellyn Clogg, he'd provided another path forward in their investigation.

"He's absolutely right about us considering not just someone who disliked Gwellyn—that list is endless—but someone who had something to gain from her death," Polly said. "I'm still thinking we need to have a chat with the guy Lady Ridgewood-Brimble mentioned, the one with a Mickey Mouse aerial ball on his *red* car. I'll have a word with Grayson about using his police skills to find him." She looked at Tim and, in a solicitous tone, added, "Speaking of dear Grayson, please, please, please convince him to stay for dinner tonight with Terrence. I'm not usually this nervous, but I don't want Terrence to think I'm ambushing him."

"Although you are sort of like a spider lying in wait for a fly." Tiara smirked.

Having the right combination of guests for dinner can be tricky, but Polly had been mixing and matching interesting and talented people to enliven her dinners most of her life. Even as a little girl, she had tea parties with Mary Poppins, Paddington Bear, Thomas the Tank Engine, and an entire stable of unicorns. Over the years, she'd learned how to weed out the dull ones and those with little to contribute to a conversation. One could never expect that the new trophy wife or boy toy of a raconteur wouldn't be a lifeless stiff, but fortunately, in Beverly Hills, there was always a steady stream of new talent to try out. In this instance, she felt comfortable combining newspaper reporter Terrence with police constable Grayson. After all, she surmised, the police and media feed off each other.

"I'd invite Sarah to make it an even boy/girl, boy/girl, boy/girl, but I don't need competition from an attractive woman who is so much younger than me," Polly said just as her toasted cheese and tomato sandwich arrived.

The afternoon flew by so quickly that it surprised everyone at Thistlethorne Lodge when the grandfather clock in the reception hallway chimed 6:00 p.m. Even Lily, who was usually a clock-watcher, had been so absorbed in dinner-prep chores that she was amazed when it was time to hang up her smock and go home. There was so much to do in the remaining hour before the guests arrived that Tim agreed, however reluctantly, to pitch in. He figured he had as much at stake entertaining Grayson as his mother had playing hostess to Terrence.

Thankfully, unlike many of Polly's dinner parties back home in Bel Air, this one was informal and didn't require fancy attire or *come as your favorite song* costumes, and thus, it didn't take hours to dress up. Tim wore the explosively vibrant new Kensington Mills shirt he'd purchased that morning. Polly wouldn't have been caught dead wearing the same cocktail dress again in front of Terrence, so she selected white slacks, a sand-colored long-sleeve cardigan, and a layered beaded necklace. Tiara, who had zero interest in fashion and was more often seen in blue jeans and button-down men's shirts, dressed with her usual lack of flair in elastic-waist denim trousers and an untucked white button-down Oxford cloth shirt. And when the doorknocker thudded at 7:00, the house and its residents were nearly ready.

Terrence was the first to arrive. He handed Tim a gift bag containing a bottle of wine, set his umbrella in the urn-turned-brolly-holder, and hung up his rain-soaked jacket on the coat rack next to the door. They made polite small talk as they walked down the hallway to the main reception room. Polly, seated on the Chesterfield and petting Mr. Boots, was a nervous wreck, but dug deep into her trove of TV characters and produced Millie DeVorzon, the passive-aggressive high school librarian whose demure façade hid her man-hungry appetite.

"Terrence, you dear man," she trilled as she received his kiss on her cheek. "Thank goodness you're here. We had oodles to talk about yesterday, and I can't wait for more."

Terrence then noticed his camera case on the floor in front of the settee. "That's where I left it," he said, grabbing the case by its strap. "I was having so much fun that I sort of lost all track of reality. I didn't come back when I noticed it was missing because I didn't want to look like the idiot that I obviously am. Don't let me forget to get a shot of you before I leave tonight."

Shortly after Tim served champagne, the doorknocker thudded again. Tim excused himself and left to retrieve Grayson. Soon, the two guests were seated in the reception room and playing polite fanboys to Polly. Tiara joined them briefly for a quick hello/welcome (and a glass of champers) and divided her attention between being the chef and adding support for Polly and Tim.

When, at last, Tiara summoned everyone to the dining room, Grayson and Terrence expressed the same look of awe as Sarah had a few days earlier. Apparently, neither had ever been in such an elegant room. The mahogany table, silver cutlery, and candelabras were as polished as ever, and soft harp music issuing through the speakers helped create a relaxed but sophisticated atmosphere. Polly deftly proved that she was an equal-opportunity diva when it came to playing gracious hostess. She maneuvered the conversation from a few reflections on her career highlights to encouraging her guests to reveal their own achievements—and skeletons.

As the soup course segued into the main dish, the small talk around the table moved effortlessly from the mediocrity of current Hollywood movies (Polly rolled her eyes at superhero films) to the stupidity of some pop song lyrics (she also winced when she considered the whiney voices of the current crop of female recording stars).

Terrence agreed with Polly that pop music was less about meaningful lyrics and more about a catchy melody and a beat to dance to.

"Which is why I like show tunes," Polly insisted. "They're

usually *about* something. They move the story's plot forward or reveal information about the characters."

On the other hand, Grayson suggested that there had always been crummy songs that were massively popular hits. In Tim's eyes, his pal had just earned a gigantic number of brownie points for contradicting Polly Pepper. Grayson didn't simply agree with everything his famous hostess had to say just to keep the debate amiable. And when Polly finally transitioned from her inexhaustible list of complaints about the sorry state of showbiz and the world in general, she deftly turned the conversation to the topic she was most interested in: who killed Gwellyn Clogg.

Polly had two local and informed men at her table whose jobs made them more aware of the people and happenings in the village than anyone else (with the possible exception of Vicar Aylsworth), and she was determined to make them share that knowledge in exchange for her hospitality.

It was getting too close to coffee and dessert time, so she took a fortifying sip of her bubbly and looked directly at Grayson. "Tell us about your meeting with the police inspector in Bristol today."

"I was going to discuss this with you in private," he said and then took a deep breath. "But since you're all personally involved, and Terrence is a friend, I'll level with you. The meeting wasn't exactly as I'd thought it might be. Detective Chief Inspector Morley did get a tip from CrimeClue. And it was about Gwellyn Clogg. But... the tipster suggested... the person accused Gwellyn... of plotting to kill... Mr. Drake."

That did it. Except for a harp plucking out Mozart's Concerto for Flute and Harp, the room was suddenly completely silent—if only briefly. Then everyone around the table simultaneously erupted in gasps of incredulity and talked over each other with questions.

Tiara picked up her butter knife and tapped the side of her wineglass until there was only a murmur among the diners. "Let Grayson finish!" she said as all eyes again turned to the constable.

Grayson cleared his throat. "The really sad and weird thing about this is that CrimeClue received two calls about Gwellyn two months apart, and the one about her plot to kill Mr. Drake came in just a day before he died. But it took CrimeClue a couple of days before notifying the authorities in Bristol. Then it had to filter to the right department and wait for a DI to be assigned. It's a bureaucracy thing. Now, of course, Alistair Drake is in the ground, and Gwellyn Clogg is in cold storage. Neither can provide more information, and there's no way to trace the tipster."

Polly sat forward and folded her hands on the edge of the table. She looked at Grayson in disbelief. "Do you mean to say that in this day and age, when that silly Siri on my phone can tell me what the weather is like on Mars and can tell nosey fans how old I really am, that the police, or Scotland Yard or MI6 or whatever your intelligence agency is here, can't track the phone number for someone reporting a murder?"

Grayson agreed it was ridiculous, but explained that the whole reason for CrimeClue to exist was for people to be able to pass on information anonymously. "Also, according to their website, they review tips regularly but state that they don't promise individual responses." That didn't quell the frustration of everyone around the table.

"So," Polly said, "it's quite possible that Abbots Clover has had *two* murders in the past couple of months. This sleepy village goes ages and ages with nothing more nefarious happening than an incident of stolen scones, and suddenly, we're London, Los Angeles, and Albuquerque all rolled into one. What are we going to do? How do we find out if Alastair died from old age or Gwellyn giving him a push over the edge of life?"

Grayson shook his head. "The medical examiner who works out of Bristol is someone I know personally. He's lazy and getting ready for retirement. He didn't even bother to call Mr. Drake's doctor after he saw the body on the floor. He took one look and immediately inferred the cause of death: age combined with whatever Mr. Drake was sick with. At the time, I didn't think much about it. I mean, he's the expert."

"Mr. Drake's illness may have been an allergic reaction to Gwellyn wanting an inheritance," Polly said flatly. "Gwellyn told me she was expecting something from Mr. Drake. Stan Carpenter confirmed that today. My intuition tells me she wanted the money she thought she was getting sooner than later."

Terrence nodded as he agreed with Polly's conclusion. "Mr. Drake's death happened two months ago," he said. "I did a brief story about it at the time because he was famous locally. Or at least his castle was famous. He was a rich layabout, so there wasn't much to write about. No organizations or clubs that he belonged to. No awards in recognition of charitable work. I think he had a rather boring life." Terrence looked at Grayson. "You would have taken a statement from Gwellyn Clogg when you came to retrieve the body. Was there anything unusual about her behavior or something she said that made you uncomfortable?"

Grayson shrugged. "I'm always uncomfortable around dead people. I'll reread the report I filed, but I didn't think anything nefarious had happened." Now Grayson was starting to second-guess himself. What if he'd jumped to the most obvious and expeditious conclusion, just as Constable Towers and the medical examiner had done? He was quiet for a long moment as he considered the events of that day. "I remember that Gwellyn seemed sort of unsentimental about the whole thing. She just said, 'The angels have visited Mr. Drake and taken the good man away.' Mr. Drake didn't have any family and only a few friends, which made it a bit of a challenge to report the death. Thankfully, he had an old-fashioned address book—no phone or computer that needed password-protected access to find contacts—which was how I could get in touch with his solicitor to help sort everything out relatively quickly."

Terrence nodded, recalling his own inquiries in order to write Mr. Drake's obituary in the *Abbots Clover Overview*. The only people he could find to interview for the piece were Gwellyn, Merv, and Vicar Aylsworth.

"They all had the usual nice things you say about someone after they die; that Alastair Drake was a 'fine human being' who would be sorely missed," he said. "But there weren't any specifics about why he was a 'fine human being.' Gwellyn said he was always 'friendly.' Merv called him 'loyal.' And Vicar Aylsworth said he was 'likable.' No one seemed to really know him very well, so I didn't have much to write about. That was a shame because there should be more than just a perfunctory, ashes-to-ashes and dust-to-dust sermon at the end of life."

Polly looked closer at Terrence and realized he was the author of the obituary of Alastair Drake that Solicitor Wainwright had given her. This further impressed her.

"I remember something in the obit you wrote that was completely memorable," she said, looking admiringly at Terrence. "It was something that you said he had highlighted in yellow marker in a book that Mr. Drake apparently reread frequently. It was a line from a character talking to the spirit of someone who had died. The dead person says, 'It is misleading to speak of people as having passed away. It is the world that passes away.' Oh, my goodness!" Polly gushed. "That has stayed with me! It's so comforting. Yesterday, we were talking about favorite quotes. That may be the one!"

Terrence beamed. "That's amazing! I mean that you remember a line from an obituary! Nobody reads obits closely. They scan them and look to see if there's a familiar name. Then they look at the person's age and cause of death. That quote is actually from a book by Frederick Buechner. Gwellyn told me it gave Mr. Drake a bit of peace about his destiny."

Tiara said, "If old Mr. Drake was murdered by Gwellyn, I hope he got a big fat laugh in heaven when he looked down and saw Gwellyn's face the moment she found out that she'd killed him for nothing. Not only didn't she get any of his money, but she was also on her way to losing her job. But if we can circle back to what Grayson said a little while ago about someone calling CrimeClue the day before Mr. Drake's death, who would have known about her plans? To whom would she have confided that information?"

Everyone at the table had the same realization: since Gwellyn didn't have many friends, the pool of potential snitches was tiny.

"Maybe someone told Vicar Aylsworth about her plans, and that's why he had the heated conversation with her that Lily described," Polly said. "Maybe it was that guy Lady Ridgewood-Brimble said had been sweet on her."

Polly thought for a moment and realized it was now more imperative than ever to find that one person who might have liked Gwellyn and had been her confidant.

"Grayson, dear," she said, "may I please impose upon you and your big, important crime-investigating skills to track someone down for me? I don't have his name. But he drives a *red* car."

Grayson winced. "That's like saying, 'My son is in the Navy, too. Maybe you know him.' It's incredibly vague. However, as only about 9% of cars in the UK are red, I can run a search through the vehicle registration database and narrow it down to red cars here in the Southwest."

"It has a black Mickey Mouse aerial ball, too. Or it did a year or so ago," Polly added and watched as Grayson's face suggested the additional information was also of little value.

By the time Tiara served coffee and the spotted dick dessert she'd made from scratch, they were all offering opinions about not only who killed Gwellyn but who could have known in advance about her plan to kill Mr. Drake and tried to stop her with a call to CrimeClue. And since Polly referenced the guy that Lady Ridgewood-Brimble had suspected of being potentially romantically linked to Gwellyn, everyone piled on their most cynical thoughts about her motives and for being fond of someone other than herself.

"There's someone for everyone, or so they say." Tiara offered the truism as she sipped her coffee. "Gwellyn wasn't attractive, inside or out, but there are as many reasons for hooking up as there are people. And maybe there was something appealing about her that we all missed or overlooked. We can't all be as shapely and tempting to the eye as my bootylicious self."

But as the others laughed and Tiara looked around the table, a dull wave of melancholy wafted over her. She began to think about her lifelong lack of a special somebody. Or at least the type of special someone songwriters and poets daydream about. Polly and Tim were currently pursuing relationships, but she herself had zero prospects. And not for the first time, she doubted her desirability. She had long ago decided that she had to be too selfish or her standards too high to attract the right mate. She'd convinced herself that romance didn't really matter because she was her own best company and that living and working with Polly Pepper was all the excitement she needed out of life. After all, she had a grander life than most people because she not only traversed the most interesting social circles but also traveled the world and was now living—if only temporarily—in Europe. Tiara was used to having these feelings every once in a while and knew that by morning, she'd be her old forward-looking self again.

And then Mr. Boots jumped on the table and attacked Polly's spotted dick.

24

Friday morning arrived, and Polly was becoming glum. It was unusual for her to feel this low, but it was another drizzling gray day—in a seemingly endless stretch of sucky-weather days—and last night's dinner had failed to not only shed new light on who Gwellyn's killer might be, but another mystery had been thrown into the mix: was Mr. Drake murdered too? And there had been no crystal-clear signs of further romantic interest from Terrence, either. Not that he could have made any obvious overtures in front of the others. But everything in Polly's life seemed in limbo.

"What's wrong with this picture?" she mumbled to Tiara when she arrived at the breakfast table and slumped down in her chair. "In a small English village, exposing a killer should not be this hard! These Brits are sneaky," she said, then polished off her first Prosecco in one long pull.

Tiara knew from experience that it was no use merely telling Polly to cheer up or offering a long list of reasons for her to be happy. The old *you've got your health and a roof over your head* adage had lost its therapeutic potency years ago. It could take hours or even a full day for Polly to come round to her usual buoyant disposition. Tiara knew she had to completely take her boss's mind off whatever bothered her. In Los Angeles, that could be done simply by schlepping her off to boutique stores on Rodeo Drive in Beverly Hills for a few hours of retail therapy. Or changing her hair color. Or getting Polly's lazy agent, JJ, to book her as a guest on an afternoon TV chat show. Here in Abbots Clover, however, she wasn't sure what might do the trick for mental health recovery. Then an idea popped into her head. She'd been thumbing through the *National Trust Handbook*, listing places of historical interest and importance, and wanted to check out famous local landmarks. If castle ruins or Palladian manor houses couldn't do the trick to rekindle Polly's positive attitude, she hadn't a clue what might work.

"We're going sightseeing!" Tiara announced.

Polly rolled her eyes as she slathered butter on a croissant. "I'm not in the mood to see the Crown Jewels unless His Royal Highness wants to slip the Koh-i-Noor diamond into my purse. Let's just find Gwellyn's killer so we can go back to Hollywood," she said. "I don't even care anymore if Mr. D got whacked. I think I've had enough of this old place. And the crummy weather. And…"

Tiara could be just as stubborn as Polly. She wouldn't let anything get in her way when she decided about something. With hands on hips, she declared, "Millions of people would love to be visiting England, and we're actually here! Thousands of years of history are right here on this little island! The Romans came in AD 43! Shakespeare wrote *Hamlet* just up the road! Don't forget James Bond! And fish and chips! We should take advantage of all there is to do and see!"

At that moment, Tim wandered into the breakfast room. "Did I hear you say we should take advantage of James Bond? Which one? I vote for Pierce. No, Sean. No, Roger. Okay, Pierce."

"As usual, you came in on the tail end of the conversation,"

Tiara sassed as she poured Tim a cup of coffee and set a plate of freshly made blueberry scones in front of him. "Your momma's down in the dumps, and I was saying there are a gazillion things to do here in England to take one's mind off their problems, so why aren't we playing tourists? We could go to Stonehenge. Or the Roman baths. Windsor Castle could be a fun day out."

"We definitely should be courting William and Kate and Charles and Camilla," Tim agreed. "If only so that Polly can boast about it to Bette and Barbra."

And then "God Save the King" blared from his phone. Tim looked at the caller ID and smiled. He answered and quickly left the room for privacy. When he returned, he was beaming.

"This will cheer you up," he said to his mother. "Grayson thinks he's found the car you're looking for in the registration database. There's a picture in the file of a red Vauxhall Vivaro with a Mickey Mouse aerial ball. It's a van, not a car, but it's the only registered vehicle of that color in the whole area. He's texting me the name on the registration and the address. He said to warn you not to contact the owner but knows that you won't listen to him, so why bother to say anything? But it's his job to point out a bunch of potential illegal things like trespassing, stalking, and harassment. And something called malicious communication."

"I'm usually the stalkee, not the stalker!" Polly said as she slugged back the last of her Prosecco, threw her napkin on the table, and tightened the belt on her robe. She looked at the grandfather clock in the corner of the room and said, "Right-o! We have to see a man with a van!"

A fine mist was varnishing the countryside. Tim followed the guidance from the voice on his GPS and cautiously maneuvered their car down narrow country lanes to the village of Tuescomb for a surprise visit with Andrew Stanton. Constable Grayson had warned that although there weren't any police records associated with Mr. Stanton, safety should still be their utmost concern. And if there was any sign of hostility or danger, they were to leave immediately and call the station. Of course, those instructions went in one of Polly's ears and straight out the other—just as Tiara's earlier suggestion of sightseeing had. She figured that since she'd once survived an entire week of rehearsing her TV show with pugnacious guest star Chevy Chase, she could probably endure almost anything.

The voice inside Tim's phone said, "Turn left. Then you have reached your destination."

Open fields bordered the small, unpretentious house. Tim pulled into the driveway behind the Vauxhall van, which had oxidized to the color of burnt orange. Set on blocks and missing all its wheels, it also had an aerial ball that might have once boasted rodent ears, but was now just a round piece of disintegrating rubber.

Their unanimous nonverbal first impressions of the property: *ghastly*. Overgrown, tall weeds and winter-dormant plantings against the front of the house made the whole property look shabby. The outside walls were an unattractive brown stucco, which made it even more depressing. And it looked like bedsheets were used for drapes in the windows.

"Looks like the gardener went on holiday and never came back," Polly sneered as she opened her door and stepped onto the tall, wet grass.

When the trio assembled at the front door, they braced themselves for something creepy. In their respective minds' eyes, they pictured a fat, bearded, hillbilly thug with a can of beer in one hand and a gun in the other, as well as a steady stream of foul language and threats to leave the property or risk getting their heads blown off. If they were still in America, he'd almost definitely have a shotgun. But this was England, where guns were rare. So when Tim knocked on the door like someone offering religious tracts and the tenant answered, they were surprised and delighted to find that only one of their visualizations was accurate. He held a can of beer.

The quartet didn't say a word for what seemed a very long time but probably only lasted two seconds. They looked at each other, wondering what to do next. Although Polly and company's eyes were focused on the man who was probably Andrew Stanton, they could peripherally see into the house and beyond into the back garden. The whole place was a mess.

Finally, the man at the door barked, "Wah?"

Doesn't anyone in England pronounce their Ts? Polly thought as she heard his common accent. But she smiled and took charge of the greeting. She stepped closer to the door. "We're here to see Andrew Stanton. I suspect that's you."

"Only me mum calls me Andrew. Me mates call me Fingers," said the man, softening his tone and gradually transforming into a less unfriendly bear. "*Fingers* 'cause I was born with an extra one on me left hand. Had it removed when I got old enough to make my own decisions. Mum wanted me to have the choice. You can come in if you're that American movie star, which, by the looks of you, you are. I heard you travel in a pack and might visit."

Polly and her team slipped past Andrew and entered his small bungalow. They couldn't help surreptitiously looking at Andrew's left hand. Polly was relieved to see that it looked the same as anyone else's. But maybe she was looking at the wrong one. She always got confused about which was left and right on someone opposite her. The trio stood in the main room and glanced around at the disarray. Andrew Stanton obviously seldom had guests and didn't feel obliged to keep his place tidy. The furnishings were old: a leather settee and two fabric-covered reclining chairs surrounding an oak coffee table with a jumble of newspapers, coffee mugs, and unopened mail on top. The fireplace looked not to have been cleaned in ages, and an empty metal bird cage hung from a hook on a wrought-iron stand. Although it didn't house a bird, the tray was lined with newspaper, and birdseed was scattered on the floor below.

Andrew saw Polly looking at it. "Birdie's gone," he said wistfully.

Despite his unrefined accent and behavior, Andrew Stanton was not an unattractive man. Nor was he an ungracious host. Although Polly and her team had developed ideas of how someone who might have fancied Gwellyn might look or act (not a pretty image), they found him pleasant, in a diamond-in-the-rough sort of way. He looked to be in his mid-forties, and at nearly six feet, his weight seemed appropriate for his height. A missing canine tooth caused him to self-consciously avoid smiling more than he had to, but he became more cordial as he warmed to Polly and the others. He even offered them tea and biscuits, which they politely declined as they imagined being served in unwashed cups.

As often happened to Polly, and she thought this was likely true for most people, preconceived ideas and fears failed to live up to their anxiety-inducing expectations. How many times had she lost sleep over an upcoming audition or stage appearance, only to have a great result? Dreaded dinners that had been agreed to in haste sometimes turned out surprisingly entertaining. And charity events that she tried to avoid almost always turned out to be heartwarming and philanthropically lucrative. At this moment, Polly was thinking about how unexpectedly pleasant Andrew turned out to be. He even knew (of course he did) that she lived at Thistlethorne Lodge, where his old friend

Gwellyn Clogg had worked, and he had been sorry to learn of her death.

"We were saddened, too, and just want to know more about Gwellyn, which is why we're here," Polly half-lied. "What was she like as a person? What were her dreams and aspirations? That sort of thing."

Soon, Andrew was providing corroboration of most other assessments of Gwellyn. But he also offered a few contrary judgments. Yes, she could be vile. "I sometimes called her Sullen Gwellyn," he joked. He also agreed that she was a thief. "I wouldn't drive her anywhere when she was carrying something hot." They were sometimes physically intimate. "She thought she was fat and ugly. I couldn't lie and give her that old crap about beauty being in the eye of the beholder. But I told her that 'ugly' wasn't my perception of her. And that was true. There was something to like about her. Maybe not her looks. Definitely not her meanness. But I can sometimes see beyond them things. She had plans to retire as soon as possible. Of course, I told her that was daft unless someone left her some money because she didn't have no savings or rich relatives. She couldn't give me a straight answer when I asked where she would live if she left Mr. Drake's service. It certainly wasn't going to be with me, although she hinted she wanted to move in. I wasn't *that* into her. Just wanted me a bit of fun from time to time."

As the interview continued, Polly and her team took turns asking specific personal questions, and Andrew was happy to be forthcoming. He seemed genuinely sorry when he didn't have an answer to a question. When he had an opinion, it appeared well considered.

Finally, Polly asked the most important question of the day. "If I were to suggest that Gwellyn was murdered, who would you point your finger at?"

It didn't take Andrew any time at all to answer. He agreed

that she could have been killed, but as everybody else had said, the list of possible suspects was long.

"I could be a suspect myself," he admitted. "Gwellyn threatened to publicly accuse me of using her to steal from her employer, Mr. Drake."

During the next few minutes, Andrew recalled the day after he'd first made love to Gwellyn. He said that she had seemed so grateful for his physical attention that she gave him an antique gold ring set with three small rubies. He said he hadn't questioned where she'd gotten it from or how she could have afforded such an extravagance. He thought maybe it had been a family heirloom. Then, each time they'd meet for a liaison, Gwellyn would present him with another trinket. He admitted he liked the gifts. He'd never had a gold pocket watch. Or a sapphire stick pin that he would never have the occasion to wear. He swore he wasn't using Gwellyn for the valuable gifts but said he didn't reject them either. And he didn't mind that Gwellyn seemed to feel that she had to pay him for the experience of physical intimacy.

"I was worth it. She got what she wanted from me, and I did too, plus a sort of bonus," he said.

However, he revealed that several months ago, he'd met another woman and told Gwellyn they couldn't see each other anymore. Gwellyn was shattered and threatened to go to the police with the accusation that he'd stolen the jewelry she had given him. She'd told him that the ploy had worked before to get rid of a maid she didn't like when she worked for Lord and Lady Ridgewood-Brimble. Andrew admitted that he'd been a secret guest of Gwellyn's at Thistlethorne Lodge when Mr. Drake was confined to his room.

"She liked to show off the place where she worked. Lily could vouch for that, and so could Vicar Aylsworth, who had seen me there a couple of times. Gwellyn told me it would be easy for her to claim that I'd cased the place and then stolen the watch, rings, and things. And she knew where I hid my valuables and could tell the police where to find my safe box. It's possible that I could have killed her to keep her trap shut," Andrew suggested. "In the end, I gathered everything into a plastic bag and gave it to her."

Neither Polly, Tim, nor Tiara thought Andrew was a killer. They'd had enough experience with aggressive personalities in Hollywood to know when someone was dangerous. However, they also knew some people excelled at concealing their mental disorders. Heck, hearing Andrew's description of his transactional relationship with Gwellyn and her obvious low self-worth and problems with interpersonal relationships made *her* more likely to be the mental case capable of murder.

Nope, Polly thought, *this ain't the guy*. On the one hand, although she was happy that she could confidently cross Andrew's name off the list of possible suspects, she was deeply disappointed that she'd come to yet another dead end. Unless she'd overlooked something, her investigation had reached an impasse. She was completely out of dubious characters to look into. And she was crushed.

Andrew had been as helpful as possible, but there was nothing more to reveal about Gwellyn or her death. When asked for his opinion on the guilt or innocence of others, he had nothing more to offer than what Polly and her troupe had already uncovered. And when they drove away from Woodbridge Lane, Polly's eyes began to moisten with a veneer of tears.

Polly was tired of fighting. She was tired of following clues that led nowhere. Tired of being a hack criminal investigator. Why, she wondered, had she had success in the past, and now her nose for sniffing out killers had plugged up? It was like her early career in showbiz when there had been great and relatively easy triumphs, and then it had all faded away. She was despondent because she didn't know, or maybe never really knew, the potion or incantation to recreate those successes. She decided that perhaps life really was just a random series of accidents and that she had no control over her fate the way she once thought she did. Polly used to believe she held some magical secret for creating her successes. She'd done exceedingly well with her positive thinking and, perhaps, with her naivete. When she hadn't known the challenges of creating a meteoric acting career from nothing or connecting dead people to their killers, she was fearless and somehow had massively fruitful results. However, having gone through what she thought were all the proper procedures for replicating those master strokes of achievement, she was at a total loss.

The trio rode home in silence.

Polly spent the afternoon writing in her diary and making notes about everything she wanted to do when she returned to Hollywood. She decided to have a serious conversation with her agent, JJ. Although she'd been his client since the beginning of her career, if he couldn't find more work for her, it was time to cut bait and look for representation elsewhere. There was also the possibility of downsizing her home and moving to Palm Springs or Santa Barbara, somewhere comfortable and pretty, where she could spend the last years of her life as a big fish in a smaller-than-Hollywood pond. Although she wasn't ready to retire completely, she had friends in those areas, and maybe if she palled around with her has-been peers, she wouldn't feel so lonely and out of place. She had to find a purpose in life again. *Perhaps I didn't fully appreciate success when I had it*, she wrote. *And maybe it will never come again. But I must find something that makes me feel less redundant than I do now.*

When Tiara brought her champagne at six o'clock, Polly was ready to bid adieu to cold and rainy England.

And then the telephone rang. It was Terrence! And yes, she'd absolutely have dinner at the Fox & Hare with him the next night.

"It's probably not going to amount to anything more than a meal," she said to Tim and Tiara at dinner. "And I don't care what the villagers say about me anymore. I'll probably never see them again, anyway. Or Terrence, for that matter."

25

The morning light seeped into Polly's bedroom, and the pall that had shrouded her temperament started to lift. During the night, she'd relived the events of the previous day and decided that it no longer mattered to her who killed Gwellyn Clogg or if the housekeeper had been murdered in the first place—or even if she'd killed Mr. Drake. Death by heart attack or zombie suicide squad made little difference to Polly now. *She's dead, and there's nothing I can do about it. If something nefarious happened, that's for the police to determine.* It was time for her to butt out. Her current priority should be to consult with Solicitor Wainwright about finding an estate agent to put Thistlethorne on the market, collect the £££s, and get the heck out of town. *Who needs a castle, soggy England, or ghosts, for that matter?* She thought, as images of the sun setting over the Pacific Ocean were wafting through her head.

By 10:00, Tim had left the house to spend the day shadowing (his word, which Polly suspected was a euphemism) Grayson as he went about his police work. Tiara had sequestered herself in the kitchen to supervise Lily's chores and to bake Polly's favorite treat, a triple chocolate and peanut butter layer cake. Polly was alone, reading in the study. Her thoughts drifted from the Peter Boon cozy mystery novel she was enjoying to what Andrew Stanton had said the previous day about Lily and Vicar Aylsworth being able to corroborate his frequent visits to Thistlethorne. She realized that when Lily had listed the possible men in Gwellyn's life, she'd never mentioned Andrew Stanton. She'd identified Oliver, the milkman and the unnamed lorry bin driver, and Christopher Bradshaw, the village chiropractor. But she'd left out Andrew, who actually owned a red vehicle. This seemed odd, and despite her resolve to forget about her investigation, she summoned Lily with the pull of the servant's bell cord.

Now, standing in the library with her back against the door, Lily was visibly shaking when Polly bluntly asked why she'd never mentioned that Andrew Stanton had been a friend of Gwellyn's and a visitor in the house. Lily was speechless. She stood mute and squirming, her eyes darting around the room, trying to avoid looking directly at Polly.

"Sorry, mum. I forgot, I guess," she said in obvious panic and on the verge of crying.

Polly shrugged, shook her head, and let out a sigh of impatience. She sat down behind Mr. Drake's large mahogany desk and calmly talked about how she couldn't understand why, when asked specifically about the possible men in Gwellyn's life, Lily had lied that she hadn't been aware of anyone in particular. Clearly, there was one man who came around frequently enough to be accused of pilfering from the house.

"You didn't forget," Polly challenged. "You intentionally tap-danced around my question and deliberately offered up names of other people Gwellyn might have been interested in. The milkman. Really? The lorry bin driver. Not bloody likely. Why didn't you want me to know that Andrew Stanton was a friend of Gwellyn's?"

Tears of fear began to drip down Lily's cheeks.

"I can accept almost anything in another's personality, but not lying," Polly said, trying to remain composed. "It always gets you into more trouble than telling the truth. Don't you agree? People lie for a reason. Maybe they want to get something. Maybe they want to hide something. There's always a self-serving motivation behind lying. What was yours?"

Lily wiped her runny nose on the hem of her smock. "I don't know why, mum," she answered with a catch in her throat as she tried to talk. "Gwellyn threatened to sack me if I told anyone about Mr. Stanton's visits, and I guess my promise was just so far down inside me that it stuck even after she died. And then I couldn't change my story because you'd know I wasn't truthful in the first place."

Lily rambled about what she'd observed during Andrew Stanton's visits. She said Gwellyn was always in a better mood when she was expecting him and was usually nicer for the rest of the day after he left. Each time he visited, they'd disappear into one of the bedrooms for an hour. Lily had strict orders to care for Mr. Drake if he rang for something while Gwellyn was occupied. One time, Mr. Drake got up and wandered around the house while Gwellyn and Andrew were together. Mr. Drake was in one of his wistful moods and wanted to enjoy the other rooms in his beloved home. He walked into the bedroom where Gwellyn was re-dressing, and she convinced him that the man who was also putting his clothes on was really just taking measurements for new drapes.

"I don't think Mr. Drake was dumb enough or sick enough to buy the explanation," Lily said. "And he probably didn't believe Gwellyn when she explained why his humidor of cigars in the library was empty and his cognac carafe, too. And why certain mementos like his Limoges porcelain antique pillboxes were not in the places where he'd once set them. I think Mr. Drake was as afraid of Gwellyn's bullying and that he probably just let her indiscretions pile up without consequences."

As Lily recalled Andrew's visits and the deceptions perpetrated on Mr. Drake, Polly felt a wave of sadness for the old man. This was his house, for crying out loud. But he had been a prisoner, and Gwellyn had been his jail matron. He undoubtedly knew that hanky-panky was going on under his nose, but he couldn't risk complaining about it. Mr. Drake was utterly alone and had no one to serve as an advocate for his well-being. Gwellyn had even seen to it that Vicar Aylsworth no longer came to visit. Polly was grateful that she had loyal and completely trustworthy Tim and Tiara in her life. For all of Mr. Drake's financial independence, he had no other freedoms or true and faithful friends.

When Lily had exhausted herself describing the visits from Andrew, Polly sighed heavily and summed up Mr. Drake's final months. "Your employer was captive in his own home and not as well cared for as he should have been. His own staff were sneaking around and lying to him. He must have been miserable. Perhaps he even wanted to die just to be done with this life." She looked at Lily, crossed her arms, and said matter-of-factly, "Gwellyn killed Mr. Drake for an inheritance, didn't she?"

Lily looked down at her shoes. "I think so, but I wasn't here, mum. Gwellyn told me that Mr. Drake died during the night. That's all she said when I came to work that day, and it's what I heard her tell Constable Jenkins and the medical examiner, too. She never actually said, 'He died in his sleep.' But everyone presumed that. Like his heart was so old that it just wore out like a battery.

"I know she thought she was going to inherit from him," Lily continued. "Merv and me, we thought maybe he'd remember us in his will, too. One day, just before Mr. Drake died, Gwellyn got particularly angry about something—Mr. Drake wouldn't eat the meal she'd made, I think—and I heard her say, 'This is taking too long. The geezer's got to die soon. Do I have to do everything myself around here?' Or some words like that. She was talking to herself, but when you say your thoughts out loud, they're probably your true thoughts. I know she was glad when he finally died 'cause she had less work to do, and she could make definite plans to move back to Wales. Or so she thought. It made me happy when she didn't get any inheritance. I didn't think she deserved anything from him. Bad behavior shouldn't be rewarded."

Polly nodded in agreement. She'd been almost giddy imagining Gwellyn's initial response to finding out that whatever her plans had been for her post-Thistlethorne life, they had to be scrapped.

"What did she say when Solicitor Wainwright told her the news?" Polly asked.

"It was only when Gwellyn got the letter that you were coming to the house that she realized something wasn't right," Lily said. "She'd been waiting for news of her inheritance. I remember how excited she was that day when the post arrived with an envelope with Solicitor Wainwright's office address. She had to sign for it, and she was quick to shoo away the postman so she could enjoy the moment in private. When she opened it and read the paper, her face turned red hot. She looked stunned. Like when someone doesn't get an award they are sure they'd win. Then she called Mr. Wainwright. I was eavesdropping when I shouldn't have and heard her argue that she'd done some research and read that when someone is dependent on someone who dies, they can't be overlooked regardless of a will."

"She was only dependent on him for a job," Polly interrupted.

"But she didn't see it that way. I don't know what Mr. Wainwright told her, but she put the phone down on him and started destroying things. You probably would have liked the vases that were on the fireplace mantel in the main reception room. And I guess they were actually yours by then. She broke 'em, then yelled at me to clean up all the mess. Even Mr. Boots was so scared that he disappeared for a couple of days. Then I watched from the window when she stormed out to talk to Merv. I couldn't hear what they were saying, but they both made a lot of angry gestures, and he threw down a shovel. I wanted to run away because it was like when my mum and dad used to fight, and I wanted to hide or disappear."

Polly imagined the scene of Gwellyn Clogg on an angry tear. That would have been terrifying to witness, especially for someone as mousy as Lily. Gwellyn had demonstrated an elevated level of rage that day when Polly said that she was moving into the house, and now, knowing the backstory of Gwellyn's expectation of being an heiress, her nasty attitude made more sense. Gwellyn truly believed that she was owed something from Mr. Drake merely because he was rich, and she was in his orbit.

"How did you and Merv react to the fact that you weren't inheriting anything from Mr. Drake's estate, either?" Polly asked.

Lily made a face and shrugged. "I never really expected anything. It would have been a nice bonus to get a keepsake of one kind or another, like the little painting of lilies in a pond that I liked. But in the end, it didn't really matter that much. But it did matter to Gwellyn." Lily added that Gwellyn had started coming to work later and later and had stopped keeping the place up to Mr. Drake's standards. She pushed Lily around more, too. "Then, one day, everything changed," Lily said. "It was like Gwellyn decided to stop being mad. I could tell she had something up her sleeve. She said she was making big plans for another life."

Polly shrugged and brought the dialogue to a close. She

dismissed Lily with the suggestion that she give serious consideration to why being honest was important. "Truth and lying and subterfuge are a matter of one's personal ethics," she said.

As Polly sat alone in the library, the otherwise quiet atmosphere was interrupted by the sound of rain on the window. She glanced outside, and even though the weather was foul, Merv was, as usual, pushing a wheelbarrow containing debris caused by the wind. As Polly watched the gardener, she was once again impressed with him and him not seeming to care about the challenges of his work. He did what he had to, and since he couldn't control the weather, he just got on with life. In a moment of clarity, Polly realized that was what she needed to do with her own life.

"Pick yourself up, Polly!" she demanded. "No more moping around. The world won't end if you don't find Gwellyn's killer!"

And then she decided to take a long, hot bubble bath before dressing for dinner with Terrence.

Polly sifted through the clothes hanging on the rod in her wardrobe. She complained to Tiara that she had nothing suitable for her date.

"Now I know how Tim feels about his meager wardrobe," she grumbled as Tiara set out Polly's mascara and eyeshadow palette on the vanity. "I've noticed that British women of a certain age tend to favor boring black, brown, and beige." Polly sniffed. "Most of my things are pink or purple or fuchsia. I don't want to wear anything that Terrence will think is too eccentric. I don't want the locals to think I'm from another planet."

"*Think* or to have the rumor *confirmed*." Tiara sniggered with a loud, sarcastic laugh.

Polly ignored her maid and selected a collarless embroidered jacket from a hanger. Then she began rummaging through her jewelry case for a necklace to complement the colorful glass beading in the coat. She stopped for a moment and studied herself in the wardrobe mirror.

"Why am I nervous?" she said pensively. "Why do I care what I wear? I'm merely going out for pub grub. It's not like we're dining at Le Bernardin in New York or that Terrence is really anything more than a chum. In a few months, I'll be back in Bel Air. He'll only think about me when he brags to friends about interviewing Polly Pepper for his dumb paper and shows them clips of my old show on YouTube or when he receives a card from me at Christmastime. And even that'll stop after a couple of years."

Shaking her head, Tiara said, "When did Polly Pepper become such a pessimist? You never used to be this way. Frankly, your negativity act is wearing thin. Stop demanding that the universe do its job *your* way. Your job is to be your charming self to Terrence. Let the gods do the rest. Stop projecting. You don't know what you don't know."

Of course, Polly knew that Tiara was right, and she agreed that she had always been well served by letting life unfold organically without too much fuss or interference.

"But I think I really like Terrence," Polly purred softly like someone yearning for an expensive bauble in a shop window but presuming it was probably beyond their budget. "I was perfectly happy being on my own until I met him. Now, I think it would be nice to have a cuddle bunny."

"Whatever Lola wants, Lola usually gets," Tiara sassed. "Just remember the truism about being careful about what you wish for. Don't forget how cuddle-worthy you thought Mr. Polly Pepper one, two, and three were at first." Then, in a moment of self-examination and her own lack of anything remotely cuddle-bunny-*ish*, Tiara said, "Don't end up like me. I obviously set the bar too high."

As Tiara helped Polly put the final touches on her outfit (she'd rejected the too sparkly embroidered jacket in favor of a simple hand-knitted, blue, and ochre-tipped Merino wool poncho, accented with a necklace of faux pearls), Tim knocked on her bedroom door.

"Mummy! Mummy! We need to talk!"

Polly looked at Tiara with a wink that suggested Tim's excitement might be about picking out engagement rings for himself and Grayson. When she opened the door, Tim practically flew onto the bed and drew himself into the fetal position. He cradled a pillow and whined, "Grayson doesn't want me to play in his sandbox!"

Polly and Tiara moved to either side of the bed, confused by Tim's declaration.

"Your sandbox analogy always sounds a tad psychosexual, sweetums," Polly said without much sympathy. "Now, tell Mummy what happened and how she can help."

If she and Tiara had held their breaths waiting for additional information, they'd surely have passed out. Tim remained quiet.

"Sweetums, you know that Mummy's never been a very good mind-reader. What's really the matter?"

"Work," he groused. "Grayson has to work tonight. It's Saturday, for Pete's sake! Only bartenders work on Saturday nights!"

"Has it occurred to you that someone has to be on duty if one of those bartenders calls 999?" Tiara said, shaking her head.

"That doesn't make it fair!"

"What about Grayson's so-called *sandbox*?" Polly pressed. "Did he actually say that he didn't want to see you anymore?"

"Not in so many words," Tim conceded. "But what am I supposed to do all by myself on a Saturday night? I'm all alone over here in dreary England!"

Polly and Tiara deftly returned to their task of prepping for Polly's date, and their resident crybaby's lamentations began to die out. The room was filled with an anticipatory buzz as Tiara delicately applied a streak of blusher to Polly's high cheekbones, then clipped an elegant string of pearls around the star's neck. The distinct fragrance of her signature perfume, a blend of rose, vanilla, and a hint of citrus, wafted through the air, filling the room with an intoxicating scent.

Tim finally seemed to take notice of something other than himself. He sat up and turned to his mother, his gaze growing more focused.

"Wait a minute," he grumbled, his eyebrows furrowing in accusation. "I smell perfume. And you're all... dressed up."

A lightbulb seemed to flicker on in Tim's mind.

"Oh, right!" he exclaimed with a snort. "You have a date! Brilliant! Just what I need in my time of grief and despair: my own mother flaunting her love life while I nurse my broken heart. Thanks for rubbing it in my face!"

With a huff and a dramatic roll of his eyes, he turned over again and buried his disgruntled face into the soft pillow.

Terrence arrived to collect Polly at 7:00 p.m. He looked handsome in his forest green turtleneck and Harris tweed sports jacket. Polly silently approved as she accepted a kiss on her cheek and furtively sniffed the fragrant air around his face. *Burberry? Paco Rabanne? Montblanc?* She wasn't sure, but it was intoxicatingly pleasant.

"I genuinely appreciate people who are punctual," she trilled.

Terrence explained that after years of having to meet copy deadlines for work, if he were now five minutes late for an appointment, it would be appropriate to call the police because something tragic must have happened to him.

"Oh, I brought you something," he said, holding out a large envelope.

"My interview!" Polly screamed as she looked inside the envelope and flipped to the middle of the *Abbots Clover Overview*. "Look, look, everybody! I'm famous!" she exclaimed to Tim, Tiara, and even Mr. Boots, who had wandered into the entry hallway to check out who was visiting.

Polly was nearly jumping up and down with enthusiasm as she gave the two facing pages a cursory examination. "Where on earth did you get that old photo?" she playfully chastised. "Obviously, something you found online. We never got around to doing a shoot."

Terrence admitted that in order to meet his publishing deadline, he'd had to make do with stock images of Polly from when she was getting her star on the Hollywood Walk of Fame and a publicity photo from her starring role as Mamma Rose in a touring company of *Gypsy*.

"You look pretty much the same now as you did then," he complimented her. "Still glamorous."

"And seductive?"

"That too," Terrence agreed.

Although the evening air was cold, the rain had stopped, and the moon and stars were occasionally visible as clouds drifted overhead. The countryside was quiet. Quiet was one of Polly's fears, particularly a two-person silence. She had a deep uneasiness during the space between subjects in a conversation and had developed the art of always having a reserved topic of something interesting and clever to say to avoid such an unnerving situation. During her early days in Hollywood, she'd memorized current events from newspapers and magazines before dinner parties so she could seduce a table of people into thinking she had deeper thoughts than Aristotle or Confucius. Polly could easily have been a chat show hostess. She liked to keep the party going. But she needn't have worried about a lack of things to discuss with Terrence. He brought almost as much to the table as Polly did herself, and the short drive to the pub went by in a flash.

The Fox & Hare on a Saturday night was always crowded. Terrence had reserved a favorite table in an alcove away from the busiest part of the pub, but he still had to queue at the bar to order drinks and food. And by the time their meals arrived, both were having so much fun that they were more interested in talking than eating. Polly merely picked at her deep-fried fish and chips, and Terrence just nibbled on the pastry crust of his steak and ale pie. When he returned to the bar for the second round of fruit cider (for him) and Prosecco (they didn't have champagne) for her, Polly started thinking that she might have been wrong about Terrence being a temporary distraction. There was something very satisfying and surprisingly calming about being with him. Although she couldn't put her finger specifically on what that was, it made her feel settled and optimistic. Yes, he was physically attractive, but honestly, at this stage in Polly's life, she was more interested in men whom she could trust and who made her laugh than in the height and girth of their physique. She was keenly aware of how, when she was younger, her libido had too often distracted her from the red flags right in front of her. Even though they were from different social worlds, she found they had fundamental values in common. And by the time Terrence delivered Polly back to Thistlethorne Lodge and supplied a long and intense kiss, she was pretty sure she was falling in love.

❧

The playful cross-examination from Tim and Tiara when she arrived in the reception room lasted more than an hour and covered everything from what Terrence's astrological sign was (Aries) to whether or not he'd be willing to sign a prenup (they didn't think it was too early to discuss his views on their respective finances) and when their next date would be (Monday night for a meal he'd cook at his place).

"You're both jumping the gun!" Polly argued devilishly as she revealed the highlights of what they'd discussed.

Terrence had modestly said that his character strengths included always trying to improve himself as a human being, but his weaknesses included avoiding confrontations and, therefore, giving the impression that he was a wuss.

Polly had confessed to Terrence that she was a strong woman when it came to her career and was, therefore, sometimes considered a diva, but in her personal life, she thought of herself as sensitive to others' thoughts and feelings. They silently agreed that if the other had submitted an application for partnership, they each had ticked all the right boxes for the other.

When Polly had finally knocked back her last glass of champagne for the night, she opened her arms wide for a tight hug with Tim and gave Tiara a peck on the cheek. Then she retired to her bedroom. The house's silence was suddenly unsettling as she slipped into her bathrobe and washed the makeup off her face. Although she knew Tim and Tiara were mere steps away, she started to feel a deep anxiety. Surely, she thought, this was probably because she'd just returned from a gloriously fun evening with a potential paramour, and she was afraid that her romantic thoughts would disappear. Great emotional highs are often followed by equally great lows. Polly knew this, but the odd sensation she was experiencing was somehow foreboding.

As she sat before the three-panel mirror on the vanity and

stared at her reflection, Polly could almost see a dark cloud drifting over the room and absorbing all the optimism she'd felt only a short while ago. Where was the light-hearted buoyancy she'd felt with Terrence at the pub? She suddenly and inextricably thought that her life was about to take a dramatic turn. She couldn't exactly isolate her feelings, but she sensed change on the horizon.

Mr. Boots, who had followed Polly upstairs, was now occupying one of the bed pillows. He raised his head momentarily, looked around the room, meowed once, and settled down again. Polly suspected he was sensitive enough to know what she was feeling. And what she was feeling at the moment was rather crummy.

26

The night was a long one for Polly. She tried to sleep but couldn't turn off her kaleidoscope of thoughts. Her head was crowded with a million competing abstract images, sounds, and fragments of conversations, ideas, hopes, and fears. Even with her eyes closed, she saw a montage of dead and alive Gwellyn Clogg and could hear the housekeeper's strident voice in her head. She revisited their final altercation and then shifted to the moment when Gwellyn had been placed in a body bag and wheeled away on a gurney. She recalled what had been said about Gwellyn by her enemies and her secret lover. Hated by this one. Detested by that one. Resented by another. In the end, pretty much disliked by all.

Those thoughts and memories were eventually crowded out by Polly's concerns about her budding friendship with Terrence Marks and her ongoing and never-far-away fears of possibly not being wanted in Hollywood anymore—or worse, winding up as a question in the *National Intruder*'s popular monthly Dead or Alive celebrity quiz.

As she lay under several layers of covers and watched the parade going on in her mind's eye, she recalled the one simple reason she'd come to England in the first place: to take possession of an inheritance. Easy-peasy. Waltz in. Sign a few papers. Look around. Waltz out again. She'd accomplished her mission. That should have been the end of the story. Then a dead body had gotten caught in the wheels of life and gummed up the gears. *Whose fault is that?* Polly asked herself and simultaneously answered that it certainly wasn't hers. She was free of responsibility and obligation, and if she wanted to, she could be on the next flight from Heathrow to LAX. *Maybe that's what I need to do. I've had enough of being a fish out of water here in Abbots Clover.*

"I'm Polly bleeping Pepper, for pity's sake!" she whispered into the darkness.

But what about the other part of this Disney fairy-tale equation: Terrence? A knight in shining armor, if ever there was one. But could there be a happily ever after? There's no such thing as a castle without a prince and his lady fair. Everyone knows that! And what about my dream of finding just one more meaningful relationship before I die? Terrence could be the one. Maybe. Am I nuts?

As Polly's thoughts finally started to pivot away from the problems of the present to what her next plan of action should be, she made a mental list of whom to call to make a smooth transition back to America—if leaving England was what she'd ultimately decide to do. She'd text her travel agent and set a departure date. Then she'd tell Tim and Tiara, who'd jump for joy. They could return to the California sun and the sparkling lights of Hollywood. Next, she'd employ Solicitor Wainwright to find an estate agent to sell Thistlethorne Lodge. Who cared what price she got for the place or the amount of UK and US capital gains taxes she'd have to pay? Or the unfavorable exchange rate between the dollar and the pound? Polly just wanted her life to be as semi-settled as it had been before well-meaning Mr. Drake turned her into a reluctant heiress.

But again, there was Terrence. Her thoughts were filled with the what-ifs of Terrence. Terrence. Terrence.

Terrence Marks was certainly a potential *Someone Special.* Polly imagined having an attractive man on her arm for film premieres and special public appearances. A man who was all hers, not just a friend she'd invited to share the fun. He was the only man she'd met in ages whose easy laugh was contagious, whose hypnotic eyes she wanted to stare into, and whose lips practically begged to be kissed, and who gave her a curiously pleasant feeling around her tummy whenever she thought about him. Still, there was no way to predict their compatibility in the long run. She'd known other celebrities in her age category who believed they were in love with what, in show business, they call a "non-pro." Most of the relationships had turned out to be less than fulfilling. Her darling Elizabeth Taylor marrying Senator John Warner and construction worker Larry Fortensky instantly came to mind. What was Liz even thinking? Oh, right. John had some political power, and Larry was charming and oh so good-looking. But then she thought of the Jesse Tyler Fergusons, Pierce Brosnans, and George Clooneys of the world who had successfully partnered with commoners. *These things do, sometimes, work out*, she told herself.

Finally, Polly felt herself giving in to sleep; the next thing she realized, it was morning.

Dear God, I can't face the day, Polly said to herself as the anxiety from last night crashed into her morning. Her eyes started blinking to focus on her surroundings.

She looked up to where the walls joined the ceiling and saw the cracked—and in some places missing—ornamental plaster cornice. Then her attention was lazily drawn to the shabby drapery hanging in front of rotting window frames. The chifforobe was a beautiful piece of mahogany furniture, but not practical for someone like Polly, who had a massive wardrobe. Even the Oriental carpet, a portion of which she could see from her pillow, had obviously been a meal for moths and wool-eating worms and needed to be cleaned or chucked and replaced.

Nothing about the house, except for its history, was appealing to Polly anymore. She was suddenly decided about her nocturnal thoughts of leaving England. Her beloved Pepper Plantation in Bel Air needed repairs and upgrades, and the bucks from a sale of the old castle—whatever the price—would be a windfall and enable her to maintain her California house and lifestyle.

But... Terrence...

~

"This is insane!" Tim erupted with shock and disappointment at the news that Polly was saying that they should sell their castle and abandon Gwellyn's murder investigation. "Only a few hours ago, you were practically skipping down the aisle and rushing off to a honeymoon in Bora Bora! Now you're telling us that we should go back to California. What the heck?"

The pushback was unexpected.

"We can come back to England anytime," Polly insisted as she looked at the surprised expressions on Tim's and Tiara's faces. She had summoned her team into the library merely to discuss the potential for a return to Bel Air, and now that the words had slipped between her lips and she'd heard her own voice, she wasn't feeling the relief that she'd anticipated. Where were the whoops of joy and the "thank goodness, you've come to your senses so we can finally go home and have breakfast poolside in the garden every morning for the rest of our lives" sighs of relief? In Southern California, they could plan outdoor meals years in advance and be certain that the weather would be lovely on that future day.

"You'll be able to stop bellyaching about how cold and wet and dreary it is here," Polly said.

She looked at Tiara, who was obviously dazed by the news.

"I'll set us both up with profiles on Plunder when we get back," Polly said, offering an incentive. "And you don't have to wear your French maid uniform ever again. As for Grayson," Polly said, looking at Tim, "you really haven't invested a lot of time in that relationship. He's really just a friend."

"You don't know that!" Tim snapped at his mother in an unusually nasty tone. "Just because I tell you everything doesn't mean I tell you *everything!*"

Polly sighed in frustration. "It's only been eleven short days since you two met. He can come back with us if he wants to. I'll sponsor his US citizenship. Otherwise, there's FaceTime and Zoom. You'll find other distractions on your dating app. Don't look at me like I've just told Kim Possible that she can't do anything, for crying out loud."

"I'm not interested in Plunder anymore," Tim said, his voice the same sad tone as Tiara's. "I deleted the app from my phone. I didn't think I needed it anymore. And I'm just getting used to weird things in England, like fish fingers. Fish don't even have fingers, so it's a dumb name, but still kinda funny. There's a lot about the UK that I don't understand but that I'm starting to like."

"What about you and Terrence?" Tiara interrupted, giving Polly a curious eye. "What happened between last night's dinner and this morning? I went to bed thinking that you guys looked like a happily-ever-after fairy-tale couple, and I woke up to find that you've taken the *L* out of *lover* before you even got started."

At the mention of Terrence's name, Polly's gaze shifted to an image that only she could see: Terrence, seated opposite her in the Fox & Hare. His seductive smile. The crow's feet at the sides of his eyes. The scent of his aftershave. Polly's past and future collided when she pictured him. Now, with her family balking at the wisdom of her judgment, everything was a jumble, including her decision to pack up and head home for the greener pastures of California.

And then a knock on the door jolted the trio out of their respective disappointments and resentments. It was Lily.

"Mum," she said with her usual trembling voice and holding out a business-size white envelope, "this came. It was under the main gate, but the post was already delivered today, and it doesn't have a stamp, so someone probably brought it personally."

Everyone could see that the envelope was addressed to:

27

Polly Pepper
Urgent!

Annoyed by the interruption, Polly snatched the envelope from Lily's hand without her usual "thank you" and quickly unsealed it. She withdrew a trifolded sheet of letter-size paper and read the one typed sentence in the middle of the page:

Objects in the mirror are closer than they appear.

"No kidding!" Polly mocked the sentence.

Tiara plucked the page from her hand and silently read the message along with Tim. "A riddle," she said.

"A warning," Tim added.

"A driving metaphor," Lily suggested, instantly realizing it wasn't her place to comment.

"A clue," Polly said, nodding at her own conclusion as she considered the meaning and significance of the message. "This has to do with Gwellyn Clogg's killer," she added.

Then, deep in contemplation, she began to drift casually around the room, making faces that transitioned from grimace to scowl to smirk. Polly was in her own bubble of rumination, but the others could tell that the cryptic message had sparked her curiosity, and she was again thinking about her nearly abandoned investigation. Tim hoped the message was the prompt Polly needed to re-engage with her pursuit of a killer. He and Tiara were guardedly optimistic.

"There's no name or return address," Lily said, expanding the mystery. "So it's totally anonymous and can't ever be traced."

"Don't bet on that," Tiara insisted. "You should know Polly Pepper better by now. And don't you have a kettle to boil for tea or cobwebs to dust away?" she added as Lily reluctantly left the library.

"It has to be from someone who knows something about our investigation," Tim said, intentionally prodding his mother to change her mind about leaving England.

Although Polly didn't agree directly, she continued to make ambiguous facial expressions, and the others could tell she was trying to figure out the answer to all their questions—and her own.

"It's definitely a sign of some kind!" she proclaimed. "No one sends anonymous notes unless they're kidnappers—or wives exposing their cheating husbands' mistresses. Someone is telling us we're close to finding Gwellyn's killer. I feel it. But it's probably someone who can't risk revealing themselves or who can't even go through CrimeClue. They're saying that we have to be cautious about someone nearby. 'Objects in the mirror are closer than they appear.'"

"Maybe it came from the vicar," Tiara said. "You thought he couldn't make an obvious or specific accusation of anyone in the village because of his position in the community."

"Mary Radcliff or Sarah Rogers might be clever enough to

give us a hint like this," Tim suggested. "And see this? It was typed on an old-fashioned typewriter," he added, holding the paper up to the light from the window to demonstrate that the words on the page were not from a laser printer. "Does anyone know if Mary used a computer or an old manual or electric typewriter to write her book? We didn't see her writing desk, but she's old enough to have probably learned to type on a typewriter, and maybe she never gave it up. I hear some writers are superstitious that way, like wearing lucky sweaters when they're working or skipping chapter 13 in their books."

Polly and Tiara shook their heads in uncertainty, their thoughts running circles around their assumptions and theories. "Mary's probably the logical choice, at least from a duplicitous writing point of view," Tiara agreed.

"But she and Sarah would be smart enough to know that old typewriter print can be traced by the police," Tim said. "I saw that once on an old episode of *Murder, She Wrote*. Angela Lansbury was so clever! She found the old typewriter and read the killer's message on the ribbon itself!"

"Rest in peace, Angie," Polly said, thinking about her legendary friend and wishing desperately that a producer would reboot that long-running murder mystery series and hire Polly herself to step into Lansbury's role. "Modern laser printing can probably be traced too," she said. "There aren't many ways to hide things from the FBI or Scotland Yard anymore. Not like the good old days of Jack the Ripper or the Zodiac Killer. That's why I never looked at those naked pictures of Justin Bieber circulating online a few years ago. I was afraid of being caught!"

"You waited for me to download them on my computer," Tim teased, recalling his mother's clandestine review of the risqué photos.

"Enormously impressive!" Polly giggled. Then she realized what she'd just said, and her face turned red. "I mean, Bieber's *career* was impressive," she stuttered. "His *career* is enormously impressive!"

When she'd recovered her composure, she returned to the subject of the mysterious note. "I suggest the message came from someone who didn't have access to a computer or a printer or didn't know how to use one. That seems obvious to me."

"In this day and age, only someone ancient wouldn't know how to use a computer," Tiara said. "Today, babies come out of the womb with tablets! I always say, if you need tech support, call an eight-year-old."

"That eliminates the vicar," Polly agreed. "He'd write his sermons and church notices on a laptop or iPad. And when we went to pick up *Lust Among the Bluebells* from Sarah, she told us to tell Josh the book was in her office next to the computer. So it's not from her."

"Don't forget Terrence," Tim added. "But he's a writer, so of course he has a computer."

They all agreed that everyone they'd previously suspected of possibly being involved with Gwellyn's death had alibis, and none of them was a plausible killer.

"That leaves only Mr. Boots," Polly lamented in deep frustration. "But who cares? We're leaving as soon as I make all the arrangements."

28

———

The afternoon was freezing cold, but the rain had stopped, and Polly decided to take her mind off the calamitous morning with a stroll around the castle garden. As her departure from Thistlethorne and England was imminent, she wanted what would probably be among her last memories of the place.

"It'll be good exercise, too," she convinced herself as Tiara helped her into her heavy coat and cashmere scarf.

Polly stepped outside and was so cold that her nose immediately started running.

"This was a stupid idea," she said, but decided to forge ahead for remembrance's sake.

The sky remained steel gray, and the bare tree branches swayed in the breeze. A few blackbirds were pecking at the earth for something to eat, and Mr. Boots raced up to Polly for a scratch behind his ears. As she wandered the walled courtyard garden, Polly admired Merv's work preparing for the upcoming planting season, and decided to tell him so. She thought she should let him know that she appreciated his diligence and devotion to Thistlethorne, even if she wouldn't be around for the spring blossoms. Polly tucked her cold hands into her coat pockets and meandered down to the potting shed.

The door to the shed was slightly ajar, and Polly pulled on the rusted handle, but there was no sign of the gardener.

"Merv, darling?" she sang out as she stepped into the shadowy space.

Mr. Boots had followed her, and she picked him up and cradled him in her arms until he wriggled away and landed on the top of the tool-littered workbench. There, among the clutter, Polly noticed the hasp that should have secured the shed door, with its padlock still clasped in place. The cat put his paws on the dusty, cobwebbed windowsill and meowed at a pigeon cooing on a nearby tree branch. As Mr. Boots turned to retreat, his tail brushed up against a porcelain teapot, which had been precariously set on the narrow sill. The teapot started to wobble, and Polly caught it just as it fell toward the worktable.

"Is there something you need, mum?"

Polly jumped. Merv's voice completely startled her, and she nearly dropped the teapot. "Just rescuing this lovely old thing," she said as she regained her composure. "But I swear the handle was already gone when I came in." She held the teapot for Merv to see it was broken and then set it back on the windowsill. "I hope you don't mind me popping into your workspace and having a peek. The door wasn't locked."

Merv looked at Polly, then at the teapot. "Why would I mind? Everything here belongs to you. I'm just your devoted servant." Then he turned his attention to a wicker basket. "Bin collection tomorrow," he said, reaching for the basket and hefting it from its place beside a bag of potting soil. "I'd best be hauling this out." He looked again at Polly as if to suggest she should be on her way, too. "It's starting to rain again. You might want to get back to the house before you're drenched."

Polly glanced out through the dirty window. "Yes, it's time for a cuppa champers—I mean cocoa," she said and picked up Mr. Boots.

Together, they dashed across the castle courtyard toward the house. The moment she opened the door, a clap of thunder rattled the earth and her nerves, and she quickly scooted inside and closed the door.

The lack of a reliable broadband connection at Thistlethorne Lodge always made watching the BBC or a Netflix movie frustrating at best. Therefore, the evenings at the castle had become increasingly monotonous. Tiara tried in vain to coax Polly and Tim to play Scrabble or Trivial Pursuit, but everyone seemed too lethargic to care about anything more than how depressed they were about leaving England and wondering what they could have done differently to solve the mystery of Gwellyn's murder.

As the trio sat listening to Shirley Bassey—all of Mr. Drake's CDs seemed to be recordings by Shirley Bassey, Judy Garland, or Rosemary Clooney—singing through the sound system about big spenders and the eternality of diamonds, Polly started thinking about the bag of valuables they'd found. Particularly, she thought about the key ring that had been among the prizes. Of course, she recognized the key to the secret passageway, but what about the other two?

As the idea of keys and their locks filtered through her thoughts, she decided to make use of the boring evening and try to find the right slot for the other two. With nothing else on their agendas, Tim and Tiara listlessly followed her as she wandered around the house, searching for rooms, drawers, and storage places bolted, latched, or otherwise locked. A secured desk drawer and an ancient wooden trunk, none were responsive to Polly's attempt to slide, shove, and jam the key shanks into the locks' cylinders. And by the time they'd exhausted all the secured parts of the main floor, Polly grumbled the lines to a poem she'd once heard:

Locks without keys, the secrets they keep.
In whispering winds while children sleep.
In dreams, they dance; in tales, they spin.
Opening doors to worlds from within.

"I give up," Polly said wearily and suggested they all hit the sack.

But something about the keys, one of which was small, still shiny, and looked relatively new, puzzled Polly. She continued to think about them as she lay in her bed, staring into the darkness of the room. Then, just before drifting off to dreamland, Polly opened her eyes and sat up. She slipped out of bed and into her bathrobe and slippers. Following behind the beam from her smartphone's torch, she made her way downstairs. She picked up the jailer's key ring that she'd left on the coffee table in the reception room and then proceeded to the entry hallway. On the mahogany console table by the door, she picked up her own set of keys and made a side-by-side comparison.

"Duh!" She castigated herself for not recognizing before that the cut notches in the blade of the largest key matched the one to the castle's main entryway that Solicitor Wainwright had given her. Now, two of the keys were accounted for: the one to the passageway in the larder and the one to the castle entrance. She returned to bed with a theory about the third key and an eager desire to test her supposition first thing in the morning.

~

Dawn arrived, and although the sun still couldn't penetrate the thick gray clouds and fog, at least it wasn't raining. The first to awaken, Polly dressed, put on her heavy coat and scarf, and quietly slipped out of the house, eager to test a suspicion about the third and smallest key and the lock it was mated to.

It was an eerily quiet morning. The fog made the castle grounds seem insulated from the outside world. Polly made her way through the courtyard and headed for the potting shed. When she arrived, she found the unlocked door closed and buttressed with a rock set against the opening to thwart the wind, badgers, or foxes from getting inside. She was there to collect the hasp and padlock that she'd seen the previous day. She snatched her prize from the workbench and quickly stashed it in her coat pocket.

"You're up before the birds." Merv's disembodied voice wafted out from behind the veil of misty fog.

His voice unsettled Polly. She turned toward the sound to find him standing in the doorway with a pitchfork.

"I can't waste such a beautiful day," Polly said, flustered to daftness. "I love this time of morning," she lied, having seldom been up before 9:00. "But now it's time for my meditation and yoga exercises."

Polly noticed Merv was looking at her like a nosey neighbor keeping a distrustful eye on a trespasser. She was pretty sure that she knew why.

"Ta!" she said tentatively and scuttled back through the fog to the house.

Lily was already at work in the kitchen when Polly returned. "Breakfast is on the sideboard, mum," she said as Polly withdrew the padlock and hasp from her pocket and hung her coat and scarf by the door. "Your other maid is making herself right at home... as she always does when you're not around."

Polly gave Lily a tight smile and thought, *Brown-nose Barbie.*

When she arrived in the breakfast room, she proudly dropped the padlock and hasp at Tiara's place setting.

"This came off the potting shed," she said.

Tiara picked up the hardware and examined it, then gave Polly a quizzical look. "You're scavenging for scrap metal?"

"It's locked."

"I can see that. Where's the key?" Tiara asked, examining the Stanley padlock with more scrutiny.

"If I'm right, it's on the key ring we found in the dungeon."

"That would mean... "

"Whoever hid Old Man Drake's valuables in the dungeon had Merv's keys. I noticed he had to take this off the shed door!" the star said triumphantly.

Tiara looked at Polly and shook her head. "How'd you ever get rich and famous and navigate the shark-infested waters of Hollywood with a birdbrain like yours? If the key to Merv's potting shed is on the key ring that we found in the dungeon, which also has the key to the larder door, it means the keys belong to Merv!"

Polly grabbed the padlock and hurried through the main reception room with Tiara and into the front entrance hall. As Polly picked up the key ring from the console table and fitted the small key into the lock, she looked at Tiara. They both held their breaths. Then she turned the key. The U-shaped shackle popped up! The two women looked at each other with astonishment and trepidation.

"These are definitely Merv's keys," Polly said. "He needs to know that someone left them in the dungeon!"

"One guess who that someone was." Merv's voice came from behind, startling Polly and Tiara, stunning them into terrified silence.

29

———

As a light rain continued to fall on Abbots Clover, Tim was starting to realize that ever since meeting Grayson, the UK didn't seem so dreary. He'd gotten up early to meet the constable for breakfast, and if things between them continued to progress this way, he felt he could probably be persuaded to give up surfing in sunny Southern California in favor of throwing darts at the Fox & Hare in squelchy England.

"It must be weird to have a famous mum," Grayson said as they chatted idly over coffee at Bound to Read.

"It's major weird to have Polly Pepper as my mother, period." Tim laughed. "Sure, it's kind of glamorous, and I get to live in a mansion and go to amazing restaurants, and a lot of famous people are around all the time, but it's like living in a zoo—with Polly as the endangered species and the whole wide world ogling and pointing. And forget about dating. I never know if guys want to hang out because they really like me for me or if they just want to meet my mother and try on her Bob Mackie costumes."

"I kind of know the feeling," Grayson continued. "I'm never

sure if it's the police uniform that guys find attractive or if I'm sexy all on my own?"

Tim smiled evilly. "Speaking for myself... it's definitely both. And don't get me started on your adorable foreign accent."

"Foreign accent?" Grayson feigned insult. "I live here, buddy, so you're the one with the foreign accent. But I think it's pretty cool that you had to come all the way from America for us to meet. Some people in the village have never even been up to London, which is only two hours away by train, let alone traveled out of the country. When I was a kid playing around your castle, I used to pretend that a time machine brought me to Thistlethorne, and my mission was to rescue the evil king's prisoners from the dungeon. I actually found a secret entrance to the castle that led to the real-life dungeon!"

"At the back of the castle? I found it, too! And there's a passageway that goes all the way up to the bedrooms. It's really cool! I didn't think anyone knew about it!"

Grayson grinned and said, "There's a lot more to the castle than meets the eye. I've gotta show you the trapdoor in one of the cells. It was probably another hiding space for the king or whoever lived here. Or maybe it was a torture chamber. Whatever, it's pretty spooky. Of course, I'll protect you."

"You'd look pretty good in a suit of shining armor," Tim said, giving Grayson a lecherous smile.

It was nearly time for Grayson to start his work shift when he texted Ella Towers and asked her to cover for him. He wanted to spend the day exploring the castle with Tim. They'd only walked a short distance down the high street toward Thistlethorne when Grayson's phone rang. The caller identification said *ET*.

"Ella wouldn't call if it weren't important," he explained as he answered the phone. A moment later, he said, "Right-o. I'm on my way." He looked at Tim. "It won't take long, I promise. Then I'll be free to spend the rest of the day with you."

They agreed to meet back at Thistlethorne, explore the secret passageway, and maybe have a sleepover that night.

"Remind Polly of how scary it was so she doesn't join us!" Grayson sniggered as they exchanged a quick hug and went their separate ways.

Tim nearly skipped along the cobblestone road leading to the castle, and he couldn't help but smile and fantasize about playing the role of the Lord of Thistlethorne Lodge, with Grayson by his side. He pictured the two of them reigning over the village and giving lavish banquets with the guests wearing Renaissance-era costumes and dancing pavanes and galliards to live music with lutes, harpsichords, tabor drums, and other period instruments. He would be a benevolent nobleman. The villagers would bow to him and praise how he and Grayson ruled over their loyal subjects. Songs and poems would be written about them, and they would live happily ever after together in the castle. Then Tim's phone rang, jolting him out of his reverie.

Tim looked at the screen: *PP*. With a sigh of irritation, he answered and explained that he was on his way home. However, his mother didn't respond. He decided that she'd probably accidentally pocket-dialed him. As he listened closer, he heard someone shouting in the background.

"We finally got a Wi-Fi signal for Netflix! What are you watching?" he said into the phone. But again, there was no response. "Okay. Not sure if you can hear me, but I'll be home soon." Then he hung up.

30

────────

As Tim approached Thistlethorne Lodge, he quickened his pace, eager to get home and freshen up before Grayson arrived. When he reached the short drawbridge over the empty moat, Mr. Boots appeared out of nowhere and nuzzled his ankle. Tim kneeled to scratch the pet behind his ears.

"There's a bay-bee!" he murmured. "Catch lots of mice during the night? Yes, you did! I bet you did!"

Tim discovered that the heavy gateway door was unlocked and slightly ajar. He pushed it open farther, and Mr. Boots scooted past him and disappeared into the courtyard.

Entering the house, Tim was aware of how unusually quiet it was. He glanced at the time on his phone screen and subconsciously noted that it was odd that Polly and Tiara weren't fussing around or bickering or listening to music on the radio. He proceeded toward the breakfast room.

"Mummy! Tons to tell you!" he called out, but Polly didn't respond. No one did. The house seemed frozen in silence. He frowned when he saw the homely dish containing scrambled eggs and sausages on the sideboard and plates with bits of cold food on the table. He noted that Polly's flute of Prosecco was half full. She'd never in a million years leave that much in a glass.

Maybe you're at the kitchen table, working on that thousand-piece jigsaw puzzle that Tiara talked you into starting.

"Mummy?" Tim called again as he walked through to the kitchen. But it was empty, and the lights were off. He was bewildered.

Then, in the darkened corner, he noticed a weak strip of light leaching from under the door to the larder. *Still searching for more Gwellyn clues*, Tim said to himself as he flipped the switch to the kitchen light and walked to the larder door. He reached for the handle but instantly stopped when he heard an angry voice that sounded like Merv's penetrating the door. As Tim cocked his head and listened closer, he also heard Polly's distinctive voice.

"You'll never get away with this!" she said and seemed to be making a speech—as if she were playing the role of Mildred Picklechurch, the bumbling lady detective character in a popular comedy sketch on her old TV show. It sounded to Tim as though his mother was explaining the finer points of a crime and laying out a pronouncement of someone's guilt.

Polly's theater-trained voice was clear, though muted by the door. "Actually, until this morning, I didn't really suspect you as Gwellyn's killer," she said. "Last night, Lily became my choice. 'Quiet people have the loudest minds,' they say." Polly continued on about how she'd come to realize that Lily wasn't necessarily the pea-brain she'd originally assumed. "I'm fascinated by her elevated vocabulary. When she said I was an 'oppressive American capitalist,' I was impressed. And after, she used a string of colorful adjectives to describe Gwellyn: 'malicious, despicable, loathsome.' I suspected a savant disguised as Alice from *The Brady Bunch*.

"Then yesterday, Lily brought me that anonymous note. She

said the cryptic message, 'Objects in the mirror are closer than they appear' was 'a driving metaphor.' Metaphor was a curious word for an undereducated person like Lily to use. But even more curious was that I hadn't read that message aloud. Neither had Tim nor Tiara. So she only could have known what was printed on the page if she'd written it *herself*. 'Objects in the mirror are closer than they appear.' A clever warning about *you*, Mr. Gardener!

"My darling Timmy pointed out that the note was typed on an old-fashioned typewriter," Polly continued. "Other than Tom Hanks and his famous collection, no one uses a typewriter anymore. But Mr. Drake did. During the night, I suspected that someone had used his antique Smith Corona to write that note. You didn't have direct access to the house and stationery supplies in the library, so I guessed it was Lily who typed it. And now I also recall some of your other trail-of-crumbs clues. I remembered last week at the Fox & Hare, when I came looking for the key to the door hidden behind the shelves here, you said that you didn't know anything about a concealed door that led to a secret passageway. That was odd because I never said the door led to a 'secret passageway.'

"Then, when you came round for tea, you said that your money was on Lily doing something less creative than you to get even with Gwellyn for all her bullying. But that was right after you insisted Gwellyn hadn't been murdered. Want to hear my theory about how Gwellyn ended up in the medical examiner's fridge?"

Tim heard Merv's voice again. "Oh, absolutely, Ms. TV Star. Take me to Fantasyland. I'm all ears."

There was a long pause before Tim heard his mother's voice again. "Over the course of Mr. Drake's illness, when you were invited into the house to sit with him in his room, you took the opportunity to steal bits and bobs," she said. "You hid what you pilfered down in the dungeon. But for the longest time, I couldn't figure out how you—or whoever stashed the loot down there—could get out of the passageway if they'd locked themselves in. Then I figured you made your way out through the opening in the wall we found at the back tower. You must have realized that you'd dropped the key ring or left it in the dungeon at some point. You were in a jam because without the keys, you couldn't get back into the dungeon through the larder door, and you couldn't risk being found making your way through the outside opening now that we're living at Thistlethorne. And without the key to the potting shed to get to your tools, you had to remove the hasp and lock to get in. Am I right?"

Tim heard Merv's voice again. "Not bad. But you're wrong about a couple of things. I wasn't the one who ripped off Mr. Drake. I wouldn't have done that to him. He was nice to me. That was all Gwellyn's handiwork through and through. And I wasn't the idiot who left the keys behind in the dungeon, either. That was the brilliant Lily."

Tim recognized the next voice as belonging to the maid. For once, she sounded more assertive and self-confident—unlike the little frightened fawn who couldn't look directly into anyone's eyes when speaking to them.

"I'm far from an idiot," Lily said proudly. "And I'm very observant, too. I watched Gwellyn nicking stuff from Mr. Drake. Little things that she didn't think he'd miss. A ring here. A watch there. That wee painting with the water lilies—I was named for lilies—and I'd hoped he'd leave it to me in his will. I thought Gwellyn had been selling everything. But then, after she found out that Mr. Drake didn't leave her anything in his will and that Polly Pepper was coming from America to take the house, I saw her and Merv in the larder sorting through all the stuff she'd pinched. I could tell from her smug attitude that she was gloating and showing off, making Merv see how clever she'd been to plan for her financial future and retirement. Then they noticed my shadow and knew I'd been spying on them. They put everything back into the bag real fast and pretended they were just talking about nothing in particular. Merv knew better. Later, he took me into the old chapel and said that he and Gwellyn had merely been taking an inventory of Mr. Drake's stuff for the solicitor and that he might share some of it with me.

"I'm pretty good at pretending about a lot of things. I pretended to believe Merv when he said he was acting on behalf of the estate. Just like I pretended I was scared of Gwellyn. I pretended to be surprised when I found her body. Merv told me he had a good plan. He wanted me to help him trick Gwellyn out of the valuables. He knew that I knew where Gwellyn's secret place for hiding things was. There's a wood panel inside the kitchen's dumbwaiter that conceals a niche where we think servants used to stash wine and spirits in the old days. He said that if I helped him, he'd make sure that Gwellyn was out of the way and would give me a share so that I'd have security when the castle's new owner came and sold it and I was out of a job."

Lily paused momentarily, and Tim wondered if it was time for him to intervene. But then he heard her continue her confession.

"Merv," she said, "I purposely left the keys behind in the dungeon. I'd worked it all out in my head. You'd get rid of Gwellyn, then the police or CrimeClue would figure that out, and you'd be arrested. Then I'd collect the stuff from the dungeon for myself. But I didn't expect the castle's new owners to find out about the secret passageway and discover all the stuff I left down there in the cell. They completely spoiled my plans."

"You're both so common," Polly said. "Gwellyn was killed because you're rapacious thieves, just like her."

"*Rapacious: aggressively greedy or grasping. Rapacious,*" Lily proudly recited like a contestant in the Scripps National Spelling Bee competition.

Tim could hear Merv offer a chuckle and imagined the gardener shaking his head and wondering how much more information he should reveal.

"Gwellyn boasted to me about all the loot she'd taken from Mr. Drake, and since Solicitor Wainwright hadn't come to search for the things that went missing, I figured it was finders, keepers all the way. After Lily grabbed the bag from the dumbwaiter and stashed it in the dungeon, I had a good laugh when Gwellyn discovered it was missing. She confronted me, and I played innocent. Just like I did with the fish guts. Then I decided to take my final revenge.

"I got a really fun idea," Merv continued. "I'd found a false widow spider making a home for itself in that old porcelain teapot in the shed—the one you miraculously spared from shattering yesterday. It was well known that Gwellyn was absolutely petrified of spiders—even the little harmless ones that hang around ceiling corners. I called her up and said I was feeling generous and had decided that she could have half the loot back. See, I'm the generous type. I said I'd hidden her share in a teapot and left it in the larder, and since she was probably going to be sacked the next morning, she had to come right away, in the middle of the night, to get her reward."

"Oh, she was a greedy one, all right," Lily continued. "She was here in no time. She must have raced over. We were outside and watched from the window. She picked up the teapot like it was a Ming dynasty vase, lifted the lid, and shoved her piggy hand inside. Then bam! The spider attacked! Its venom might not have been enough to kill her on the spot, but she had a bad heart, and Merv was pretty sure that the combination of freaking out when she saw that thing crawling on her skin, as well as the bite, would be enough to cause a heart attack. He was right. When she dropped to the floor, her hand was stuck inside, and she clenched that damned teapot handle so tight that it snapped off."

Merv spoke again. "As I watched and waited for her to die—she sure screamed and convulsed a lot—I saw Mr. Spider casually wander away, free and easy, totally unaware that it had just killed something scarier than itself. Now I see he's made a nice new home over there."

Tim imagined Merv was pointing to the spiderweb he'd seen in the window. He listened in horror as he thought about Gwellyn's reaction to the creepy spider. He'd probably literally go insane if a scorpion crawled on him or if he were buried alive in a box.

"I also remember the teapot in your shed with its missing handle. I found this... " Polly reached into the pocket of her cardigan and retrieved the piece of ceramic she'd found on the larder floor. "The tiny blue flowers match your teapot."

"The racket we heard that night," Tiara said. "It was poor Gwellyn trying to get our attention. We maybe could have saved her life."

"She shouldn't have put the idea of ghosts into your heads," Lily said. "You thought it was a haunting. She did sound like a banshee when that spider crawled on her hand and bit into her."

"Funnily, I would have gotten rid of the teapot altogether," Merv said, "but I remembered that you took a picture inside the potting shed that second day you were here, and I figured you might notice it missing if you compared the picture with the scene as it is now. That might have called attention to me. Plus, the teapot was legally yours, so I hesitated to destroy it."

"Now you consider legalities," Polly said. "Also funny—I played photo editor and deleted that picture, so I wouldn't have put two and two together. But I suspected that the red spot I saw on Gwellyn's hand the day we found her was from a bite or a sting, although the police constable suggested it wasn't anything more than a scratch or rash."

Then Tim could hear Lily confessing that she didn't mean to be a party to murder.

"Shut up, you little good-for-nothing dogsbody," Merv told her. "Now that I've got my stuff, you can join Gwellyn, who's probably cleaning the devil's personal toilet right this very minute." Merv laughed at the image he'd conjured in his head. "Lily, move the shelves away from the door! Now!"

Next, Tim could hear the scraping sound of the shelving unit being pushed aside to reveal the door to the passageway. Knowing he had to do something right away to save his mother's life, Tim looked around the kitchen and picked up the first weapon he saw: an eight-inch steel chef's knife. For a fraction of a moment, he thought about trying to access the hidden entrance into the dungeon and launch a surprise attack. Then he thought about calling Grayson for help. But again, time was of the essence and quickly running out. He couldn't risk waiting for his friend to come to the rescue. Tim had to act now. And fast. He had no choice but to confront Merv. In America, a killer like Merv would surely have a gun. But he'd learned that in England, very few people had firearms, and it was a long and difficult process to legally own one. And having been previously arrested, Merv wouldn't be eligible to legitimately own a gun.

At that very moment, Tim pulled open the door to the larder and dashed into the room, brandishing the knife. But Merv did have a gun! And he pointed it directly at Polly Pepper's temple.

"Perfect timing," he said, cocking his head, indicating for Tim to stand with the others. "Drop the knife, or I'll shoot your mother. You're all about to take a little trip to explore the old dungeon again."

As Tim moved toward Polly and the others, he bluffed that

he'd already called the police and that they would be swarming Thistlethorne Lodge at any moment.

"I know all about your policeman friend," Merv spat sarcastically. "He's not much of a cop, and in this bloody village, he won't have any backup unless it's that pathetic old crone he hangs out with. And by the time anyone gets here, you'll all be dead and sealed up inside these walls where you won't be found for probably a hundred years."

"Polly Pepper is an American icon," Polly shot back. "If I go missing, they'll quickly find that Thistlethorne Lodge was the last place I was seen alive, and they'll take this place apart stone by stone until they find me. You won't get away with killing us the way you almost got away with killing Gwellyn."

"It'll take 'em a while to figure it all out, and by then, I'll have disappeared," Merv countered. "Probably can't track me 'cause I don't have a mobile. And no one will be alive to say exactly what happened to you." Merv tossed the key ring to Tim. "Open the door and get on down to your tomb! Move!"

"Do as he says, dear," Polly encouraged. "We all have to die sometime. It'll only hurt for a second."

"You've been shot dead before, have you?" Tiara asked.

"I'm using my imagination as an actor," Polly said. "And being the victim of murder won't be so bad. At least not for me. It guarantees the front page of *Daily Variety*. Surely, the *New York Times* and the *Times* of London, too. Stars who tragically die young are immortalized forever. Perhaps there'll even be a docudrama starring Mercedes Ford. She'd never portray me as well as Meryl Streep, but I'm not one to criticize Oscar winners."

"You're too *old* to die *young*," Tiara quipped as she followed the others into the darkened passageway.

Merv turned on a flashlight he'd retrieved from his back pocket, which was clearly not up to its task, as it cast a weak, yellowish glow.

"FYI, batteries are in the top drawer next to the sink in the kitchen," Tiara sarcastically offered.

"I can hardly see the steps!" Lily cried as she gingerly led the descent.

When they finally reached the space that had once been used for monstrous acts of cruelty hundreds of years ago, Merv separated them into pairs and forced them into the adjoining cells. The increasingly weak beam from Merv's light made the place look even more sinister.

"If I were the decent sort, I'd just leave you here to rot," Merv said. "A dungeon is built to muffle the screams from tortured prisoners so no one would ever hear you calling for help."

"Yes! That's much better than blowing holes in our heads," Polly said with a hint of hope.

"Either way, you'll be a meal for the rats," Merv said. "I can practically hear their dinner bell ringing. Ding! Ding! Ding! Come and get it! Now, tell me how it works," he said, pointing his gun and the increasingly ineffective light at Polly. "Do you get top billing and die first? Or do you take the final bow after the minor players have left the stage?"

No one could see Polly rolling her eyes, but they couldn't miss the derision in her voice. "You're the director, Merv. You decide. But you won't go very far in Hollywood if you don't have a clear vision for the project and are not in control of your cast and crew. But before we do the whole kick-the-bucket, final-act, curtain-coming-down scene, I'm still curious about something. Did Gwellyn kill Mr. Drake for an inheritance?"

"Yep. She told me she was going to suffocate him and claim that he died in his sleep. And I'm the one who called CrimeClue and told them about her scheme," Merv confessed. "My original strategy was to get her out of the way by having her arrested and locked up on suspicion of murder. But CrimeClue took forever! Days and weeks passed without the police showing up. When you moved in, and I'd heard you were going to sack her, I called them again and left another message. I decided I couldn't wait. I had to take her out myself that very night. Now, enough questions!" he demanded. "Give my regards to Gwellyn and tell her…"

Just then, an unexpected noise in the distance startled Merv. He turned around and waited silently as he and his captives tried to peer into the darkness. He pointed his ever-dimming flashlight beam down the corridor.

"What the hell?"

His weak flashlight beam caught Mr. Boots, who dropped a dead mouse at his feet and began devouring it.

"Damned cat!" Merv snarled and kicked the mouse to the wall. "I swear to God I should have taken him out a long time ago. Especially since he was the one thing on the planet that Gwellyn actually liked and was nice to." Then he fired a shot into where he thought the cat was eating in the darkness.

Merv's flashlight beam was now so dim that he could hardly see his intended human victims and realized he had to finish them off right away. He raised his gun once again and pointed it at Polly. But he was momentarily distracted by the flickering of the bulb in his flashlight. Then he heard another sound in the distance.

"Meow!" came from out of the darkness. But this time, it was a human imitation.

"They have nine lives," Polly said.

And then Merv's flashlight went dead.

"Who's there?" he demanded. He listened for a sound indicating where the voice had come from. The subterranean chamber was now in complete darkness. No attempt at adjusting his eyes successfully provided even a glimpse of the surroundings. The total darkness had completely disoriented the gardener.

"I have a gun!" he shouted. "I'll kill you! I will!"

"It's Gwellyn's ghost!" Lily cried, totally believing that the dead woman had returned to seek revenge.

Another barely perceptible sound came from the darkness, and Merv nervously shot his pistol in that direction.

"Not even close," the voice stated as another shot instantly rang out from Merv's gun.

Tim recognized the voice. It was Grayson's! Tim instantly had an idea as Polly and the others shivered with cold and fright. He'd seen their cell phones tossed together in the larder, but Merv hadn't remembered to take his phone away. He thought that if he could just give Grayson a quick indication of where Merv was standing, the policeman would have a chance to tackle the killer. A brief flash of light would be all that was needed, but Tim feared that Merv, who was already agitated, might shoot toward the light. He decided he had to take the biggest risk of his life. He retrieved his phone from his back pocket and touched the home button. Just as expected, the illumination caused a jittery Merv to react and fire his revolver again.

Polly found her voice, and although it was quivering with fear, she couldn't resist deriding her captor.

"Merv, darling," she said, "I've counted the shots, and you don't have enough bullets left to finish your job here."

"Teacher, you forgot to give us our homework," Tiara mocked Polly in a smart-alecky singsong.

Silence filled the stone chamber. Everyone knew Merv was considering what Polly had said and was reviewing his options.

"Has Mr. Boots got your tongue?" Polly teased.

Suddenly, another shot rang out and ricocheted off the stone walls.

"Damn. I was always lousy at math," Polly confessed.

Merv offered a gleeful chuckle, which instantly squelched

everyone's hopes for safety and freedom. "I'm packing plenty of ammo."

However, in the nanosecond after his gloating, a physical struggle erupted in the darkness, and another shot rang out. Then... silence filled the chamber. The prisoners held their breaths in fear and expectation.

"Gray!" Tim called out in panic. "Gray!" he called again, then hit his phone's home screen again and touched the flashlight icon.

In the next instant, Polly and the others exhaled with a collective sigh of relief as they saw Merv laid out on the stone floor, a silver candlestick by his side, and Grayson standing over his body. Merv was still breathing but incapacitated, and Grayson was on his phone, calling the police in the next village.

Mr. Boots, too, was busy finishing his mouse meal.

31

Morning arrived, and Polly literally skipped into the breakfast room to join Tiara at the table. The sun was shining, and the sky was clear for the first time since they'd come to Thistlethorne Lodge. Instead of seeing Merv puttering around the castle courtyard, they now viewed a quartet of magpies scavenging for a meal.

"One for sorrow, two for joy, three for a girl, four for a boy." Tiara recited the old nursery rhyme about magpies.

"Everything seems utterly fresh today, doesn't it?" Polly trilled, kissing Tiara on the top of her head and scooping Mr. Boots into her arms. "All those negative vibrations from Merv and Lily—it's like the hellhounds have been cast out, and the whole place has undergone a thorough cleansing!"

"No more demons," Tiara agreed. "The only scary noises I heard last night were the ones coming from Tim's room." She looked at Polly, and they both grinned evilly.

As they exchanged lascivious smirks, Tim wandered into the breakfast room, wearing only the bottom portion of his PJs and looking like a confused scarecrow with a bedhead of straw hair. He plopped himself down at the table.

"I heard that," he said, smirking and lethargically grabbing a warm croissant from the silver muffin basket.

"She only meant that sometimes sounds from alive people are creepier than those from dead ones," Polly deadpanned as she looked up to see Grayson entering the room, wearing the same jeans and flannel shirt he'd had on the day before. "Our savior!" she exclaimed and began applauding wildly. "You deserve a knighthood, young man! Yes, you do! I'm calling Sir Elton to put in a good word to Charles and Camilla!"

Grayson blushed. "All in a day's work. Tim deserves just as much credit as me." He sat on the chair beside his friend and reached for the teapot. "And who knew he had such perfect aim throwing a candlestick? If he hadn't knocked Merv out cold—from inside a dungeon cell, no less—I might not have been able to overpower him."

"Candlestick?" Tim said, shaking his head. "I didn't have a candlestick. I thought you clobbered him."

"Don't play modest," Grayson said as he leaned over and gave Tim a flirtatious fist bump to the gecko tattoo on his biceps.

The table conversation quickly detoured to their near-death experience the night before. Tiara imitated Lily wailing to the police about her innocence and that Merv had coerced her into aiding in Gwellyn's murder.

"And that look in Merv's eyes," Polly recalled with a shudder. "His voice has been an earworm in my head all night: 'I'll get you for this if it's the last thing I do!'"

"We also have to thank the police team from over in Wyre Piddle," Tim added. "It's almost a miracle that Grayson's phone got a signal from down in the dungeon to call them."

"Speaking of police—or wannabe police—Ella Towers deserves a commendation, too," Grayson said. "She called me just in the nick of time. I was at the front entrance of

Thistlethorne, but nobody answered the door. I looked in the windows. I even pulled the bell by the main gate. But there was no sign of anyone around, even though Tim was definitely expecting me. I was about to ring his phone, but Ella interrupted, which was good because if I had called, it might have spooked Merv and made him follow through with his plans faster. Ella told me that Gwellyn's autopsy report had come in and that her cause of death was still inconclusive, but venom from a false widow spider was present in her blood. I don't know; I just had a hunch that something wasn't right. Maybe I'm starting to get the hang of my job after all. I remembered reading Gwellyn's file and her complaint that Merv had once threatened her life. When I didn't see him around the castle grounds—he's always around—I took an educated guess that you all might be in trouble. That's why I snuck in through the secret entrance. Playing around here when I was a kid finally paid off."

"Since applause is going around, don't forget that I was the clever one for speed-dialing Tim before Merv confiscated my phone," Polly bragged. "The moment I figured we were in the presence of the British Norman Bates, I knew I had to send up a smoke signal."

As they all discussed the possible dire alternate outcomes that could have occurred, Polly became less concerned with the past than she was with the future. "When will I get my bag of treasure back? Evidence or not, the price of gold is going sky-high, and if I'm supposed to live in this castle and maintain it too, I'll need all the funds I can get my hands on."

Tiara and Tim abruptly stopped eating their croissants and sipping tea. They looked at each other, then turned and gaped at Polly.

"Live in the castle?" Tim said.

"Maintain it too?" Tiara parroted her boss.

Polly shrugged and handed her empty glass to Tiara for a top-up. "Just a thought," she said. "It's been on my mind. I mean, what is there for me in Hollywood anymore? I can't bear to say the words aloud, but let's face it: I'm now a has-been. Of course, that's way better than being a never-was, but I'm starting to realize that maybe I've stayed too long at the fair, so to speak."

Tim and Tiara kept staring at Polly and suddenly felt deeply sad for her. They recalled the untold number of times fans had asked when she would be returning to television, and her stock reply was always a vague *"I'm considering several exciting projects."* But there weren't any projects to consider, exciting or otherwise. It was a dismal time for the older star, whose entire life had been devoted to her career. Now, she was finally admitting that the phone seldom rang with opportunities anymore, and she was ancient history.

"I've been searching for a second act, and maybe it's staring me in the face," Polly said, trying to sound optimistic but feeling the soul-crushing, end-stage-of-grief acceptance. "Heck, I don't want to be one of those divas whose only public appearances are at charity events and lifetime achievement awards banquets. Let Molly Ringwald have all that fun. Anyway, I'm tired of the summer stock amphitheater circuit and playing Mama Rose, Auntie Mame, or Dolly Levi in the humid heat of Missouri in July. And I'm certainly not butch enough to play Edna Turnblad in *Hairspray!*"

"My grandmother loved you and your old show," Grayson said, trying to offer encouragement but only reinforcing what Polly was saying—that she was from another generation and no longer of any social or artistic relevance.

Polly gave him a wan smile and a slight shrug. "Your grandmother has excellent taste, dear," she said graciously. Then, determined not to wallow in self-pity, she gleefully said, "Hell, we just got a new lease on life! Yesterday, we were this close to being shipped back home in the cargo hold, and today... it's like we've been reborn! There's a hell of a lot more to life than the glamour of Hollywood! And I might even be falling in love. Don't forget I have a date with Terrence tonight!"

Exclamations of "Hear, hear!" and "Absolutely!" resounded from around the table.

"Goldie Hawn would kill for your second act!" Tim praised his mother.

"But what about Pepper Plantation and your reverse mortgage commercial?" Tiara said, appealing for a return of Polly's practical side.

"I don't know," Polly said. "I don't know anything, really. I'm just thinking out loud. But I suppose we could rent out the house for a small fortune. I hear the Sussexes' Montecito neighbors are petitioning for them to find a different mansion to raise their runny-nosed non-prince and princess. And there's that amazing mode of transportation called air travel that can whiz me to commercial or TV locations anywhere on the planet—if I ever get another gig. As for seeing friends, we can catch up with chums over Zoom, Skype, or FaceTime! Anyway, it's something to think about."

"I'm thinking about the rotten weather here," Tim said. "I've already lost my tan."

"Not to mention how provincial this village is," Tiara added. "You're not going to find anyone as sophisticated as you are."

"The people of Abbots Clover aren't really much different from the ones in Hollywood," Grayson said, feeling a need to defend his village and its residents. "They might not be as fashionable or worldly, but you attract like-minded people wherever you go. Maybe you could even start a film festival or create an arts community. You could give concerts and have some of your famous friends as guest stars. We've got lots of talent right here in Abbots Clover."

"Yeah, Mae Billings can be your opening act." Tim laughed. "The vicar says she does an awesome 'Supercalifragilisticexpiali-docious.'"

Polly grimaced, but quickly gave Tim a wide smile. "And maybe there's a special someone here for Tiara to date," she said.

"Hang out with us at the pub, and you'll definitely catch someone's eye." Grayson grinned and gave Tim a look that suggested he was proof of the possibilities for romantic encounters in Abbots Clover.

Polly raised her glass of Prosecco and proposed a toast. "To a new life! I'm up for the adventure! Who's with me?"

Suddenly, the French doors in the breakfast room blew open, and a gust of stiff wind rushed in. Everyone at the table turned simultaneously to the sound of someone weeping upstairs. A thud, like a bowling ball landing on the roof, caused them to jump. The heavy silver candlestick that had somehow found its way back from the dungeon fell over on the mahogany sideboard. Mr. Boots, who had been dozing on Polly's lap, leaped away with a loud meow and dashed from the room.

Then they all distinctly heard a disembodied voice whisper, "Heh, heh, heh. Fresh blood to liven things up around here."

Upon hearing the ghostly chuckle, the room became still. However, rather than showing fear, Polly seemed to repress laughter.

"Our resident spirit seems to have a taste for theatrics." She raised her glass in a toast. "Here's to Casper the Comic! Who knows? If it's got such a cracking sense of humor, maybe I've found my next co-star!"

Everyone stared at her in surprise, prompting her to elaborate with a mischievous glint in her eyes, "Think about it! Polly and the Specter starring in *Keeping Up with the Cadavers*! Now that's a reality show that Netflix couldn't resist!"

THE END

ALSO BY RICHARD TYLER JORDAN

<u>Polly Pepper Cozy Mystery Series</u>

Remains to be Scene

Final Curtain

A Talent for Murder

Set Sail for Murder

A Corpse in the Castle

<u>LGBTQ+ Titles</u>

Overnight Sensation

Strangers in the Night

Gay Blades

One Night Stand

Breakfast at Timothy's

ABOUT THE AUTHOR

RICHARD TYLER JORDAN is a novelist and nonfiction writer. His books include the cozy mysteries *A Corpse in the Castle, Remains to be Scene, Final Curtain, A Talent for Murder, Set Sail for Murder,* and the Christmas novella *Naughty or Nice.* His LGBTQ+ titles include the romcom/mystery *Breakfast at Timothy's,* as well as *Overnight Sensation, Strangers in the Night, Gay Blades* (which was #1 on the InsightOut Book Club Bestsellers List), and *One Night Stand.* He has also contributed novellas to the anthologies *Summer Share* and *All I Want for Christmas* (both of which earned Lambda Literary Award nominations) and *Man of My Dreams.* Jordan is also the author of *But Darling, I'm Your Auntie Mame,* a history of the fictional icon Auntie Mame created by Patrick Dennis. As a senior publicist and staff writer with The Walt Disney Studios for thirty years, Jordan worked on the marketing campaigns of over 500 live-action and animated feature films. Now an expat from America, Richard lives in England in a cozy 16th-century cottage (with his husband and an amiable ghost).

You can contact Richard at **www.Richardtylerjordan.com**.